BETWEEN TWO WORLDS

Also by Olivier Norek in English translation

THE CAPITAINE COSTE INVESTIGATIONS

The Lost and the Damned

Turf Wars

Breaking Point

OLIVIER NOREK

BETWEEN
TWO WORLDS

Translated from the French by
Nick Caistor

MACLEHOSE PRESS
QUERCUS · LONDON

First published in the French language as *Entre deux mondes*
by Editions Michel Lafon, Paris, 2017

First published in Great Britain in 2024 by

MacLehose Press
An imprint of Quercus Editions Ltd
Carmelite House
50 Victoria Embankment
London EC4Y 0DZ

An Hachette UK company

A CIP catalogue record for this book is available
from the British Library.

ISBN (HB) 978 0 85705 921 5
ISBN (TPB) 978 0 85705 922 2
ISBN (Ebook) 978 0 85705 923 9

This book is a work of fiction. Names, characters, businesses, organisations,
places and events are either the product of the author's imagination or are used
fictitiously. Any resemblance to actual persons, living or dead, events or
locales is entirely coincidental.

10 9 8 7 6 5 4 3 2 1

Designed and typeset in Garamond by CC Book Production
Printed and bound in Great Britain by Clays Ltd, Elcograf S.p.A.

MIX
Paper | Supporting
responsible forestry
FSC® C104740

Papers used by Quercus Books are from well-managed forests and other responsible sources.

*To my grandfather Herbert Norek,
an immigrant from Silesia who became
a French citizen*

Confronted by the violence of reality, I have not dared invent anything. Only the police investigation, based on true facts, has been fictionalised. My thanks to the people and police of Calais, to the Renseignements Généraux, the journalists, my sources in the CNRS and Sciences-Po, the aid workers, but above all to those men and women who, fleeing the horrors of war, opened their hearts to me.

The child

To avoid creating a disturbance or panic, the man at the tiller opened the throttle so the noise from the ancient outboard motor covered his words. He ordered his companion:

"Throw her overboard."

"Now?"

"We can get rid of her more easily at sea than in a car park. She's been coughing the whole time. We don't want to get caught when we've put them on the trucks in Italy."

The boat was filled with two hundred and seventy-three migrants. An assortment of ages, sexes, origins, skin colours. Tossed about, soaked to the skin, freezing cold, terrorised.

"I don't think I can do it. You go."

A sigh of irritation. Nothing more. The trafficker let go of the tiller and shoved his way through to a woman in the depths of the boat. As he drew closer, she tightened her grip on the body enfolded in her arms. She pressed her hand on the little girl's icy mouth, praying for her to stop coughing. Frightened, the child dropped her threadbare fluffy purple rabbit. Without even noticing, the man crushed it underfoot. He shouted at the woman.

"Your little girl. You have to push her overboard."

The madman

Calais migrant camp
October 2016
Final day of dismantling the Jungle

The diggers were clawing insatiably at huts and tents, reducing them to debris that a little further on was piled into mountains of plastic, fabric and clothes, destined to be consumed by flames once the wind died down.

Virtually nothing remained of the shelters hope had built.

A digger's prongs were raised as it began to cross this vast stretch of no-man's-land. The engine roared, the digger bumped over the uneven, frosty ground, heading straight for its next target, an old hut made of wooden pallets with a cardboard roof. One of the last.

A few years earlier, this area had been shared by a municipal rubbish tip and a cemetery. Then the French state decided to use it as a place to park migrants who dreamed of reaching England. This morning, it was once again a rubbish tip. But when the digger's powerful claws dug into the ground, it was the cemetery that resurfaced.

Three arms became visible, so the workmen concluded there must be at least two bodies in the hole they'd dug at the edge of the camp. To judge by the length of the smallest of them, it belonged to a child. Somebody called the foreman on his walkie-talkie.

Hidden about twenty metres away, a shadow flitted among the trees bordering the Jungle, keeping the comings and goings of the machines in view. Unaware of this presence, the workmen gathered round the hole, stupefied by horror.

A workman looked up and saw the silhouette emerge from the forest. Dressed in rags, long greasy hair, skin that was black, brown, or simply filthy. The figure held a rusty machete pressed against his thigh. He advanced slowly, tapping the blade against his leg. None of the men was brave enough to block his path; they all took several steps back.

Reaching the hole, the menacing-looking stranger kneeled down and began scraping at the earth still covering the corpses. Frenetically at first, his gestures accompanied by animal grunts, more calmly after a while. He touched a leg, stroked a hand as though it were still alive. He raised the child's arm until it was right under his nose, sniffed it, and let it drop again. Rigid in death, it stayed pointing to the sky for several seconds before slowly easing back onto the earth.

Although it was broad daylight, the stranger remained barely more than a silhouette. A jumble of repugnant scraps of clothing, arms plunged into what was proving to be a mass grave. Suddenly, as if he had lost all hope, he abandoned his search. He stood up, his face a mask, and shambled away with the machete, vanishing into the forest once more.

The first police officer with concrete information called the public prosecutor, who was still hesitating over coming to the scene.

"Forensics are talking about seven bodies."

"Adults?"

"Not all of them."

"Complete?"

"Not all of them."

When the officer had finished his report, his colleague ventured a question.

"Why didn't you tell him about the guy with the machete?"

"I'm keeping that for the lieutenant. He's the only one really interested in this shithole. If I tell the prosecutor there's a strange guy with a machete here, we're going to have to find a strange guy with a machete. And going into that forest at night doesn't exactly appeal. Besides, we've been closing our eyes for almost two years – why open them today?"

PART ONE

ESCAPING

I

Damascus, Syria, June 2016
Section 215: Military Intelligence
Interrogation Room in the detention centre

The last blow had opened a deep cut above the man's eyebrow. He was naked, tied to a chair in a basement room, where his howls couldn't be heard through the thick walls. Blood trickled down to the dusty ochre tiles of the windowless room. Taking the prisoner by the scruff of his neck, Adam pressed his forehead against his own. Their sweat mingled.

"You will talk. No cause is sacred enough to help you bear the pain in store for you. Do you understand?"

At the far end of the room, Salim put a bottle of water warped by the heat down on a wooden table and wiped his mouth on his sleeve. Rising to his feet, he picked up a thick black electric cable. Solid and heavy; more effective than a baton. Walking round the prisoner, he said to Adam:

"Your sentences are too long, and there are no questions in them. It's obvious you have a desk job. He's knows what we want to hear. There's no point talking to him anymore."

He lashed out at the man's already swollen left knee, torn open and bleeding. The cable was raised twice more, brought down on exactly the same spot, where the nerves were raw. The pain was so intense the prisoner couldn't even cry out.

Slumped over, he kept on muttering the same phrase directed towards God. And since they both worshipped the same deity, this enraged Salim even more.

"And anyway, we're not getting anywhere just hitting him. I've been telling you for an hour we ought to use the acid . . ."

"Do you want answers, or just to destroy him?" Adam asked. "Acid makes them black out. There have to be moments of respite, otherwise it doesn't work. Acid attacks the skin for a long time afterwards, so they can't tell the difference between being tortured and being allowed a break from it."

Salim seemed surprised.

"So this isn't your first time? I thought you people at headquarters didn't like to do the dirty work."

"This one's special. He's mine. I don't want to miss a minute," Adam retorted, turning back to the prisoner.

Gripping the man's shoulder, he whispered in his ear:

"Can you hear me? I won't let you go."

Salim glanced at his watch and decided it was time for a cigarette break. When he returned to the room, he was accompanied by his superior officer, who complained how slowly the interrogation was going and dismissed Adam without even looking at him.

"Tell the ministry we don't need a chaperone. This one will talk, just like the others, whether you are here or not. And we're not going to break him with our fists."

Obeying orders, Adam allowed himself to be escorted to the door, but before it closed, he plucked up the courage to ask Salim:

"The acid?"

"No. *Basat al-reeh*."

The prisoner would be tied to a board, feet in the air and head hanging down. For an hour, the blood would accumulate in his skull, compressing his brain until he felt his eyes popping out of their sockets, about to explode. Only then would they start to kick him in the head.

And if that didn't make him talk, the acid would. Nobody could withstand the acid.

Adam returned to the ground floor in the private lift that only went to the building's basement rooms. Out in the open, he took a series of deep breaths to expel the rotten air still fouling his lungs. However hard he tried, the smell of blood and stale sweat remained embedded in his uniform.

To either side of him stood the Faculty of Medicine and the Faculty of Arts and Humanities, both situated in a neighbourhood of Damascus protected by the regime and left almost intact by the war as a result.

He thought of Aleppo, only three hundred and fifty kilometres further north. Its skeletal homes, where you could see inside rooms as if they were doll's houses. Its buildings devastated as far as the eye could see, none of them higher than two storeys. Its avenues lined with burned-out vehicles. And in the midst of the chaos, in the midst of all the police, the military, the noise of the army's vehicles and tanks, its terrified, cowed population was trapped in a game of Russian roulette.

Damascus. Adam was on the right side of the country and on the right side of those in power. A police officer for more than fifteen years, and now a loyal member of Bashar al-Assad's military police. No-one would have suspected him. He might even succeed in saving his wife and daughter before he was caught. There was very little time left.

He hailed a taxi and dived into it.

"Muhajirin, the main street."

"That's a very long street," the driver complained.

"The bottom of the hill will do fine."

Adam no longer trusted anyone. There was no way he was going to give his exact address to a stranger.

2

Six years earlier, when he had bought this apartment in a middle-class district of the city, Adam had not paid much attention to its name: *Muhajirin.* Those who travel. The migrants.

Turning the key twice in the lock, he swept in like a gust of wind. In the kitchen, Nora heard him and her heart beat faster. Even before she saw his face, she knew the moment had arrived. The moment they had been preparing for. The moment their lives depended on.

"Well?" she asked.

"He's been transferred to Section 215. He won't be able to stand it. Where's Maya?"

"In her room."

"You know what to do. Two suitcases, one each. I'll leave you to it, I have a call to make."

Nora kissed him on the mouth. Her lips were still moist from her tea. Adam's were dry with anguish. He turned on his heel and went into the hall. Removing the wooden panel over the water heater, he slipped his hand under the cylinder and pulled out a phone held in place by two sturdy lengths of tape. He dialled a number, dispensing with any greeting.

"This evening. For Nora and Maya. Is it still possible?"

"Aren't you going with them?"

"I'd only make it more dangerous for them. Tarek's been arrested."

"I know. Do you think he'll talk?"

"Of course he will. Now they've got their hands on someone from the Free Syrian Army, they'll take their time."

"Do they know we were behind Operation Pavel?"

"I hope not. I was with Tarek this morning, in the torture chamber, and he was resisting. He saved my life. But when they break him, because I promise you they *will* break him, he'll let slip my name and I'll be a target. My wife and daughter as well. They have to leave without me. I'll join them later. I'll do whatever I can."

"*In shaa Allah.*"

"Yes, he better had."

Nora finished packing her suitcase in less than a minute and came out to put it by the front door. As she reached the point where the two narrow corridors of their apartment met, she bumped into the hall desk. A framed photograph fell to the floor, smashing the glass. The memories spilled out, as if it was only the glass that had kept them in.

Maya's sixth birthday party.

Nora, her long, perfectly smooth black hair like a river of ink down over her shoulders. Maya with those curious eyes of hers, passionate about everything and incapable of keeping still, even for a simple snapshot. And the broad figure of Adam, his arms round them both. His athletic build had been particularly appreciated when he was a student at the police academy. The same academy an Isis bomber disguised as a policeman had blown up a few years later. Adam had picked up the remains of colleagues, former instructors, and some civilians.

Until then he had been a model policeman, perfectly

formatted, loyal to his country and its leader. Full of hope when a democratic wind had blown through Syria during the Arab Spring. Just as in Tunisia or Egypt, all of a sudden, the people realised it was possible to fight for their freedom.

But however noble this movement's aims, it was quickly stifled at the cost of thousands of lives, and Syria was engulfed in a civil war. Taking advantage of this weakness, Isis sank the claws of violence and obscurantism even deeper. There were now two executioners for one and the same victim: Bashar al-Assad's dictatorship and Isis fighting over the unarmed Syrian people.

It was following the army's violent suppression of the peaceful revolt that Adam had made his choice. Refusing to be nothing but a witness to his country's death agonies, he joined a rebel cell in the Free Syrian Army and became an opponent of the government in the most risky way. By infiltrating it as a member of the military police.

Whether it was chemical, in the same way that animals can sense anxiety and fear, or intuitive, as when one can understand one's loved ones without a word being spoken, for once Maya didn't make a fuss. She did as she was told, aware despite her young years that something serious was happening, and that she should keep her demands and questions for another day. From her bedroom, she could hear her father's voice.

"Spend the afternoon at Elyas's. This evening, he'll drive you to Beirut along the military road, and then you take a night flight to Tripoli in Libya. That will be the easy part. Go and fetch Maya while I call a taxi."

"Are we going to Uncle Elyas's?"

Nora turned to look at their daughter laboriously dragging her suitcase out of her bedroom, so small and innocent. She was suddenly aware how hazardous their imminent journey would be.

Adam went into the living room. Despite his size, he had to stand on tiptoe to reach the three volumes of *Fantômas* in French on the top shelf of the bookcase. Paris and its mysteries and intrigues, as written by Souvestre and Allain – with a passport hidden in each of them. He gave two to Nora and slid his own into his back pocket. From now on, the need to escape could arise at any moment.

At the bottom of the hill where the Muhajirin neighbourhood had sprung up, Adam repeated the instructions to his wife. More for reassurance than because it was strictly necessary – Nora already knew them by heart. They stood waiting for the taxi to arrive, suitcases by their sides like well-trained dogs. Maya remained unusually quiet, and her two parents couldn't help thinking their daughter had grown up all at once. Well-behaved. Determined. They asked themselves how much she understood of the situation, and how much escaped her. Suddenly their daughter's eyes widened, full of resigned sadness.

"Maya?" asked her worried mother.

The little girl hesitated a moment. Her father was bound to say she was being childish, but she couldn't keep it in very long.

"Monsieur Bou!"

Seeing no sign of their taxi anywhere in the distance, Adam gave in to his daughter's desperate plea. He sprinted up three floors and stood panting in her small pastel-coloured bedroom. He searched under the sheets and bed until finally, between two pillows, he found Monsieur Bou, a threadbare purple fluffy rabbit.

Ever since she was born, he had called his daughter by the

nickname Arnouba: my little rabbit. She had soon wanted a real one, but as Nora was allergic to animal fur, the fluffy Arnouba had appeared as a consolation. Maya never let him out of her arms. And in the way children have of mangling names, Arnouba was soon rebaptised Monsieur Bou.

Adam innocently imagined he would protect Maya during her journey through the most dangerous countries on the planet.

With Maya safely installed in the taxi and their suitcases in the boot, Nora and Adam kissed goodbye. Neither of them wanted to make this embrace especially intense. It had to be a normal kiss, as if it were unthinkable that it could be the last. But the tears that sprang unbidden to Nora's eyes put paid to that. They were desperately afraid for each other.

"I'll join you soon," Adam promised, opening the taxi door for her. "Call me from the hotel as soon as you reach Tripoli."

Maya breathed on the window and drew a heart in the condensation. When the taxi pulled away, she read an "I love you" on her father's lips.

PLANNED ROUTE FOR NORA'S
AND MAYA'S JOURNEY

ITALY

GREECE

Pozzallo

TUNISIA

MEDITERR

Tripoli

LIBYA

300 km

300 mi

1. DAMASCUS – BEIRUT
113 KM
2 H BY MILITARY ROAD

2. BEIRUT – AMMAN
238 KM
1 H 10 BY PLANE

3. AMMAN – TRIPOLI
2,147 KM
3 H 30 BY PLANE

4. TRIPOLI – POZZALLO
450 KM
1 TO 3 DAYS AT SEA

5. POZZALLO – CALAIS
2,585 KM
MANY DAYS AND WEEKS

TÜRKIYE

NEAN SEA

EGYPT

SYRIA

Beirut

LEBANON

ISRAEL

Damascus

Amman

JORDAN

3

Tripoli, Libya
Awal Hotel, in the city centre
Three a.m.

"What's the hotel like?" asked Adam.

As soon as they had arrived, Nora freed herself from Maya by plonking her in front of the television. But it had only taken ten minutes for her daughter to tire of the music channel's quickfire clips. She stepped down on to the thick fitted carpet and began to explore her luxury four-star hotel bedroom. Silky sheets, spacious bathtub and big windows through which she could see the lights of the Red Castle Museum on her right and the three-storey Ottoman clock tower on her left. Somewhere in the city a long burst of machine-gun fire blasted out, echoing off the walls of houses and apartment buildings. Any European child would have taken this for firecrackers or fireworks, but Maya, instinctively aware of what it meant, drew back sharply from the window.

She continued her explorations, heading for the adjoining room with the double bed where her mother had unpacked the things needed for a short, one-night stay. As she was about to enter, Nora, phone wedged between shoulder and ear, pushed her out with her foot and shut the door in her face.

"The hotel? It's perfect. But it's strange, all this luxury, when we know what's ahead of us."

"Is Maya alright?" asked Adam.

"Yes. More or less. But I think she caught a cold in the airport lounge during the stopover in Amman. We had to wait more than two hours there with the air-conditioning on full blast. She hasn't stopped coughing from the moment we took off."

"You should never have made this journey on your own. But getting you away from Damascus was the only way I could protect you. I'm so sorry."

"I forbid you to be sorry, *habibi*. You're doing all you can for us."

Adam remembered organising the trip three months earlier, when Operation Pavel had been launched and they had been forced also to envisage its failure. And with it, the evacuation of his family.

"Why not via Turkey?" Nora had objected, her finger on a map of the Middle East. "From Damas to Aleppo, then from Turkey to the Balkans. We won't even get our feet wet, and it's a much shorter journey to Europe."

"Do you know how many checkpoints there are from the south to the north of Syria, from Damascus to Aleppo?" Adam had objected. "Between the government and Isis, dozens of them. There are random checks as well. Whether all three of us travel, or if, for whatever reason, you and Maya have to go on alone, it'll be the same: I'm a Syrian government officer and at the first Isis checkpoint I'll be shot. And Maya and you . . ."

He found it hard to continue. In that case, death would be the kindest outcome.

"No. You have to take a civilian plane to Tripoli in Libya, then cross the Mediterranean and reach Italy. From there, you travel through Europe and join your cousin in England. Half a million migrants reach there every year, so there's no reason we shouldn't make it. The real problem is I'm part of the Bashar government, which means France will never give us refugee visas."

"But you're fighting against his government."

"Yes, that's true, but from inside, and discreetly enough for there to be no proof. So to reach England we'll have to do it illegally, via Calais. It'll take time, but we'll be patient. You've seen on Internet there's somewhere we can stay. They call it the 'Jungle'."

"It looks more like a refugee camp."

"Maybe, but the important thing is there's protected huts for women and children. I'll make sure I find a trafficker who can get us a place in a car or lorry, and we can take the ferry or the Eurotunnel. Your cousin will be waiting on the other side of the English Channel. He's promised to help us."

"I know you'd have preferred to stay in France."

"We don't have any family there. And I don't think France is the country I once knew. England will be perfect for us."

Back then, poring over the map of the Middle East in the warmth of their living room, with Maya's bedtime music in the background, it had seemed possible.

Now, in Tripoli, on her own with her daughter, Nora was terrified.

"Did you manage to see Tarek again?"

"Tomorrow afternoon. I've made another request to be present at his interrogation. I only hope I haven't drawn attention to myself. It feels as if the whole world has its eyes on me."

"It's normal to be paranoid, *habibi*: you're a hen disguised as a fox in a pack of wolves."

"I should never have described myself as that," Adam chuckled. "Now you're making a joke of it."

4

Port city of Garabulli, Libya
Five a.m.

After a few hours of disturbed sleep filled with nightmares, Nora gently shook her daughter's shoulder. When Maya opened her eyes, she smothered the child with warm kisses.

"Up you get, sweetheart. Today we're crossing the Mediterranean."

Maya clambered slowly out of bed and dragged herself to the bathroom, carrying Monsieur Bou by one leg.

Then they repacked their suitcases, which they had hardly disturbed.

In less than half an hour, the taxi picked them up from the hotel lobby and drove the forty kilometres from Tripoli to Garabulli, where they had a rendezvous at the exact time the driver dropped them off.

As day was dawning, they found themselves alone a few metres from a beach that seemed to stretch on forever. On one side, white sand dunes; on the other, a rocky promontory lashed by the waves. To anyone who didn't know its history, it looked wonderful. But six months earlier, when the migrants on board had rebelled against their traffickers, a boat coming from Egypt had capsized a few kilometres off the Libyan coast, and those same waves had deposited two hundred and forty-five dead bodies on Garabulli beach, as if returning them to mankind as a reproach for its stupidity.

An hour later, Ferouz, their contact, had still not appeared. They waited and waited, anxiously scrutinising the few people coming and going at that early hour, hoping on each occasion that somebody would approach them and identify them by their first names, as agreed. But no-one did.

In the distance down the bumpy road a cloud of dust appeared, announcing the arrival of a pick-up with a massive machine-gun mounted on the back, a handful of soldiers clustered round it. As the vehicle rolled by, Nora pushed Maya behind her and adjusted her veil so that her hair was properly covered: something she hadn't done since she married Adam. The pick-up continued on its way, but even though she lowered her eyes, she realised she had been noticed, assessed, judged.

At a quarter past six, migrant workers (most of them Nigerian) officially began the day, heading for back-breaking building sites or poorly paid odd jobs. At the same time, the first café opened its doors. They went in. If they contacted Adam now, he would only worry, and since they didn't have much choice, Nora decided it would be best to carry on waiting.

At seven o'clock, a man walked past the café window as if looking for someone. His advanced years and heavy belly gave him a weary look; the early morning heat threatened to make this even worse as the day progressed. When he went by a second time, still glancing all around him, Nora got up from their table. She made Maya promise not to move and stepped outside the café. The little girl watched her mother through the plate glass window. At first Nora kept a respectful distance from the stranger; then they exchanged a few words, and Maya saw her mother come to a halt and run her hands twice through her

30

hair. She knew these gestures well, and understood immediately their journey had hit an obstacle.

Coming back inside the café, Nora collapsed onto her chair and rummaged in her pocket for her phone.

"Aren't we leaving?" asked Maya.

"Let me call your father."

Adam's phone rang while he was in the shower. They had agreed Nora would call him as soon as she met their contact in Garabulli. He emerged from a cloud of steam and, so as not to risk losing the call, didn't bother to put on his bathrobe. Sitting naked on the sofa, he answered, pressing the handset to his soaking hair.

"Their boat was confiscated last night by the Italian coast-guard," Nora told him.

"Damn and blast it!" Adam exploded.

"Ferouz is suggesting we go in another boat, a Zodiac. This evening. It seems he knows the organisers. Do you trust him, Adam?"

"Ferouz? I barely trust the person who recommended him to me, and now he's passing you on to strangers. We didn't choose just any old boat. You were supposed to travel in the hold, protected from the weather all the way across to Italy. I find it hard to believe he's managed to find two places on a seaworthy craft overnight."

"He says the people with the Zodiac miscalculated, and they have too many Afghanis."

"Is that a problem?"

"Yes, apparently it is. They try to mix nationalities. If there are too many people from one country and there's trouble on the journey, they could gang up and take over the boat. So they're going to get rid of about twenty Afghans and they're looking for Sudanese and Syrians to replace them. The good thing is they also take responsibility for the journey from Italy up through Europe as far as Calais. Perhaps I could wait for you in that Jungle place, where women and children are protected? That would be safer than staying in Italy, where we'd risk being picked up and sent back to Syria. It seems there are no police in the Jungle – at least, that's what Ferouz says."

She heard Adam sigh. He sounded perplexed, at a loss. She could just picture him.

"No," he decided eventually. "That's too many changes, too much uncertainty. Go back to the hotel and wait for me to call. I'll think of another way."

"I know you'll find a good solution. Don't worry about us."

"You're asking the impossible, Nora."

Just as he was about to enquire after Maya, the doorbell rang. His heart skipped a beat.

"I have to go. Don't go anywhere else – return to the hotel straightaway. Don't accept anything from anybody, be suspicious of everyone. I'll contact you in an hour."

At the second ring of the bell, Adam wrapped a towel round his waist; at the third he opened the door. Standing there was a soldier of lower rank than him.

"Captain Sarkis?"

Adam nodded, eyeing him coolly to demonstrate his superior status.

"You're wanted at Section 215."

Adam immediately thought of Tarek. Had he cracked? No-one can withstand torture indefinitely: it makes even the innocent confess. Though his brain was racing, he was careful not to let it show.

"Two minutes. I'll put on my uniform."

Closing the door, and trying desperately not to make any noise, he lifted off the wooden cover over the water heater and took out his secret phone. The soldier was waiting patiently outside the front door, just a few metres away. Holding his breath, Adam carefully replaced the cover, and headed into the kitchen with the phone, removing the SIM card on the way. He opened the microwave, put the card in and turned the heat to maximum. In four seconds, the card began to swell and give off sparks. At 800 watts, all the information stored on it was trashed. He threw it in the bin and went to put on his uniform. If the day was going to end badly, no-one would be able to trace the number that kept him in contact with his cell in the Free Syrian Army.

He picked up his everyday phone, looked himself over in the mirror, and opened the door again.

"I'm ready."

5

Section 215: Military Intelligence
Command post

He hadn't been ordered to appear; he'd been escorted. A nuance. Besides, Tarek's session wasn't due to start until five that afternoon, and it was only ten in the morning when they passed through the first checkpoints outside the government building on 6th May Street in Damascus.

All around them were busy-looking hotels, boutiques and shopping centres. It was as if the darker side of the capital was nothing but an urban myth. A torture centre? In the heart of the city? You'd have to be crazy to think that.

A military salute. Identity check. A soldier swept a pole-mounted mirror under their vehicle to make sure there was no bomb. A second one inspected the interior, then their saloon car could set off again. Adam stayed calm even when they didn't head for the interrogation block but towards the building for officers and NCOs.

An escort, an unexpected time of day, and an unexpected destination. Too many surprises: things didn't look good. For an instant, Adam imagined himself whipping out his gun, putting a bullet in the driver's head, grabbing the wheel and racing out of the compound as fast as he could, hoping to avoid the gunfire aimed at him. As this last desperate scenario flashed through his mind, he realised he still had his gun. Did that mean they trusted him enough to keep it? If they were suspicious, wouldn't they have taken it from him at the entrance? He concentrated on controlling his breathing.

When they reached the command post, the soldier asked Adam to follow him. They went down corridors and past offices until he found himself in the waiting room of the general in charge of Section 215. The man who, twenty-four hours earlier, had ordered him out of the torture chamber because he was getting nowhere.

Uncomfortably seated on a metal chair beneath the official portrait of the Syrian president, Adam counted the seconds as if they were miniature eternities. Then the door opened.

"Captain Sarkis!"

Adam sprang up, snapped to attention and addressed his superior officer.

"At your orders, General Khadour."

As the senior officer stuck out his hand, Adam studied him: genial-looking, radiant from pink-cheeked good health, his paunch testifying to an easy life.

"Take a seat in my office, captain. We have a lot to talk about, don't we?"

Blinds down, a cigarette expiring in a stone ashtray, and on the back wall a huge black-and-white photograph of 1960s Damascus. Adam managed to take this much in before the other man spoke.

"If I'm to believe the report I received, you wanted to be present at the questioning of a prisoner?" said Khadour.

"Affirmative, General sir. Tarek Jebara."

The general wrinkled his nose as if the room had suddenly been filled with manure.

"You give him too much importance by naming him. Prisoner 465 is sufficient, don't you think?"

The fact that all the general's statements ended with a question reminded Adam of how the affable, welcoming person sitting opposite him operated. Over months and years, prisoner after prisoner, asking questions, extracting answers through fear, threats and violence, again and again. And today, he was the one facing the questioning.

"Yes, Prisoner 465, General sir. This afternoon, if the information I have is correct."

"It is. Your information is reliable," the general said amicably. "Unfortunately, the same can't be said of your prisoner. We brought forward his interrogation for internal organisational reasons. He didn't survive. Tedious, isn't it?"

Adam was facing one of two possibilities. Either Tarek had talked, or he had held out. Either Adam would live, or he would spend the next few days answering more questions from General Khadour. His pulse racing, a knot in his stomach, he kept his hands on the chair armrests to keep them from trembling. He had no choice but to continue playing his role.

"Did we at least get the information we wanted?"

"Not really. I was impressed by his courage and tenacity. He even earned the right to special treatment. The treatment I reserve for honourable prisoners. 465 is the kind of man I'd have liked to have on our side. Despite all our best efforts, he revealed only one thing."

The general said no more, and for the first time his sentence did not end with a question. As if he knew.

He knew: Adam was sure of it.

"Since 465 is dead, your timetable is quite empty, and I'd like to take advantage of that. You have no objection, I hope?"

Before Adam could reply, the general removed any hierarchical difficulties.

"Don't worry, I have informed your commanding officer. You are . . . how did he put it?"

He pretended to be thinking this over for a moment, then declared:

"At my disposal. That's it! He said: 'Captain Sarkis is entirely at your disposal.'"

With this he lapsed into what for Adam was an excruciating silence. Khadour drew a file closer, leafed through the pages, and came to a stop at a sheet which had a photograph of Adam pinned to the top corner.

"Father a diplomat, handling Franco–Syrian relations," he read, as if this was the first time he had seen the CV. "Sixteen years with the police, ten as an officer. In 2012 you requested a transfer to the military police, where you have had a distinguished career for four years. Numerous citations, a medal for bravery, wounded in service. You must be proud of your record?"

Adam unconsciously raised his hand to his face to touch the deep comma-shaped scar on his left cheekbone. A grenade, according to his file, and that wasn't far from the truth. A booby-trapped car while Adam was ordering a takeaway coffee. A blast that blew in the café window and sent shards of glass flying like tiny harpoons. Six dead. He was a police officer, and the press needed a hero. Adam was promoted to captain. He wasn't proud of his medal, his promotion or his wound.

"Do you know what worries me more than a service record littered with dismissals, cautions and warnings?" continued the general. "It's a file that has none of them. I don't like good students, those who come first, the favourites. They often conceal manipulators. And on top of that, you're a Christian."

"At least that means you can be sure I'm not an Isis militant."

Taken aback, the general raised an eyebrow then burst out laughing. He stared hard at Adam, as if weighing him up.

"What do you know about Operation Pavel, Captain Sarkis?"

Adam was surprised at how well he managed to control his reactions; his voice did not betray the fact that it was an operation he had instigated.

"Commander Pavel Oljenko is a military adviser sent by our Russian allies. A fortnight ago, an active cell of the Free Syrian Army made an attempt to kidnap him, but so far the only person we have succeeded in identifying and arresting is Tarek . . . I'm sorry, Prisoner 465. Your section did all they could to get him to talk. Until this morning."

Adam carefully avoided the details he was supposed to be unaware of. That Pavel Oljenko, the former head of Russian operations in Chechnya, was a chemical warfare expert, using his knowledge to help Syrian government. Kidnapping and getting a filmed confession out of him would have been a major coup, proving to international observers that Bashar al-Assad was using "dirty" weapons against rebels and the civilian population. After that, supporting his regime would have been hard to justify. Shunned like a leper, the tyrant would have seen his reign teeter. That had been the somewhat optimistic aim of Operation Pavel.

"You were assigned to the investigation into the kidnapping from the start, weren't you?" Khadour went on. "At your own request, according to my sources. What I don't understand is why you asked to be present at the interrogation sessions. It's rare for an officer from headquarters to want to visit the basement of Section 215, isn't it?"

Adam felt as if he were juggling with chainsaws. He weighed each word carefully.

"Your men are known for being heavy-handed. My aim isn't to torture, but to obtain information. I sometimes feel that aspect is secondary here. No disrespect to you or your men, General sir."

"Is that the only reason?"

On the black-and-white photograph on the wall behind the general, Adam noticed a couple holding hands among the crowd of people immortalised that day. It was enough to remind him of Nora who, if she had listened to him, must by now be safely back in her Tripoli hotel.

"Captain Sarkis?"

Adam's mind had wandered for a second too long.

"Yes. I can't see any other reason."

Without a word, the general stood up to leave the office, and Adam did the same. Outside, two armed guards were waiting for them. Adam touched the inside pocket of his jacket to feel the bulk of his phone. It wouldn't be long before the general abandoned his friendly attitude and reverted to the man Adam had met the day before. By now, his apartment had surely been turned upside down by soldiers, and the name Sarkis would be on every search list everywhere, putting Nora and Maya in danger. There was no way they should wait for him any longer. He had to make the call so they got out of North Africa as soon as possible, whatever the consequences.

Outside the building, the same saloon was waiting for them, engine idling. The soldiers opened the doors for the two officers, then sat in the front. Adam and the general did not renew their conversation, if that's what it had been.

"The military airport," ordered Khadour.

A jeep pulled out ahead of them, another followed behind. The general never travelled without such protection. Sirens wailing, the convoy travelled the twenty-two kilometres to their destination.

At the airport, its seemingly endless runways covered with weeds, the driver pulled up outside a shuttered hangar about thirty metres long by ten wide. The horizon shimmered in the heat like petrol fumes about to catch fire, as though it were the threshold of hell.

The general stepped out of the car, but when Adam went to follow him, he found his door was locked. The two soldiers fell in behind Khadour, and Adam was left on his own. By now, he reckoned his chances of surviving the day were almost nil; his thoughts turned to Nora and Maya. As discreetly as possible, he slipped his hand inside his jacket pocket, took out his phone, and tapped out a message.

Listen to Ferouz. Get out as quickly as possible. Go to Calais. Contact your cousin. He'll know what to do. I love you.

Tapping again several times, he deleted his contacts and messages as a security measure. As he was putting away the phone, his door opened and the baking heat outside flooded the interior once more. A uniformed soldier told him to follow him.

They came to a halt outside the hangar, by a metal filing cabinet with four numbered drawers. While the soldier was unlocking the nearest one, Adam looked in vain for the general.

"Weapon and phone, Captain."

Adam did as he was told. As he handed them over, the two hangar doors slowly creaked open, offering him a moment's respite. He glanced at his watch: 11.35 a.m., the exact time Maya was born. He thanked the heavens for giving him this life, however it might end.

6

Port city of Garabulli, Libya
Two p.m.

Nora had told Maya that her papa would join them later. Seeing her mother's pallid face, the little girl had pretended to believe her.

This time, Ferouz was waiting for them in the café. He was sweating, and gulped down the glass of cold water brought with his scalding hot tea. Spluttering, he got his breath back thanks to two small unpleasant belches. A stuffed-full plastic bag lay between his feet. Nora plugged her ear-buds into her phone and put them on Maya, loading her favourite lullaby, *A vava invouva*, on a loop.

"You don't look well," said Ferouz with concern.

Nora didn't raise her eyes.

"I've got the confirmation," he went on. "You leave at sunset. A Zodiac military dinghy. Libyan army surplus, with room for two hundred people."

"As many as that?"

"That's the minimum. They'll cram it full, like they always do, so it'll be more like three hundred. Places are worth more than gold, they're worth blood."

Hearing this, Nora checked her daughter wasn't listening.

"About that. Two places in less than twenty-four hours, what's that going to cost us?" she asked suspiciously.

Ferouz waved a ponderous arm for another glass of water.

"As I said, you're replacing an Afghan family, so it won't cost more than expected. Two thousand for you, a thousand for the little one. And then there's the journey overland through Europe to Calais. That's another two thousand each. Seven thousand dollars in total. Everything paid in advance, though I don't like the idea."

Nora had a little less than nine thousand dollars on her. Adam had emptied their accounts, sold everything disposable – at a quarter of its value, of course, because business done in a hurry or under duress is the worst kind. She hesitated.

"Are you sure about this Jungle? Does it even still exist? And are women and children really protected?"

"If France is no longer taking in any war refugees, I think you can forget about staying there. You've seen the camp on the Internet, haven't you, so why the doubts? I've also got this for you . . ."

He pushed the plastic bag forward with his foot. He took out two life jackets, two bowls, ten or so chocolate energy bars, a plastic wallet for their passports and money that she could tie round her waist, and another waterproof pouch for her phone to go round her neck.

"Our suitcases are full," Nora objected.

"You already have one too many, and you'll have to empty half the things out of the other one."

"That's impossible! All we have left of our lives is in them!"

Ferouz reacted indignantly.

"Don't be stupid. Your life is listening to music alongside you. Believe me, the lighter you travel, the better. Now go to the toilet and choose the essentials. I'll keep what you leave behind – it'll pay me back for the jackets and chocolate. Be quick, I'll keep my eye on the little one."

Staring into the mirror in the toilets, Nora allowed the tears to fall. If she saw the glass as half full, Adam had sent her a message: that meant he was alive and could move about freely. If it was half empty, he was asking her not to wait for him, and to go and find her cousin in England, as if he was unlikely to catch up. She smashed the imaginary glass and thought only of Maya.

After lightening her load of memories and clothes, Nora went back upstairs and sat down again at the table.

"Is your little one ill?" asked Ferouz. "She's coughing and she looks pale."

"She'll be alright."

"You must know it's not a good idea to undertake the crossing when you're ill."

"She'll be okay."

"I'm not the one you have to convince. Just think if she passes it on to the others. It's not so easy to cross Europe with a group of migrants with forty-degree temperatures. They might even refuse to take you."

"I'm telling you she'll be fine. And we'll be careful."

"It's up to you. If you're ready, all I have to do is introduce you to tonight's guides."

Nora wanted everything clear.

"How much do I owe you for all this?"

Ferouz mopped his brow, put away his already soaking cotton handkerchief, then stroked Maya's hair with a smile.

"You're about to set off on a long journey to England. And as you're going on your own with your daughter, it's even more dangerous. Keep your money. And take care."

Nora, who had been so suspicious of him, now had to restrain herself from giving him a hug. As they were leaving the café, Maya was less inhibited, and planted a child's big kiss on Ferouz's damp cheek.

7

Damascus, Syria
Military airport

By now, the ten-metre-high metal hangar doors were wide open. Given Adam's position, it was inevitable that he had contemplated death. He hadn't expected to be meeting it in person, amid the foul stench of blood, flesh, putrefaction, and clothes soiled with excrement. In front of him on huge plastic tarpaulins lay neat rows of almost three hundred dead bodies, grey-skinned, faces contorted, limbs awry.

At this hour of the day, the hangar's glass roof allowed the sun's rays to heat the interior so much it was ten degrees hotter than outside, and the stench was that much more unbearable.

"Normally they're taken to the military hospital at Mezzeh, but that's full to overflowing," said the soldier, moving through the rows in front of Adam.

"Are they all Syrian fighters?"

"Negative, Captain. Civilians. All civilians. Traitors."

A photographer pushed in front of them, kneeled down beside one of the corpses and took a series of photos. The soldier jerked his chin at him.

"He's your mission. The photographer. You have to keep your eye on him and make sure he gives you each roll of film once it's full. General Khadour will be back this afternoon. He says you're his new right-hand man."

Adam avoided asking about the fate of his predecessor.

"What about my things?"

"General's orders. You don't need your weapon, and phones are forbidden. Only rolls of photographs can leave here. Come on, I'll introduce you."

Seeing them approach, the photographer straightened up and saluted Captain Sarkis. The soldier took advantage to leave them to it.

"Good morning, Captain."

The air in the hangar was so foul Adam almost retched. The photographer saw this and commented:

"I wish I could tell you that you'll get used to it, Captain. But no, the smell will stay with you even at home."

Adam instinctively extended his hand. The gesture took the photographer by surprise, and it was a while before he reciprocated.

"Adam. Call me captain only when the general is here."

"Whatever you say. My name is Samir."

A twin-seater plane and a helicopter had been moved to the side of the hangar to leave room for this human abattoir, which filled the entire space.

"I still can't take in what I'm seeing, Samir."

"I'm glad to hear it."

The photographer walked over to another body before explaining.

"Every morning the bodies of civilian prisoners are brought here. At first it was ten or so a day, but over the past few weeks that's accelerated. Today we've received the overflow from Mezzeh Hospital. They're supposed to keep them, but they've run out of room – that's why there are hundreds here. It's going to take us all day, and most of the night too."

He stepped back to show Adam part of the dead body they were standing next to.

"Look there, level with the collarbone. They're marked with the sector where they were arrested, followed by their prisoner number, and I add my own number, take a photo and move on to the next one. When I've used up a roll, I hand it to my officer."

Adam surveyed a row of bodies and saw they all bore the same inscription: 215. Every one of them came from General Khadour's torture centre.

"Now you mention your officer, have you any idea why I'm replacing him?"

"I don't think he could stand it anymore. Khadour sacked him. I wouldn't be surprised if I have to take his mugshot in here one of these days."

"What about you? How can you bear it?"

Samir seemed taken aback by his superior officer's question.

"Because they're traitors. Because it's right."

Adam said nothing. The photographer repeated himself, as if he needed his confirmation to stay sane.

"It is right, isn't it?"

"Yes, Samir, it's right," Adam reassured him, gritting his teeth.

There in front of him was absolute proof of the secret, widespread and meticulously planned extermination of anyone who opposed the Bashar al-Assad regime.

"The next one will be number six thousand," murmured Samir.

He kneeled down and took out his indelible marker pen to

write the number on the collar bone. But the man's skin, from chin down to his chest, was so bruised and battered it would be impossible to read. Instead Samir chose the forehead, where he wrote 9/24: today's ninth roll of film, photograph 24. Adam studied the corpse. Teeth smashed. Fingernails torn out. Broken nose.

"Next to the chopper there's a table with a register. You have to note the time and serial number whenever you authorise a new roll of film. Here, I'm finished with this one."

In the palm of his hand, Adam held twenty-four virtually weightless deaths he imagined had been as slow as they were violent. He walked round the edge of the hangar so as not to have to pass through all the bodies, signed the register, and picked up a new roll, writing down its particulars. By the prisoners' numbers, he read the cause of death.

Accident.

Suicide.

Cardiac arrest.

Those appeared to be the only options: the word "torture" was nowhere to be seen. He looked up from the register, turned, and surveyed the makeshift charnel house. There was a corpse right in front of him. The man's skull was spilt open in several places, and instead of eyes there were just two black holes edged with dried blood. As far as he knew, tearing out someone's eyes was no way to gain information. This was no longer torture: it was a murderous frenzy. The only aim was to kill while inflicting as much pain as possible. With enough refinement and imagination that a certain amount of pleasure in the work could not be ruled out.

Adam approached the corpse. What he saw almost made him cry out in terror. On the collar bone was marked the

48

number 215, and beside it the prisoner's number: 465. Adam couldn't help recalling what General Khadour had said: "I was impressed by his courage and tenacity. He even earned the right to special treatment. The treatment I reserve for honourable prisoners. 465 is the kind of man I'd have liked to have on our side."

Tarek.

Samir called to him from the far end of the hangar.

"Captain? Where's the roll?"

Adam walked over to him, forcing himself to stay calm as he tried to catch his breath. His mind was in such a whirl he had to take great care with every step he took. He thought of Nora and Maya. Tarek hadn't talked, and against all expectations, he himself was still alive. That meant they absolutely must wait for him.

"How can you make a call from in here?"

"There's no line. You can't. We're searched when we come in and when we leave, and while we're in here they watch every move we make. Let's just say the atmosphere is slightly paranoid."

Adam followed the photographer's gaze. Every five metres along the roof above them were cameras, apparently covering the entire hangar.

"Think of it as the work of an archivist. We classify and register in order to leave an administrative record, like a kind of census. For History's sake. But no information can be allowed to filter out. That's why you're here."

"How long have you been doing this?"

"A little more than two years. Every day."

Adam knew he had to get out of there as soon as possible. He wouldn't be able to save his country. All that mattered now were his wife and daughter. He was going to escape from Syria by whatever means possible. And let those who might say he could have stayed to fight for his people go screw themselves. Or come here, to this stifling hangar, and count the suicides with their burned feet and torn-out teeth.

8

Port city of Garabulli, Libya
Six p.m.

Ferouz had taken care of the payment and reassured himself about the crossing. The Zodiac dinghy was more than fifteen metres long and seemed almost new. The two Libyan people traffickers had said there was a depression moving away and the tail of a storm that was blowing itself out. The window of opportunity was brief, but they were used to it. On a marine map they showed Ferouz what they said was bad weather followed by an anticyclone. All he could make out was a series of coloured blotches between Libya and Italy.

They spoke the same language, and yet *"No danger"* was constantly on the smugglers' lips, a kind of linguistic tic everyone could understand.

"You might get thrown around a bit," Ferouz summarised for Nora's benefit. "You'll need to expect waves, but they'll be calming down. If everything goes well, the storm will have passed by the time you're out at sea."

As Ferouz spoke, Nora was doing up Maya's lifejacket. Steady, mechanical movements, even though her entire body was shaking.

"Above all, wear your veil properly. Hide your face. You're pretty, and so is your daughter. You mustn't let anyone see that.

Don't ever take your lifejacket off, and go to the middle of the boat, with Maya between your legs."

The little girl left her mother's arms and rushed into Ferouz's embrace. He was far more touched by this show of emotion than he would have cared to admit.

"Aren't you coming?" asked Maya.

The traffickers enlisted the help of some of the stronger migrants, and as night fell, they were positioned on both sides of the Zodiac to push it down the beach to the water. Suddenly, an army pick-up truck appeared at the top of the dune concealing the boat. It braked in a cloud of sand and a powerful spotlight was trained on the migrants, picking them out as if it were broad daylight. Everybody on board the dinghy held their breath, reluctant to believe their journey could come to such a precipitous end. One of the traffickers raised an arm towards the soldiers, whose palms had been generously greased that morning. The spotlight was abruptly extinguished, leaving them all blinded. The next few seconds passed in complete darkness; the threat slowly subsided as the noise of the pick-up engine died in the distance.

As more passengers were crammed in among the already compact mass of refugees, a wave struck the boat side on, throwing a dense spray of several hundred litres of salt water over them. They were still by the beach, but they were already drenched and freezing cold. It was five hundred kilometres to the port of Pozzallo in Italy. It might take one night, just as easily three.

Nora was crushed in the depths of the boat, trying to protect Maya from the chaos with her arms. A woman and her daughter sat right on top of them, but she didn't dare protest.

They were the mirror image of her and Maya: another story, another country, another war. Two young black kids pushed in on her left, while another tried to slide underneath her. When he didn't succeed, seeing Maya was terrified and about to burst into tears, he began to play the big brother and sat down to shield them, head between his knees. Some of the migrants began to complain the boat was full, that they were going to topple overboard, so the traffickers shouted that everybody was to remove their lifejackets and store them between their legs. Everyone agreed reluctantly, and the boat set off without any further protests. The start of their journey was accompanied only by prayers of hope murmured in different languages and dialects. Maya tried hard, but she couldn't stifle her hacking cough. One of the people smugglers shone his torch over the huddled passengers, searching for where the sound was coming from. Nora pressed her hand so tightly over her daughter's mouth Maya could hardly breathe.

Crossing from Libya to Italy
Eleven p.m.
Fourth hour of the journey

There was no need to have the slightest notion of navigation to understand what the problem was. The waves had been against them from the start; they progressed only slowly, metre by metre. If this was the tail of a storm, it must have been a massive one.

The cold seemed to have lodged itself right inside their bodies, in their flesh and bones. The slightest spray lashed their skins with icy water.

One trafficker was at the tiller; the other was sitting a few metres from Nora and Maya. He kept hearing the sick girl coughing, but so far he'd had been unable to pick her out. He was on the alert, waiting for it to start again. Maya was almost suffocating; she was trying so hard to stifle her cough that when it came, it shattered like glass fragments. The trafficker's gaze alighted directly on her.

To avoid creating a disturbance or panic, the man at the tiller opened the throttle so that the noise from the ancient outboard motor covered his words as he ordered his companion:

"Throw her overboard."

"Now?"

"We can get rid of her more easily at sea than in a car park. She's been coughing the whole time. We don't want to get caught when we've put them on the trucks in Italy."

The boat was filled with two hundred and seventy-three migrants. An assortment of ages, sexes, origins, skin colours. Tossed about, soaked to the skin, freezing cold, terrorised.

"I don't think I can do it. You go."

A sigh of irritation. Nothing more. The man let go of the tiller and shoved his way through to a woman in the middle of the boat. As he drew near, the woman tightened her grip on the body enfolded in her arms. She pressed her hand on the little girl's cold mouth, praying for her to stop coughing. Frightened, the child dropped her threadbare fluffy purple rabbit. The man crushed it underfoot without even noticing. He shouted at the woman.

"Your little girl. You have to push her overboard."

Nora refused to respond. The black kid who had tried to protect them seemed to understand their language because he stood up, ready to defend them. The trafficker kicked him violently in the face, almost knocking him out. The other woman and her daughter who had squashed in on top of Nora wriggled as far away as possible from the danger. The man went up to Maya, arm outstretched.

The trafficker made his way back to the rear of the boat, hand raised to his scratched cheek, blood on his fingers. The other man looked at him in disgust.

"Did she do that?"

"I'll try again when she's asleep."

"A woman . . .' the first man mocked him.

"Shut the fuck up."

Two a.m.
Seventh hour of the voyage

Seven hours of cramps and cold.

Every five minutes, Nora's body slumped, her mind went blank, her eyelids drooped – until her subconscious jerked her awake again. The night was black as ink, and her eyes could pick nothing out around her. All she could hear was shivering breaths and clothes rubbing against each other as the boat juddered, the ever-taller waves lurking around them like invisible monsters, occasionally snapping at the hull and spitting out foam.

Another five minutes went by and she again let herself drift into a soothing swirl of sleep. But this time it was Maya's coughing that roused her from her torpor. A torch immediately pointed in their direction. Bodies stirring, groans. Blinded, Nora could only listen with anguish as the noise drew closer to them. Two arms seized a child first by an arm – a cry of fear – then by a leg – her heart stopped beating – and sent her crashing into the water, flung overboard like a sack of ballast.

Between Nora's legs, Maya had another coughing fit; the smuggler realised he'd made a mistake. The other mother struggled to her feet and rushed to the side, balancing on the dinghy's rubber skirt. She plunged her hands into the water, shouting the name of her child, already swallowed by the towering waves. She didn't jump in after her. Perhaps she couldn't swim. Nor did she turn to face the smuggler. Perhaps she didn't have the courage. Instead, she threw herself at Nora, whose sick daughter had made her lose her own. Grabbing her by the hair, she hurled insults at her from the depths of her despair. Two men quickly separated them before they provoked a general tumult and capsize the Zodiac.

The trafficker didn't make the same mistake again. Maya was torn from the bottom of the boat, her hands clutching uselessly. A moment when she floated in mid-air, an instant of weightlessness, then her body struck the surface of the water.

Seeing her daughter disappear overboard, Nora was unable to make a sound. She flung herself onto the side of the boat, thrust her hands into the water searching for a body, a piece of clothing, a lock of hair to grab on to, but in vain. She recognised the voice of the other woman, still hysterical, still screaming and insulting her. She felt two hands pushing at her back, lost her balance and toppled into the water. A huge wave lifted the boat and dropped it again ten metres away. In the icy water she saw the torch beam become fainter and fainter, before it was snuffed out completely. On board the Zodiac, things returned to normal: the danger had been averted, and order restored.

In the water, Nora shrieked Maya's name a hundred times, then gave up. She hadn't moved from the same place in the boat for seven hours; her limbs were so numb she found it hard to stay afloat. When her calf muscle cramped, Nora slowly began to sink. She held her breath for as long as she could, but finally surrendered and inhaled deeply, filling her lungs with salt water.

*

Her hand brushed gently against the Mediterranean seabed, followed by an arm, then the rest of her body, until finally her head settled as though on a pillow of sand, her hair a garland of black flowers.

9

Damascus, Syria
Military airport
Two a.m.

The camera flash lit up the hangar for the three-hundred and sixteenth time. Adam understood a little better how Samir had been able to put up with this for such a long time. By the end of his first day, the dead bodies were already nothing more than abstract compositions, the work of a painter with a hugely perverse monochrome red palette. Thinking like this was probably the only way to avoid losing your mind.

Another full roll. The fourteenth. Adam no longer smelled the blood, he had its metallic taste on his palate, in his nostrils, on his tongue. All at once, the doors of the hangar slid open behind him far enough to allow in a 4x4 with tinted windows. General Khadour stepped out as soon as the vehicle door was opened for him.

Samir and Adam straightened up and stood to attention like dutiful soldiers. The echo in the hangar added a slightly theatrical touch to the general's already deep voice.

"Captain Sarkis! I knew I could count on you!"

He strode over to Adam.

"A man who isn't afraid of watching his own prisoner being

tortured is capable of anything. And we should be capable of anything in this war, shouldn't we?"

"At your orders, General sir," was all Adam replied.

"You need to be back here at six tomorrow morning. The morgue at Saidnaya prison is also asking for a helping hand."

"That leaves barely four hours' sleep for our photographer," Adam said, in a tone that suggested he was already invested in his new role.

This took the general aback: he was not accustomed to his men contradicting him. Adam tried to justify himself:

"The greatest military leaders know they have to look after their troops to win wars. From Caesar to Napoleon."

"Caesar," Khadour repeated to himself, flattered by the comparison. "Fine, be here by nine o'clock – that is Caesar's decree," he told the photographer.

With that he climbed back into his 4x4, the doors slamming shut.

Outside the hangar, Adam headed for the cabinet where his personal possessions had been stored. The soldier handed him his weapon and then stood on guard again.

"What about my phone?" asked Adam anxiously.

"It's being sent tomorrow to the service department. To be returned within forty-eight hours. General's orders."

Adam stifled a strong impulse to push the man up against the wall and show him who was boss. He clenched his fists helplessly: there was nothing to be done but follow orders. Walking past him, Samir could see how vexed he was.

"It's nothing personal, Captain," the photographer assured him. "You're just being checked. Everybody working here has to go through the same process. I told you how paranoid this place is."

The two men walked together across the tarmac. A few metres further on, Adam asked Samir a favour.

"Could you lend me your phone a moment? I just need to call my wife. I didn't think I was going to finish in the middle of the night, and she must be worried sick."

Samir glanced at him, and for the first time Adam saw fear mixed with embarrassment in his eyes.

"I'm really sorry, Captain. I prefer not to. You haven't been authorised yet. I hope you understand?"

Adam forced himself to smile. He realised that by asking this favour he was like one of those people who beg you to take a bag through customs for them at the airport. The photographer was right to be suspicious.

"With General Khadour on our case, I reckon it's best to follow instructions. Don't worry, my wife can wait," he said lightly.

He was taken back to his neighbourhood by an army driver. The two men didn't exchange a word all the way through the sleeping city. When they reached the bottom of Muhajirin hill, Adam got out and pretended to walk up the street to his apartment. As soon as the jeep turned a corner, he retraced his steps and hailed a taxi. He glanced at his watch: half past two in the morning. After travelling for three kilometres, he had the man drop him in front of a cybercafé. He pushed open the door. The manager, a man in his thirties wearing a T-shirt and headphones round his neck, took a good look at him then gestured for him to step into the back room, even though at that time of the morning there were only two insomniac internet users surfing the net, oblivious to their presence. As he went past the sound system, which was playing haunting electronic music, he turned up the volume.

Adam didn't have a second to lose, and stress made him gabble his words.

"Tarek is dead, there was nothing I could do, I tried right to the end to get him out of there. But I'm sure he didn't talk: the proof is I'm here now. Nora and Maya left this evening – I have to join them. I don't have a phone anymore, I need one now, with a sim card that allows international calls."

"Do you want an ordinary mobile?"

"No, a smartphone with Internet."

"Does Elyas know you're leaving Syria?"

"Not yet, but I hope he'll be able to help me."

The store manager disappeared for a moment, then came back with the phone and something wrapped in an oily cloth.

"Do you want a gun?"

"I'm leaving as a civilian – it would only cause problems. I have to go back to the apartment. My suitcase is packed and I have money for the journey. But I need you to write down Ferouz's number because I've forgotten it."

Adam went out into the cool night air. His watch was showing three o'clock.

His first call was to Nora, but it went straight to her voice-mail. He imagined she must have tried to call him several times while he was stuck in the gruesome hangar, and that after failing to get through she had switched off her phone to save the battery. So he called Ferouz.

So as not to wake his wife, Ferouz hauled his bulky body out of bed and sat on the floor in the corridor of his home. To reassure Adam, he promised he had waited until the boat had set off, and that by now Nora would probably be able to glimpse the Italian coast. When he also mentioned how enchanting Maya was, tears gathered in Adam's eyes.

"If they've left North Africa they must be safe. I have to call

Elyas to arrange the journey to Libya, and you need to find me a boat."

"Trust me," said Ferouz sincerely.

After this, Adam couldn't help calling his wife a second time, to leave her a message.

Three thousand kilometres away, five hundred metres under the sea, the ring tone of Nora's phone broke the silence of her tomb. There was oxygen trapped inside the airtight pouch, which was now trying to rise to the surface. Held back by the cord round Nora's neck, it danced in the water. As Adam's call came through, the screen emitted a blue-tinged halo, as if revealing a crime scene.

"Nora, it's me. I'm so sorry to have scared you, but I promise I really thought that . . . Listen, don't worry, I'll be there in a few days, a week at most. I had to change phones, so learn this new number by heart. As we said, wait for me at the safest spot, the huts for women in the Calais Jungle. I'll find you; I promise I'll find you! Then it will be our new life, Nora. Our new life!"

PART TWO

WAITING

10

Calais
July 2016

Even if Bastien leaned right out of the window of their new third floor apartment, he couldn't glimpse any sign of a wave or a blue horizon. To end up in Calais without even seeing the sea: it sucks, his daughter had declared, with all the lofty disdain of her fourteen years.

They had moved in three days earlier, and the living room was still piled high with boxes waiting to be distributed to the different rooms.

The sound of a glass smashing roused Bastien from his thoughts. He followed the noise. Leaning on the kitchen door jamb, he looked in at his wife.

"Everything all right, Manon?"

"Yes. I did it on purpose," she admitted, a smile on her lips.

Brush and pan in hand, scarf tied round her short hair, her blouse open one button too many to be worn outside the home, she explained:

"It brings good luck when you move house."

Bastien surveyed the broken pieces of glass on the floor.

"Isn't it usually supposed to be something white?"

His remark knocked her off balance for a moment.

"Okay, well then I've simply broken a glass," she admitted

sadly, before pouring the shards into the dustbin and then half-disappearing behind the open fridge door.

"You'll have to go out hunting, we've nothing to eat for this evening."

Bastien ignored the NO ENTRY sign on the door. Stretched out on her bed, eyes riveted to her tablet, his daughter paid him no attention. A pile of boxes took up most of her room, all marked with her name – a name she hated as much as she hated her life: Jade.

"Don't you want to unpack your things?"

"I prefer to wait a while. In case you change your mind."

Bastien frowned without really being upset.

"Don't make that kind of joke in front of maman, okay? Come on, we're going shopping."

"Give me five minutes. I'm sending a tweet of despair to the world."

"Okay, but in ten seconds I'm going to take the first thing in the first box I find and I'm going to throw it away. Put your jacket on."

Leaving rue Royale, they headed for place d'Armes, an immense expanse of grey flagstones presided over by a statue of General de Gaulle and his wife. A few almost deserted cafes, one in every three shops shuttered in the middle of the day, the only sign of life a small group of English tourists. Bastien suddenly felt the need for something more, something beautiful that could reassure him about their future life here.

"Should we go on a bit further, to the beach?"

"Aren't we supposed to fill the fridge? Why make us do this?"

"Because I'm your father. Because I feel like walking with

you, and even if you don't have anything interesting to say, I'll be happy. See how much I love you?"

Jade took Bastien's hand as a peace offering. The two of them left the square and, barely twenty metres further on, found themselves at the docks: stone buildings stained with green algae; quays like stranded metal whales. Calais, port city. Although this was not news to Bastien, the gloomy scene made his heart sink so obviously that Jade chose not to add any comment. It was going to take a miracle to redeem their first outing. And the miracle happened, in the form of a little wooden horse and pink candy floss.

"Erm . . . Papa? Am I hallucinating or . . . ?"

Out of nowhere, between the docks and a car park, the most absurd, unexpected funfair had appeared. A sweets stall, ten or so garishly coloured rides, with flashing lights and blaring music. But the empty aisles and the lack of any joyful cries lent the fair an unsettling atmosphere, as if it were a small ghost town that every day put on a wild party that nobody ever came to.

From the control cabin of one of the rides came the voice of a DJ on the verge of suicide, distorted by a decrepit sound system.

"Roll up, roll up! We're about to start. Happy days!"

Bastien cast a downhearted glance at his daughter.

"Beach?"

"Beach."

They crossed the car park encircling the deserted Luna Park, walked on a few metres, and came to one of Calais' beaches. Thanks to the iodine-filled air, the cries of seagulls – so alien to a city-dweller – the tangy breeze, the beach stretching to the horizon, and the warmth of the sun on his skin, Bastien finally found the picture postcard image he had been searching for.

Jade stared at the coastline, then the funfair, and finally turned to her father.

"Isn't there something that bothers you?"

"I'm starting to draw up a list."

"No, I mean right now, here, with your policeman's instinct. Doesn't it look as if we're on a movie set? There's everything: absolutely everything. Except people. The empty car park that could hold a thousand cars, the deserted Luna Park and beach . . . in the middle of July! Just think what the winters will be like. Fuck, what's the problem here?"

Bastien didn't know how to reply.

"Don't say 'fuck'."

He finally admitted to himself the outing was a fiasco, and reverted to his initial mission: to hunt down some ready meals in the supermarket. Return to rue Royale, across place d'Armes and towards Calais' historic belfry, its looming tower and four clock faces protected by a dragon weathervane. As they walked, they continued their conversation.

"You've seemed worried ever since we arrived. Is it because of your new job?" asked Jade.

"It's a posting, not a job. And it'll be fine."

"What about Maman?"

"Better, I hope. We just have to keep an eye on her. And stay positive."

Bastien heard a faint but persistent alarm sounding in the distance.

"Like, not telling her it's the wrong colour when she's trying to bless the house with a bit of broken glass?"

"Yeah, I realised that as soon as I said it."

Bastien instinctively took his daughter's hand when, as they were walking past Parc Richelieu, he realised it wasn't a momentary alarm but a persistent wail, growing louder and louder as it headed straight for them, even though the threat was still invisible. He came to a halt and looked all around them. As a protective reflex, he pushed Jade behind him.

"Papa?"

A filthy red car with a smashed windscreen and dented front wings appeared at the far end of the street, engine racing as it accelerated wildly. The tyres on one side lifted into the air before the car stabilised again, picked up speed and crashed straight through the middle of a roundabout. When it hit the kerb on the other side, it literally took off, landing on a bus shelter that exploded in all directions, like a watermelon hit by buckshot. The car horn went on blaring, until it finally died away, passing from a high-pitched sound to a low growl, then complete silence. A final segment of glass still hanging from the metal frame of the shelter hit the ground, the signal for Bastien's police instincts to kick in.

"Don't move – call the fire brigade," he told Jade.

Curious onlookers were peering out of windows, while in the street the first phones were recording the scene. After three attempts, Bastien managed to wrench open the the driver's side door. Behind the wheel he discovered a young man slumped unconscious over his safety belt, face swollen and the bottom of his shirt spattered with blood. Freeing him from the belt, Bastien lifted him out and laid him on the ground. The youngster's eyelids opened, but his eyes couldn't focus on anything, darting from left to right.

Bastien raised the shirt and saw the youngster had a deep ten-centimetre gash across his stomach. He had seen knife wounds before and this fitted the bill exactly. Taking off his jacket, he rolled it into a ball, placed it on the cut, and pressed his knee on it to keep his hands free. Fearing there might be other stab wounds, he quickly tugged at the youth's shirt. The

69

buttons went flying, revealing a hairless torso. What Bastien saw there produced conflicting emotions. The absence of any other wounds reassured him about the victim's chances of survival. But what struck, like a slap in the face or a dark nightmare, was the swastika tattooed across the right hand side of his chest.

As the fire brigade sirens drew closer, he raised the youth's legs to lessen the flow of blood and continued to press on the wound to staunch the haemorrhage.

"You'll survive. I don't know if that's a good thing, but you'll survive."

Bastien looked up and met Jade's eyes. She had disobeyed his orders and come over to him. Now she stared at her father, his forearms spattered with blood from desperately trying to keep a youngster alive.

Fucking great first outing.

The fire brigade officer who had checked Bastien's identity pointed to where he was sitting on the roundabout grass. Another policeman went up to him and saluted, seeming almost amused by the situation.

"Lieutenant Miller? Ludovic Passaro, head of the Calais BAC*. Keen to get to work?"

"I start tomorrow."

"It looks to me like you're a day early. Do you know whose life you've saved?"

"A jackass with a swastika."

"It's more complicated than that."

Bastien stood up to leave. Jade joined him, more curious at what she'd seen than shocked by it.

---

* Brigade anti-criminelle. Plain-clothes police unit based in local stations, equivalent to British CID

"If you don't mind, you can tell me tomorrow at headquarters. I'd like to take my daughter home now."

"Of course. It can wait."

Passaro stepped back, and the two men shook hands before parting.

11

Calais police headquarters

Commissaire Dorsay's strides weren't as long as his, so Bastien held back to stay level with him as they walked along the main corridor in Calais police headquarters. The commissaire kept glancing at the new arrival as if to make sure this wasn't some kind of trick. For an officer to choose to be posted here was not only rare, but almost unheard of.

"To be perfectly honest, I don't know what to expect from you, Lieutenant Miller."

He suddenly turned off, forcing Bastien to double back to follow him. Everything seemed tiny in this three-storey red brick building, including the corridors and the offices Bastien had caught glimpses of through half-open doors.

"No-one ever chooses Calais," Dorsay continued. "To the point where we've had to suspend all transfer requests. Once you're in, you can never get out. Were you aware of that?"

"Not really."

"That's understandable, it's barely legal. But if we allowed transfers, we'd lose half our personnel in the first month. Which means that seeing you come here voluntarily gives me pause. I only hope you're not bad news in disguise."

Dorsay came to a halt outside a closed door and grasped the handle.

"Your service reports from Bordeaux are good. Your former boss has given you above average marks, and you don't seem to have brought any baggage with you. So what's the catch?"

"Don't worry, there isn't one. Family reasons, nothing more."

The commissaire studied his new recruit. Thirty-five years old it said in his dossier, although he wouldn't have put him at more than thirty. Freshly shaven in his special first-day suit, unruly brown hair smartly combed. Dorsay wondered what state he would be in after a month or two.

"Ready to meet your team?"

What could he say? From the moment he had entered head-quarters, Miller had been as friendly as a Parisian taxi-driver, giving only monosyllabic answers. He knew he was doing it and he wouldn't have thought much of himself, were the roles reversed. But he preferred appearing taciturn or impolite to showing what he really was: a new lieutenant all at sea after three years in the force, about to meet his very first team as leader.

The door opened onto a room barely fifteen metres square, with three desks in it. The only advantage: one large film poster was enough to cover the wall, and considering how faded it was, it appeared to have been there from the year dot – Tim Robbins was grey-faced, and Morgan Freeman almost white. The two occupants of the office looked up and came over to Bastien to introduce themselves.

"Gardien de la paix* Loris, at your service, lieutenant."

'Brigadier Corval, at your service, lieutenant.'

Bastien shook hands with them. A firm grip from Loris. A damp, limp one from Corval. His role fulfilled, Commissaire Dorsay left them to it, claiming to have a meeting with the

---

* Gardien de la paix: police officer, equivalent in rank to British constable.

Prefect. As soon as he was gone, Bastien started from scratch with what had been presented to him as his "complete team".

"If you don't mind, let's start again, with first names this time. I'm Bastien. Not lieutenant, not sir, not Miller. Simply Bastien."

Loris came over again. Thin black pullover, tight jeans, early twenties with amber skin that hinted at a mixed background, gun on her hip in a shiny leather holster.

"Erika Loris. It's great to meet you."

Then it was Corval's turn. Sweaty, baggy trousers, dressed like a fat person trying to hide it. Forty years old or more, hair plastered back off his forehead.

"Ruben Corval – welcome."

"What about the others?" asked an astonished Miller.

"We're missing Martin, suffering from depression, and Chabert, on sick leave for nine months now due to a knee injury."

"Acquired on the job?"

"No, playing football."

"And your previous team leader? I thought you weren't allowed to leave Calais, so how did he manage it?"

"Chabert was our leader. Nobody believes him, but he gets his sick leave extended every three months anyway."

It took Miller a couple of seconds to take all this in.

"Wait a minute . . . How do you manage? A BSU* with only two officers is impossible."

"Three, including you," said Erika in an attempt to reassure him. "We get by because we only respond to calls, though the BAC has its hands full with the Jungle. Have you heard about it?"

---

* Brigade de sûreté urbaine: local police force

"It's hard not to."

"Two thousand migrants raising hell every night trying to get to England whatever way they can: that creates a lot of work," added Corval.

Bastien draped his jacket round the chair at the empty desk. He wasn't going to get to grips with his team or his job on the first day, so he reverted to what he did know how to do.

"I imagine we'll get to know one another as we go along, and the easiest way to do that is by getting down to work. So how about briefing me on the preliminary investigations and today's urgent ones . . . ?"

"Today's? Absolutely nothing," said a contented Corval.

"Not even a nice stomach wound on a Nazi?"

Corval picked up a slender file and slid it over to him.

"You mean little Kevin? With a bit of luck, the investigating magistrate will reclassify it as attempted murder. And crimes like that go to the police judiciaire. We just need to wait."

"Wouldn't you like to move the inquiry on a little in the meantime?"

"Do the donkey work and have it pinched from us, then watch the police judiciaire get all the credit? Not really."

Hearing this, Bastien gave himself a metaphorical kick up the backside. On the surface, he appeared to be nothing more than an inexperienced officer at a loss as to how to react. It was Erika who came to his rescue, but the damage had been done – Corval had been quick to spot a lack of authority that could allow him to get away with doing nothing.

"His name is Perche," said Erika. "Kevin Perche. He's one of the founders of Calais up in Arms.'"

"What are they up in arms about?"

"The migrants, mostly."

"Does this Kevin have enemies?"

"More like does he have any friends? He's had a difficult year."

"Meaning?"

"Best if I introduce you to the person who knows most about it. You don't object to meeting with a journalist, do you?"

Erika swept up her jacket, pocketed her car keys, stuffed a file under her arm, and held the door open for Miller. They left Corval surfing a travel website, even though he had never left the Pas-de-Calais region in his life. Out in the corridor, Bastien was still reeling from his first disastrous performance as team leader.

"Your bulletproof vest, gun, handcuffs and armband arrived yesterday," Erika told him. "You need to go to the gun room when you have a moment . . ." She paused. "Or send someone with nothing else to do."

Miller hesitated a split second, then realised this was a chance to assert his position before his subordinate took on the role of alpha male. Spinning on his heel, he flung open the office door.

"Corval. While we're out, I need you to get my equipment from the gun room and put it in our locker."

"I have to leave early today," the sluggard protested.

"Better get on with it then."

Satisfied that he had marked his territory, Miller leaped down the front steps two at a time with a broad smile on his face, heading for the car park. Erika was waiting for him, a roll-up in her mouth as she chatted with a group of three other officers. Even from behind, Miller recognised the impressive bulk of the head of the BAC.

"Good morning, lieutenant."

"Good morning, Passaro."

"Erika tells us you're keeping the Kevin Perche case?"

"As long as it's not reclassified as attempted murder, I see no reason to pass it up."

"A BSU that actually does something –, that'll be a novelty," said one of the men in Passaro's group. "Every time we proposed something to your predecessor, he scuttled off as if he was caught short."

The BAC chief regarded his shaven-headed colleague with distaste, then introduced him to Bastien:

"I'm sorry, lieutenant. This is Cortex, our resident wise guy. Never knows when to keep his trap shut. And over there, on the bonnet of our new car, just waiting to jump to attention, I'm sure, is Sprinter."

Thin as a rake, Sprinter hauled himself off the car and greeted Bastien with a bone-crushing handshake.

"Don't worry," said Passaro, "they have real names, but I forgot them long ago."

"And what do they call you?" Miller wanted to know.

"He's the Anaesthetist," joked Erika. "In his rugby team they say he's a demon in the tackle. A real brute."

Passaro burst out laughing, but didn't reject her compliment. Erika went over to their unmarked car and chased off a seagull sitting on the roof. Bastien got in, the bird squawking loudly.

12

Bastien followed Erika like a tourist trailing after a museum guide as they entered the offices of the local *Littoral Nord* newspaper. When they got to reception, she pulled out her police ID.

"Thomas Lizion, please."

The receptionist dialled his number, and a few minutes later the journalist appeared and led them to his office. Once again, Erika took the lead.

"Tom, let me introduce my new lieutenant, Bastien Miller."

The journalist laughed as he sat down. "So you're the one who saved Kevin? Just when karma had finally decided to take its revenge?"

"I get the impression people hold it against me," Bastien said.

"And that's precisely why we're here, Tom," Erika explained. "Could you explain the situation for the lieutenant?"

"What do I get out of it?"

"Always the same old refrain. You're as predictable as the sunrise. It's in your interest to be in the police's good books, isn't it?"

Smiling faintly, Lizion gave in, clicking the mouse to wake up his computer.

"I'll print out the articles. That way you won't need to take notes. In short, Kevin Perche was part of Calais Up in Arms until they threw him out. But if we start with him you won't get the whole picture. How much time do you have?"

"This is our only urgent case," replied Bastien.

The journalist poured two black coffees – one for him and one for the new lieutenant who, to his credit, had come to take the pulse of the town before thinking he could bring any semblance of order to it.

"The influx of migrants didn't stop with the closure of the Sangatte camp in 2003. It continued, even though there was nowhere to put them and they all still wanted to get to England. Which means staying as close as possible to the Channel ports. As a result, they began to squat in every empty house, every abandoned building, gardens, parks, under bridges – the situation soon became intolerable. So a place had to be found to put them in. On the coast, well away from the town centre, between some sand dunes and a forest, there was an old cemetery alongside a municipal rubbish tip. The State bulldozed the site and the migrants were invited to install themselves there. That was a year ago. At first they came discreetly, a hundred curious people at most; then the news spread right across the planet, and thousands came. The Jungle was born."

"That sounds a bit inappropriate. Who thought up that name?"

"Don't see it as racism – it was the Iranian migrants themselves who called it that. When they first arrived, they saw a bit of forest and so named the place 'the Forest'. In Persian, the word for that is *jangal*. Here, people thought that was 'jungle' in English. A little linguistic quirk. After that the migrants were completely forgotten about. But not for long. The media got wind of it, and soon Calais was no longer one of the treasures of the Opal Coast, but the symbol of a migrant crisis and the question of their reception in France. Tourism plummeted: even the English hesitate about coming now their tabloids have labelled this a civil war. Property prices have slumped by forty per cent and shops have begun to close. Our economy depends on the port. Ten million passengers cross the Channel through Calais every year, and it's also the number one hub for ro-ro traffic."

"Roll on, roll off – ferries that take lorries bound for England," Erika explained to Bastien, who didn't have much of the mariner about him.

"But now the truckers are scared stiff, so the haulage companies look for other ports to avoid Calais."

"Just because of the migrants?" said a surprised Bastien.

Lizion cast him a sideways glance, as if realising he had underestimated the gaps in the police officer's knowledge. His tone became almost condescending.

"You must know what they do to try to board the lorries? The assaults on the trucks and attacks on the drivers? Fake accidents as if they were holding up stagecoaches. Barricades and bonfires on the motorway. Does that mean anything to you?"

"I've seen it on TV, but that's about it," Bastien admitted.

"Well, I'll leave that for Erika to explain later on, but I'll tell you about Calais Up in Arms. Their initial aim was to film daily life in the town and put it up on social media. The difficulties the people here have with this rootless and penniless population and their sometimes violent attempts to get to England. Then extremists joined in. The "migrant breakers" who organised racist raids and "hunting the blacks". Safaris, some of them called the attacks. Kevin Perche grew up in this atmosphere of hatred, like a mosquito larva in a marsh. But there was a storm of criticism on social media, and so the group quickly calmed down and the loose cannons were turfed out. Nowadays their site just puts up videos without commentary. I'm not saying it doesn't veer towards xenophobia from time to time, but they keep it under control. Besides, they know what to expect from me."

"A damning article?" Bastien said, with a hint of mockery in his voice.

Stung by this, the journalist swivelled his chair round and ran his finger down old editions of his newspaper to find the one that would put the young pup in his place. He discovered an article going back six months and proudly dropped it on his desk. Beneath the headline THE FACES OF HATE was a series of photos of internet users, together with their racist comments and calls for violence against migrants, exactly as they had appeared on their online accounts. Prominent among them was Kevin Perche, with his piggy, close-set eyes and what he had written to cause maximum hurt: "For those who haven't drowned, and those not run over by lorries, we have to set up concentration camps #happy days." Weighed against these outrageous proposals, the swastika on his chest seemed timid by comparison.

"Those comments made Calais Up in Arms kick him out. Not that he was orphaned for long. I've heard he was adopted by Identity Generation, a far-right group with a branch in Lille."

"And you put that on the front page?" Bastien said incredulously.

"It's known as a 'Wall of Shame'. The German newspaper *Bild* did the same. Does it shock you, lieutenant?"

"Not really. But my list of suspects has just got much longer. They could be anarchist, far-left, vigilante, a migrant defending himself . . . it could be anyone."

"As I told you Bastien, in Calais Kevin Perche has been living on borrowed time for a while," concluded Erika. "At least now you know who you rescued."

Bastien and Erika left the *Littoral Nord* offices with an armful of printed material.

"Lizion is a good journalist, but more importantly, he was born here. He knows what's going on, and he knows a lot of people as well. I thought you ought to meet him."

Bastien joined up a few dots.

"You talked to him openly, addressed him as a friend, and got straight to the point. Besides, he knows you don't drink coffee, because he only served the two of us. That means—"

"Yeah," Erika butted in, not waiting to hear the end of Bastien's sentence. "Not my finest hour. It's all in the past now."

Calais police headquarters
Six-thirty p.m.

Bastien keyed in the code for the service locker. It was empty apart from a pile of sealed evidence bags with money in them and a few grams of hashish that gave off a fragrant smell. No weapon, no bullet-proof vest – none of his equipment.

Stern-faced, he went down the corridor and threw his jacket onto his computer screen. Then, just as he was about to explode, he discovered a tiny message on his desk: "A cop is always better with a gun."

Less than a minute later, Bastien knocked on the BAC door and was greeted by a beaming Passaro. Cortex was in the midst of finishing his daily report, while Sprinter was stowing bottles of water in a freezer with a BABY ON BOARD sticker on the door: what better expression of police humour could there be?

Passaro opened his desk drawer and took out everything that should have been in the safe. Gun, handcuffs, armband and bulletproof vest.

"I asked Corval to get these," complained Bastien.

"And he left the station a minute after you, bragging that he wasn't going to do it. You'll have to sign the register in the gun room tomorrow, to keep the records straight."

"Some dogs understand orders, others only kicks," said Cortex without raising his eyes from his log. "You have to act accordingly."

Bastien told himself he would need to quickly learn how to tighten this particular dog's collar. As he gathered his things, he took the opportunity to clear something up.

"I get the impression the refugee camp is at the centre of a lot of tension. Do you visit the Jungle often?"

"We're in the vicinity every day. We go to the entrance whenever there's a need, but we rarely venture inside. It's both a no-go zone and a shanty town."

"What do you have to do there?"

For a moment, Passaro's face fell. Cortex and Sprinter were careful not to reply or make a joke about it.

'I'd almost be ashamed to describe it. You have to experience it yourself. But I wouldn't wish it on anyone. We only just about manage ourselves."

13

Levallois-Perret
Headquarters of the DGSI*
The same day

The phone began to buzz on the desk twenty-four hours early. Contact was on Wednesdays, and there was no reason for that to change. Commandant Paris took time to close his office door, unscrewing the lid of his pen and opening his dog-eared notebook before finally picking up.

"You've got the wrong day," he said calmly.

"I know that, for fuck's sake," replied a youthful, stressed-out voice.

"Is there a problem?"

"Of course there's a problem! I risk being found out whenever I call you, I'm hardly going to pick up the phone just to ask you about my horoscope!"

The voice paused while its owner lit a cigarette, then continued.

"Things got out of hand last night. Sal recognised one of the Nazis from Identity Generation. A guy with a swastika tattoo. That drove him mad and he saw red."

---

* Direction Générale de la Sécurité Intérieure: Counter-terrorism group for internal security: equivalent to British MI5.

Since this information was of no interest to him, the commander screwed the lid of his pen back on and closed his notebook, slightly irritated that their protocol had been breached due to a vulgar brawl. Despite this, he did his best to remain civil.

"In all seriousness, what on earth has this got to do with me? You're straying outside your mission."

"That's why I called. If you don't help me out, I'm going to find it hard to continue."

"Explain yourself."

"At first Sal just wanted to give him a good hiding and film it to humiliate him. Except that the Nazi was built like a block of wood: the blows bounced off him. The harder he was hit, the crazier he became. I tried to separate them and got a busted nose for my pains. I can't even be sure it wasn't Sal who did it; he was punching almost with his eyes closed."

Paris smiled at the thought of his informant's face covered in blood.

"Things got worse. The other guy was on top, so Sal took out a knife. I don't know if he meant to stab him, but we all saw the blade turn red and the guy double up. So we ran off."

Already more concerned, Paris opened his notebook again.

"Do you mean he's dead?" he asked almost disinterestedly, as if simply verifying the information.

"No, it's been in the paper this morning. He'll survive. But I think he got my blood on his shirt in the tussle, and you know I have a police record. That's how you recruited me, wasn't it? So it's going to take them less than seventy-two hours to track me down. That's why I'm calling you! If you want me to go on providing you with info from the Jungle, you have to get my name out of the investigation."

The silence that followed ratcheted the tension up a notch.

"You're going to drop me, aren't you?"

"Don't get paranoid – I'm thinking."

The commandant looked up and met the eye of his superior, who was sitting opposite him and had been closely following the conversation. He nodded, as though authorising something.

"Fine. We're coming to see you. Get in contact again tomorrow at ten. I'll tell you where we'll meet. Repeat."

"Good, I've understood: tomorrow at ten."

Commandant Paris stood up from his chair and went over to a wall covered with photos. As rotund as Father Christmas, he stroked his well-groomed greying beard as he did so. Sixty-something, forty of them in the intelligence services. His superior, who until then had been silent, now addressed him.

"Remind me about your informant, Paris."

"Of course, sir. Alexandre Merle, aged twenty-seven, recruited less than a year ago."

"What did we have on him?"

"He's a member of No Borders, a far-left group. They're squatting in the Calais Jungle, trying to help migrants reach England. They were the ones who blocked the Channel tunnel. They also stormed a ferry in January this year. Merle was identified on both occasions, and accepted our offer to avoid six months in prison. He comes from a good family: his father's a surgeon, his mother a bank manager. He'd never have survived six months in jail."

"Well, he's really landed us in it now. The investigation into this knife attack is bound to be given to the police judiciaire. By the way, is there one in Calais?"

"No, it's several kilometres away, in Coquelles."

The other man joined Paris at the wall detailing their operation. In the centre, there was a photo of a red-haired youth in a woollen jersey and African pants, labelled as MERLE. His was the anguished voice that had just called for urgent help. Above it, another photo, with the words: SALVADOR, KNOWN AS SAL, LEADER OF THE NO BORDERS GROUP IN CALAIS. A thirty-something Mediterranean-looking man with long brown hair. The commandant took two steps back to get an overall view. Merle was at the centre of a galaxy of photos filling the entire wall, revealing a complex investigation that Paris's group had been working on for a year now. A mosque. A panorama of the Calais Jungle taken from a helicopter. Weapons discovered during a raid on a truck. A burnt-out vehicle next to a building with shattered windows. A list of names. A map of Africa with pins stuck all over it. And six grainy snapshots of men's faces, obviously taken with a telephoto lens.

"And your target is one of those six?" the head of counter-terrorism wanted to know.

"Shadow? Yes. According to our team in Tunisia, he's starting to act suspiciously. He hardly ever goes out, and no longer uses the telephone. As if everything were in place, and he just needs to make the move."

"Shadow. A good name for an Isis recruitment officer."

Paris glanced at the six portraits on the wall.

"One he won't have for very long when we nab him. According to our last phone tap before he dropped off the radar, he can be heard saying he'd dismissed two of his closest lieutenants."

"Dismissed?"

"I doubt we'll hear any more from them, if you take my meaning. And that's good news. It may be our only chance to identify him. With a bit of luck he'll come in person to find new recruits, and if our information is reliable, it's highly likely he'll head for the Jungle. Unfortunately, no-one can set foot in there without being spotted. That's why we need help from inside the camp: Merle and his No Borders group."

"Okay, I'll call the police judiciaire at Coquelles and let them know you'll be paying them a visit. As Merle is your contact, you're the one to go, obviously."

Paris looked down at his paunch, and realised he couldn't see his shoes.

"I haven't worked in the field for a decade, sir."

The DGSI chief sighed.

"You've been tracking Shadow since I got here, and I can only congratulate you on how close you've come," he said, resorting to flattery. "So, slip off to Calais, find a hotel room like any normal tourist, call in Merle, show him the six photos, send him off on the trail, and wait patiently. You can still manage sitting on your backside in a hotel room, can't you? Get the kid out of this knife business and put him back to work."

14

From the doorway, Manon was surveying every corner of her father's study, as though rediscovering it. It was only here in her childhood home that she could find true peace. The parquet floor behind her creaked. Manon turned, smiled at her mother, and entered the room, just as she had as a little girl. Her mother came in after her.

"I think Jade is about to fall asleep."

"You made us a real feast, maman. It would finish anyone off."

Manon paused at a framed photograph, brushing it with her fingertips.

"That was his favourite," her mother whispered.

"I doubt it. Papa hated being photographed."

The weight of his recent death held her back, like an anchor tethers a boat. But here she could pretend nothing had changed.

"It's been there so long you've probably forgotten where it came from. You took it with the first camera he gave you. It wasn't the photo he liked so much, but the look you gave him that day."

Manon smiled sadly.

"There's something I've put aside for you in the loft," her mother said. "Would you like me to show you?"

The stairs up to the loft were very narrow. At the top, Manon pushed up the trapdoor and fastened it. She stepped inside the room under the eaves, then flicked the switch on one of the wooden beams. Everything stored there over the years was revealed. Old clothes, forgotten books, a bike with a missing wheel, and at the far end all her father's things that no-one had thought to clear out, even though they took up most of the space. What's the point in having such a large house otherwise, her mother had justified herself when a distant cousin remarked on this.

"It's in the hat box. Over there."

Blowing off the dust, Manon lifted the lid. Inside she saw a jumble of photographs of Prague: the Charles Bridge, the museum dedicated to Alphonse Mucha, whose paintings could hypnotise her for hours, the Art Nouveau cafés, Kafka's quirky house, the astronomical clock, the Jewish cemetery with its higgledy-piggledy tombs. Saint Wenceslas Cathedral. Father and daughter on the trip that had left them with all these souvenirs, kept as if to fix that moment and that childhood forever. In a small hat box.

Hidden among negatives, various postcards and a few unused rolls of film, Manon found her old camera. Its weight, its shape, the world she perceived through its lens: it all came flooding back to her.

"You should take it with you."

"It will just gather dust somewhere."

"Not any more than here in the loft. Your father thought you'd capture the world with that camera."

Lost in time, Manon didn't respond to this.

"I'll leave you on your own for a while," whispered her mother, setting off down the narrow stairs.

*

She went back into the living-room, where Bastien was sitting on the sofa, stroking Jade's hair as she dozed on his lap. He had hardly said a word during dinner, and she was afraid it was because of her.

"I hope you don't miss Bordeaux too much," she said as she sat beside him, careful not to wake her granddaughter.

"I'm not sure yet. Above all, it's Manon I miss. And Jade, who's such a teenager these days. It's complicated."

"Manon and her father were very close. She meant everything to him. And it's only been three months. It'll take her a while to recover from this."

"I know. I don't hold it against her."

Jade wriggled a little in search of a more comfortable position, without really waking up.

"You know I never asked Manon to come back to Calais," his mother-in-law said. "I don't believe in shared mourning. It just means you never get your own head above water. In the end you both sink to the bottom."

"I wouldn't have resented it if you had. If she feels better here near you then that's where we have to be. The important thing is for her to shake off this depression. It's holding us all hostage."

Manon's mother placed her hand on the young lieutenant's, aware how lucky her daughter had been to find him.

"You're a good man, Bastien."

"Yeah, I know. I suffer for it. I'm going to have to work on it. Toughen up."

"The new posting?"

"I got off to a bad start."

It was past midnight, and Jade hadn't seen anything of the journey from her grandmother's house to her own bedroom. As soon as they arrived, Manon thrust the hat box to the back of a wardrobe, as though to forget it. Then she shut herself in the bathroom.

A few minutes later, she emerged from the shower wearing only a short T-shirt sticking to her damp skin. She stretched out on the big new double bed, one leg under the covers, the other on top. Bastien's hand caressed her lower thigh, then gently moved upwards. Manon smiled tenderly at him, kissed him on the forehead and turned away, wishing him goodnight. Hurt, but accustomed to it, he lay with his eyes open for several minutes before getting out of bed.

The living-room computer sprang to life, filling the room with a blue-tinged glow. Bastien typed "Calais Up in Arms videos" in the search bar and found he had page after page to choose from.

A bloody-faced trucker, staring emptily at the side of a motorway in the middle of the night. The camera shakes, there are cops, firemen, the lorry on its side in a ditch, lit by flashing lights. A voice speaks of an organised attack. The words "like savages" is repeated several times.

A brawl between migrants on the outskirts of the Jungle. An impressive mass of silhouettes, armed with sticks, machetes, stones. Hundreds of men on either side of a sand dune and then, like two cars launched at full speed towards one another, the armies clash headlong with ferocious battle cries.

A CRS* detachment fires tear gas indiscriminately. The grenades soar into the sky then land in the fields bordering the autoroute and drive a horde of migrants back away from the trucks.

Cops pulling terrified young kids from under the tarps of a lorry, blinding them with powerful torches. "No England

---

* CRS: Compagnie Régionale de Sécurité: the riot police

for them tonight! Back to the Jungle," says the voice, almost contentedly.

A weeping woman in front of her house. Her garden fence flattened, the bay window shattered. Her voice quavers: "They were being chased by the police, at least fifty of them rampaged through the house like a hurricane. Everything is smashed. I can't take it anymore, do you hear me? I can't take it anymore."

Bastien played a few more videos without learning much. He was missing something fundamental. Searching in the inside pocket of his jacket on the back of a chair, he found the list of essential phone numbers he'd been given at headquarters. Assuming Passaro would be asleep at this late hour, he decided to send a message.

I want to see the Jungle.

Against all expectations, the answer appeared on his screen less than ten seconds later.

Can't say I'm surprised. See you tomorrow, Lieutenant.

15

The next morning, Bastien walked past the custody cells to see the day's menu. In the first sat a man in torn jogging pants, his arm bandaged. Another man lay stretched out in the drunk tank, motorbike helmet on his head and a restraining belt strapping his arms to his sides, as if he were the most dangerous patient in an asylum.

"He went a bit crazy," Erika explained. "He was off his face and kept banging his head against the walls. We had to protect him from himself."

"And Kevin Perche? What does the hospital say? Can we interview him?"

"Yes, in theory, we could. But the investigating magistrate handed the case over to Coquelles police judiciaire last night. We should have known. We don't deal with attempted murder at our station."

Bastien strode past the other cells, then came back to his starting point by Erika.

"I don't understand," he said. "There weren't any yesterday, and there aren't any today."

"What are you talking about?"

"Migrants. Everyone tells me they're like a plague of locusts all over the town. I expected to see the cells full."

"We don't touch migrants," Erika informed him.

"What if they're caught red-handed?"

"If there were a case of rape or murder I dare say it would be different, but for anything else we simply drop them back outside the camp and move on."

"Without reporting it?"

"The public prosecutor and the commissaire have managed to create a kind of stalemate that suits everyone."

"I love magic tricks. Explain this one to me."

Erika collected the files on the day's two detainees and filled Bastien in as they walked up to their office.

"Right. I think we agree that all those people in the Jungle are fleeing war or famine. It's not simple economic migration, but forced exile. So it would be rather inhuman to arrest foreigners for breaking the law and send them back to their countries. How would that make us look? On the other hand, it's obvious nobody gives a shit about integrating them, because they're left on a rubbish tip on the outskirts of town. So the status of 'potential refugee' has been created for them."

"It's the first time I've heard that," Bastien admitted, inserting a euro into the coffee machine on the first-floor landing.

"Don't bother looking it up – it doesn't exist anywhere else or in any legal handbook. It's homegrown in Calais, a local speciality. Basically, thanks to this concocted status, they can't be arrested. It's only logical: if we refuse to integrate them into France, we can't then bring them into the judicial system. At the same time, they're not fully fledged refugees, because that would mean we had to do something about them. When they're designated 'potential refugees' they're neither arrested nor offered any help. They're left to stew in their own juice in the hope they go away of their own accord."

"I can see a lot of thought has gone into doing nothing."

"For the sake of my mental health, I've stopped thinking about it."

Erika pushed open the door to their office with her backside, then greeted Ruben Corval, his face as washed out as his clothes.

"Bad night?" she mocked him.

"I never have a good one," the chronic insomniac replied.

Corval nodded a greeting to his new superior, and Bastien returned the gesture, deliberately allowing his eyes to linger on him a second longer to show that the previous day's affront had not been forgotten.

"Two cases this morning," said Bastien. "You two can deal with them. A drunk and disorderly that ended up with damage to private property. And a burglar who cut his arm on a window he had just smashed. He called the fire brigade himself. New town, same old cretins."

Leading on from this last thought, he turned to his brigadier.

"Corval, I'll be out most of the morning. When I get back, I want the interviews completed, the victims' statements taken, and the charges established. I'll inform the public prosecutors: that way I'll get to meet the investigating magistrates."

Corval merely grunted, but Bastien wasn't letting him off that easily.

"That is unless you don't feel up to it and you'd prefer me to leave Erika in charge?"

This dig woke Corval up. A glimmer of hatred lit up his face.

"I'm a brigadier, she's a lower rank, so I don't take orders from her."

"Read the regulations again. If I make Erika the main investigator, that outweighs rank, and so you'd be obliged to follow her orders. Personally that would suit me fine."

96

Erika hid her smile behind a mug of tea with FBI written on it. Corval swallowed his pride and gave in.

"That won't be necessary, lieutenant," he snapped.

"I sincerely hope not, for your sake."

At the height of this heated exchange, Passaro's massive bulk burst into their office, making it look even smaller than usual.

"The Jungle is calmer in the morning, lieutenant."

"I'll walk down with you."

The police station was so tiny that every square centimetre had to be put to good use. As a result, the minuscule inner courtyard was used as a car park, though you had to be a Tetris expert to park there. Bastien was heading for the brand-new BAC patrol car when Passaro called him back.

"We'll avoid using the official car. If we don't want to be clocked within three seconds, it's to better to take mine."

At that moment, Cortex and Sprinter arrived, carrying liquid soap and sponges.

"And that way I can leave the kids on carwash duty."

"Sorry for the hard work, gentlemen," said Bastien.

"No worries, lieutenant. We live in the car at least six hours a day, so we're happy to take care of it."

It was only then, when he was up close to the BAC car, that Bastien realised something.

"Having a Nissan Qashqai for a patrol car is unusual enough, but one with a glass roof! Is it a joke? Where do you put your flashing light?"

Cortex nodded in agreement and added his two cents' worth.

"We hold it in our hand or put it on the dashboard, like in an American TV show. As long as the decisions are taken by people who know nothing about our job, this is the kind of shit we have to put up with."

"It's the same with our torches. There was only one that worked across the whole group, so we ordered two new ones. A week later we received some safety lights that fasten on our arms. The sort I fix on my kid when he's riding his bike at night. We're used to the big cheeses not giving a damn, but it gets a bit tiring after a while."

"I think that's enough for now," Passaro interrupted them. "We'll be back in an hour, two max."

The BAC chief's old car left the centre of town and skirted the docks. High-rise buildings soon gave way to detached houses. The streets widened into broader avenues, until they reached an industrial estate on a boulevard big enough for all sizes of truck to manoeuvre. Three CRS vans marked the approach to the refugee camp, which was still out of sight. Passaro parked alongside them and greeted the men in riot gear.

"How do you get on with the CRS?" asked Bastien, keeping up with Passaro as he zigzagged between the men and their vehicles.

"Pretty well. We see a lot of them here: in fact, more than you would in Marseille or the Paris suburbs. But they're replaced every few weeks by another company, whereas we're stuck here. I think that makes them respect us."

Beyond the last CRS van they came face to face with the camp.

"They see coming here as drawing the short straw. But to us it's our daily routine."

In front of him, Bastien saw a thousand square metres of sand dunes stretching to the horizon, flanked by a thick forest. The Jungle followed their outline – from where he stood it was impossible to tell what kind of ground lay beneath the tents or fragile shacks of rusted metal, planks of wood and plastic tarpaulins that covered every inch of it. It looked like a stormy sea with waves of garbage.

"Welcome to the Jungle, lieutenant. The biggest shanty town in Europe."

Campfires. Wheel-less caravans rescued from breakers' yards. Thousands of faces: from North and sub-Saharan Africa, Asia and the Middle East. Stray dogs, tails between their legs. Children's songs. Pakistani pop music somewhere in the distance. Smells of garbage mingling with the aromas of cooking. A few aid workers wearing T-shirts from the Red Cross, Médecins sans Frontières or other organisations Bastien had never heard of. Men in djellabas, with long beards, others in jeans, cigarette and beer can in hand; no women. Some grubby-looking kids on their own, laughing as they chased each other around.

Nothing here corresponded to Bastien's usual reference points. New sounds, new smells, new kinds of faces. He was rocked by a feeling of uncertainty.

The wind whipped up a cloud of sand that rose above the camp then swept down, making the canvases flap wildly, whistling in between the shacks and ripping through the tall barbed-wire fence that separated the Jungle from the main road leading to the port.

"Afghanis and Sudanese in the main," Passaro said, answering Bastien's unspoken question. "Eritreans, Iranians, Syrians, Kurds, Pakistanis, Yemenis as well. Fewer Iraqis, Palestinians and Ethiopians. I couldn't even place most of those countries on a map. According to the regional authorities, there are 5,000 of them. According to the aid agencies, 7,500 men, 1,500 women, and almost 900 children. So a total of 10,000, twice the official figure."

"Women?" said Bastien. "I can't see any."

"That's normal. With several thousand guys who haven't had sex for months, some of them from a culture where you don't exactly ask permission when you get the urge, this isn't the kind of place to wear a dress, believe me. The women and most of the kids are kept further on in a special part of the camp where they're more or less protected. Come on, let's go up for a better view."

Bastien followed Passaro as he climbed the first dune. By now, all eyes were on them. Curious, suspicious, fearful, friendly or openly hostile: Bastien was party to the whole gamut of human emotions.

"Here on your left is Afghan territory. Down there, the Sudanese. The other nationalities are clustered in micro-villages around those two main groups. And can you see that sort of avenue just over there? That's the Champs-Élysées. The commercial street, if you prefer. Apparently you can buy anything there, but I haven't explored it properly. As I was saying, you never really get to know the Jungle."

Bastien said nothing. He was taking it all in, trying to come to terms with a reality he had been entirely unprepared for.

"Are you alright, lieutenant?"

"More or less. I find it hard to believe we're in France."

"Especially as all they want is to leave it behind. Their goal is *Youké*, as they call it. The United Kingdom. England. They're convinced there's endless work in the black economy there, and that refugee status is handed out like gold stars . . ."

"And that isn't the case?"

"Five years ago perhaps, but with Brexit, England has closed in on itself. Shrunk even. Like every rich country whose greatest fear is to see the rest of the world come and wipe their shoes on its doormat. But even if being accepted over there is harder than it used to be, quite a few refugees have succeeded. That means the new arrivals want to join their relatives."

"But if they want to go to this England of theirs, what business have we got keeping them here?"

"The Le Touquet Agreement, lieutenant, which places the border with England on French soil at Calais and not in Dover. And the English pay a lot for it to stay that way. Recently, more than twenty million euros just to erect the barbed-wire fence protecting the main road and stop the motorway being stormed by migrants."

"That's ridiculous," retorted Bastien.

"Yeah. The migrants are fleeing countries at war that we can't in all honesty return them to, but on the other hand we stop them going where they want to go. Call it a stalemate, if you like."

It was the second time Bastien had heard this word used about the Jungle, and the vague feeling it had provoked then became more precise now.

"Do you believe in ghosts, Passaro?"

"I've never really thought about it. Do you mean spirits that haunt houses?"

"Exactly. Stuck between life on earth and the celestial plane. The migrants remind me of them. Souls in limbo, trapped between two worlds."

Passaro had already thought something similar, without really knowing how to express it. Bastien's description unsettled him.

"Don't think about it too much, lieutenant. It's not a good idea. We do this job holding our breath. Never try to breathe when you're underwater."

"Actually, you've still not told me precisely what our job consists of."

"During the day it's almost calm. But we'll visit the night watch soon. I'll show you."

Bastien's attention had remained focused on the anarchic dustbin city laid out beneath him, hidden like a shameful open sore. He hadn't noticed a group of European-looking young men and women with dreadlocks, wearing baggy trousers and brightly coloured T-shirts, coming towards them brandishing their phones. Whenever anyone in authority entered the Jungle, No Borders came to film them. Not aggressively, but close up, ready to immortalise any careless talk or threatening gesture that could go viral on social media.

"We'd better get out of here if you don't want to find yourself on Facebook in a quarter of an hour."

Passaro plunged down the dune in a few lengthy strides, Bastien following more cautiously. As they were leaving the Jungle under the accusatory gaze of a dozen phones, they came across a young woman wearing a vest proclaiming CARE-4CALAIS, one of the local aid agencies most integrated into the camp. She was holding a colour photo given her by a man who was standing by her side. Bastien saw a painful, almost burning, look of hope in the man's eyes. As if his life depended on that photograph.

"*When?*" the young woman said in English.

"I told you I speak French," said the man, irritated.

"So, when?" she repeated in French.

"They should have arrived at least a week ago. A mother and child."

"If they're here, we'll find them in the women's camp. Wait, I'll write down their names and we can go together to check."

She took out a notebook and Adam softly spelled their names out.

"Sarkis. Nora and Maya Sarkis. My wife and daughter."

As he watched them walk away, Bastien couldn't help thinking of Manon and Jade. None of this made sense. Where was the justice?

"We do this job holding our breath," Passaro had said.

16

The previous day

Adam had barely slept in a week. For three hundred euros, he had managed to persuade a trucker he had approached at a lay-by on a German motorway outside Mannheim to hide him in the back of his truck, among boxes of hi-fis and crates of tin cans. The driver was heading for Dunkerque, but refused to cross into France with his extra illegal cargo on board. Adam had to get out at a small village in Belgium called Abele, and then used the GPS on his phone to walk the last sixty kilometres to Calais.

Arriving in the town centre in the middle of the night, he found no-one he could ask for directions to the Jungle. He would probably not have dared do so anyway, as he didn't know how the local inhabitants felt towards foreigners, or how closely they collaborated with their police. Without much hope, he consulted Google Maps on his phone and tapped in "The Jungle" as if it were an ordinary address. Google immediately came back with: "Calais Jungle, migrant camp, at 4.2km from your present position, rating 4.5/5, 2123 Rue des Garennes." Without trying to understand how you could rate a migrant camp as if it were a restaurant, he used the last of his strength to follow the dotted line on the map. He left the town centre behind, walked past quiet houses with gardens, and finally saw a group of young Africans on a deserted avenue. He quickened his step to catch up with them.

"*Jungle?*" he asked in English.

"Jungle," came a weary voice from the group.

Adam decided to ignore the GPS and follow a few paces behind the Africans.

When he reached the camp at around four in the morning, it was still asleep. Thanks to an almost full moon, he could make out the silhouettes of thousands of tents. Somewhere in there, Nora and Maya were sleeping soundly.

He had just travelled an impossible distance: almost six thousand kilometres. Propping his heavy backpack against a tree, Adam leaned against it on the soft sand. His legs began to tremble, and muscles started to twitch all over his body. Without really expecting it, he burst into tears. At that precise moment, Adam was overcome with joy. In addition to the tears, he began to laugh uncontrollably.

He allowed himself a few minutes to stare up at the sky, its pattern of stars identical to the one he used to show Maya in Syria. It wasn't much of a reference point, but it was enough to reassure him.

When he woke up with a start, the sun was warming him at the heart of a Jungle full of colour, movement, life and noise.

Adam had already seen a displaced persons camp. More than one, in fact, which was unsurprising considering the state of his country. But being accustomed to something doesn't necessarily harden you to it. He had looked on the Internet to prepare himself for his family's arrival in the Jungle, and yet he had still hoped that a country like France might offer a more humane reception. Everybody here seemed to have been left to their own devices, abandoned far from other people, squatting around the countless campfires which left a smell of damp wood in the early morning air.

He considered shouting the names of his wife and daughter to the different groups, or following the hundreds of little sandy paths that wound their way between the tents, but he had found himself in a large town that was impenetrable to anyone who didn't know its rules, and he knew he could spend a whole week searching to no avail. Experience taught him to stay in one place, high on this little dune with a tree beside it, a hundred metres from the main entrance, and keep an eye out for anyone who seemed to be in a position of authority.

A battered old white car, its doors plastered with CARE-4CALAIS stickers, entered the camp and set off down a bumpy asphalted road that went all round the northern section. When it came to a halt, fifteen or more men in dirty, ill-assorted and threadbare clothes rushed up to it. The woman who got out was instantly surrounded, but didn't seem either overawed or worried: her broad smile showed she was used to it. Adam saw her calmly responding to the questions posed in English but mangled by all kinds of accents. Little round glasses, slightly plump, and an apple-green T-shirt with CARE4CALAIS across her chest. She looked in her element. She was the one who would know.

Adam had handed her the photo, taking it from the wallet that had accompanied him throughout his journey. He was worried about letting go of it for the first time, keeping his eyes on it as though she might steal it.

"*When?*" the young woman asked in English.

"I told you I speak French," Adam said, irritated.

"So, when?" she repeated in French.

"They should have arrived at least a week ago. A mother and child."

106

"If they're here, we'll find them in the women's camp. Wait, I'll write down their names and we can go together to check."

She took out a notebook and Adam softly spelled the letters out.

"Sarkis. Nora and Maya Sarkis. My wife and daughter."

She wrote it down in capital letters, then pointed to her white jalopy.

"Do you mind getting into a car with a woman driver?"

They drove at a snail's pace for a kilometre with the windows wound down. Migrants frequently greeted the young woman; her presence succeeded in bringing smiles to their harassed faces. Some were carrying wood, machetes slung over their shoulders, others jerricans of water, still others big bowls of rice. She had to sound the horn to interrupt a game of football being played on the road, one of the few more or less level areas in the camp. Nobody seemed to notice the line of rubbish containers full to overflowing, surrounded by dogs and swarming with rats, or the cluster of portable toilets with brown liquid seeping out from under their closed doors.

Kids, youngsters, adults. All men. Poverty. Misery. And yet dignity as well. No sadness.

Coming from the most distant and violent countries, they had ended up here, the flotsam from conflicts in Africa and the Middle East.

The car stopped at the end of the road, beside a fence surrounding a wooded park where no makeshift dwellings had been erected. The women's huts were clearly protected from the rest of the camp, and this gave Adam a surge of confidence. Taking an impressive canvas bag out of her car boot, his companion invited him to go with her. When they arrived at the guard post by the entrance, she put her bag down and spoke to another volunteer, who was wearing the same apple-green T-shirt as her, an old fellow with a ponytail.

"Hi there, Antoine!"

"Peace to the world, Julie."

"Underwear. Knickers and bras," the young woman told him. "A donation from Secours Catholique. I've also got a load of sanitary towels on the back seat."

She tore the page from her notebook and handed it back to Adam before continuing:

"And this is Hakim. He's looking for his wife and daughter."

Adam didn't bother to correct her, but headed towards the volunteer while she turned back to her vehicle. The photo passed from hand to hand, and Antoine stared at it for quite a while.

"*Do you have the names?*" he asked in English.

"I speak French," Adam told him.

"So much the better, my English is crap. I need the names. Then we'll go and ask whether they want to see you or not."

"They're my family."

"That's just it: sometimes that's what they're running away from."

Adam handed him Julie's bit of paper.

"It's not computerised; it'll take time."

"Computerised?"

"I thought you spoke French," the hippie volunteer remarked. "It's not been entered into our computer, so I'll have to type the details line by line. So please, don't hang around here."

"Can I read the names out for you?"

"No, but you can come back in an hour."

Unwilling to let the old fellow, who was his only hope, out of his sight, Adam went to sit a few metres away, trying as hard as he could not to keep staring at him, yet desperate to witness the moment when he finally found the names of Nora and Maya on his list. But after forty-five minutes, the man turned the last page and closed the register. Adam could not possibly let it go at that.

"Please, look again. I beg you."

Antoine rubbed his eyes. He realised that whatever happened, the man would not give up until he had checked the list himself. Like all husbands, like all fathers. He pushed the register towards him.

"Otherwise you'll only insist I go through it again."

As Adam approached the end of the list, the last pages were like a countdown to zero. The volunteer looked at him more sympathetically.

"Did she try to call you?"

"I had a problem. I had to change my number."

"So did you manage to contact her?"

"The last time I spoke to her, she was in Libya," replied Adam, without looking up from the register. "Just before they crossed the Mediterranean. After that, nothing."

Recalling this made Adam's head spin, forcing him to sit. The other man left his post a moment to come and join him, rolling himself a cigarette.

"You know, Hakim, no two journeys are alike. I've come to realise that here, because sooner or later everyone tells me their story. Some take a week to reach us; others, if they come from the Horn of Africa, several months. You need to be patient. As for phones . . . so much depends on those damn gadgets. They break, they let in water or sand, they get sold, or lent or stolen. It's one of the things people most want. There could be a thousand reasons why she hasn't been able to reply to you."

A map of Europe appeared in Adam's mind, dotted with its

five hundred million inhabitants. He turned the last page of the register and closed it, a lump in his throat. His heart and soul were in pieces: only his body resisted.

"They could be in danger or lost in Germany, Belgium or Italy, and I'd know nothing about it. What should I do?"

"If this was where you were supposed to meet, all you can do is wait here. You're stuck in the Jungle, Hakim."

"My name is Adam."

"And when did you arrive, Adam?"

"Last night."

The man burned his fingers with his last drag and walked away.

"Follow me. We'll find you a tent and a sleeping bag; you'll have to sort the rest out yourself."

Adam followed him, turning round several times to peer through the fence, as if Nora or Maya might appear at any moment. He imagined himself running towards them. Smelling his daughter's hair, embracing his wife as if they were alone in the world, hugging them both until it almost hurt.

"Don't worry, Adam. I've got their names, and I'll keep an eye open for them. You just have to tell me where you pitch your tent. Anyway, I'm sure you'll come and visit me every day."

You're not the first, was his silent conclusion.

17

All the men in the camp had been through the same hell, the same odyssey. Adam told himself there might be a chance, however small, that somebody had crossed paths with Nora between Tripoli and wherever she had managed to reach. And at this moment, the faintest hope was still something.

There was no need for him to speak their languages: just showing the photo was enough. He came across Afghans, who were rather cold initially, Pakistanis, who invited him to smoke a joint around their campfire, and Sudanese who offered him sickly sweet tea. Ten times a day he walked up and down the stony track that served as the commercial street dividing the centre of the Jungle in two. The relentless sun brought a foul stench from the bins and latrines that the smell of fresh bread baked by the Indian baker couldn't mask. On the ground in front of a wooden-framed stone oven, a painted sign announced: GOOD BREAD. GOOD DAY. ONE EURO. There were also cigarette sellers – two euros for a packet of ten half-filled roll-ups – and a grocer in a rusty open container. Further on, resting on two trestles, a long wooden board displayed secondhand goods sold by a pair of Iraqis, offering trainers, jogging outfits, batteries and phone chargers. One kid had even got hold of an old blender, which he used to make smoothies with the fruit provided by aid agencies.

An open-air market at the centre of town: or rather, a black market in a shanty.

But he found no news of Nora and Maya.

At nightfall, Adam pitched his tent. Behind him, the Jungle. In front of him, the cordon of CRS vans that the officers very rarely left, their air-conditioning on full blast. He chewed on the two rolls of bread he had bought from the Indians, barely even tasting them, and forced himself to rest. But despite his fatigue, he found it almost impossible to close his eyes. He could hear singing, lorry engines out on the nearby main road, canvas flapping in the wind, then all of a sudden, somebody crying out in pain. The cry was repeated three times, then faded away.

Later that night it was the sound of a brawl that attracted his attention. Voices in a language he didn't recognise, wood splintering, something toppling. Adam opened his tent flap to discover, at the foot of the dune, a group of shadows demolishing a shack and looting its contents. He slowly zipped up the tent flap and lay down again. He would be a hero for his wife and daughter only. Until they arrived he'd keep a low profile and silence his sense of right and wrong.

The next day was exactly the same as the first, and so were all those that followed. Adam always adopted the same technique: approach a group having studied its composition to work out who seemed to be the leader.

"Military man!"

Adam started, and looked round to see where the voice came from.

"I see you, military man!"

A few metres away, a tall, skinny black African was smiling

at him, hand raised in greeting, sitting cross-legged on a log. He had a woollen bonnet on his head and was wearing a thick T-shirt despite the summer heat. To avoid continuing this awkward conversation out loud, Adam went up to him. Knowing they spoke Arabic in many African countries, he addressed him in that language.

"Do you know who I am?"

"Yes. You're Adam. You're looking for your loved ones. You come from Syria. You drank tea with us two days ago. But I'm from Sudan, as black as night, and we all look the same, don't we?"

"And I'm an Arab as brown as the earth, so it must be the same for you."

"I recognise you from the scar under your eye. And the story you told us surprised me. Men usually arrive alone. They try to get across to *Youké*, look for a job, a house, and only then send for their family. But you've done the opposite."

"I was obliged to."

"I'm not judging you, *military man*. We do what we can with whatever God offers us."

Overcoming the differences between the Arabic spoken in Sudan and Syria, the two men soon understood one another.

"What makes you think I'm from the military?"

"The way you observe things. You analyse everything. And your gestures and attitude. You're calm. You've known war, I can tell. You're not intimidated by the Jungle."

He held out his hand.

"My name is Ousmane. It means young snake. Adam and the serpent, we were bound to meet, weren't we?"

"The Jungle isn't the Garden of Eden, Ousmane."

"That's true. You'd have been expelled before you had time to bite an apple. You're as filthy as a stray dog and you stink just as bad. I bet you don't have any soap?"

Adam ran his fingers through his bushy beard, looked down at his black fingernails and the palms of his hands, where his life, head and heart lines were encrusted with dirt. It had been days since he last washed.

"Come on. I'll take care of you. You can't find your wife in this state."

They strode towards the centre of the camp until they came to the commercial street the aid workers called the Champs-Élysées. Ousmane took on the role of guide.

"This is the souk, but you probably already know that, as you've been all round the camp. You can buy anything here. If you have money, you won't go short. Do you?"

Adam instinctively folded his arms across his stomach to feel the bulge of the pouch tied round his waist. In it were his money and passport, and he never took it off.

"Not a lot," he said.

"Not a lot for whom? Not a lot is already something. I know you must have money because you've only just arrived here. Like everyone else you sold everything you had to make this journey, and you've kept enough to pay your passage to *Youké*, if that's what you want. But you must always reply, 'No'. 'No, I don't have money.' Understand? And anyway, if you're smart you can get free food."

Adam was pleased at the idea of a change of diet: he was growing tired of Indian bread. Ousmane came to a halt right in the middle of the Champs-Élysées souk.

"The Djalfari centre is at the far end of the Jungle, next to the women's camp. You can recharge your phone there. It's a hut with twenty or so electrical points powered by a generator. But I warn you, you need to be patient. Everybody here has a phone – it's the only link with their countries – so twenty sockets isn't much. It's also at the Djalfari centre that they hand out food officially, but you shouldn't go there. You have to queue for hours, and you risk getting beaten up by the Afghans, who see us as inferior and push in to get served first. You have to keep an eye out for them. They're no worse than anyone else, but as there are more of them, they think they can lay down the law. It's natural. A question of survival. We all become monsters when History gives us the opportunity. We even manage to find enemies among our own brothers. In your Syria you have Aleppo, and I have Bentiu and Darfur in my Sudan."

Ousmane pointed to two long lines with about a hundred people in each.

"Going back to food, the best for you is the Calais Kitchen, in that blue caravan over there, and the Belgium kitchen, just behind it, in that bus with no wheels. Two meals a day, and sometimes it's almost good. We Sudanese prefer to go to the Salaam Association to get food boxes. Cooking gives us something to do. It's important to keep busy."

They walked off down a sandy path, turning this way and that so often Adam no longer knew where he was. Passing a shack made from wooden pallets, they came upon a group of ten or so tents pitched around a campfire encircled by stones.

"Welcome to the home of the Sudanese, my friend. I'll introduce you to everyone, and you can come back whenever you wish. You can also bring your tent here with us. It's not safe on your own. This way you won't have to keep your backpack on so it won't be stolen. You're not a tortoise, Adam."

"I prefer to stay near the entrance. When they arrive, they're bound to pass through there."

A kettle was boiling on the embers. Ousmane approached the fire. A youngster was laying tobacco and cannabis on a long cigarette paper.

"Tea and hashish?" the Sudanese man proposed.

"I wouldn't enjoy it," said Adam. "I mustn't stop looking."

"So you're one of the few who has something to keep him occupied in the daytime. That's good, it'll stop you going crazy. There are lots of madmen in here. Because of what they've lived through, or seen, or lost. The only thing they have to do is go out at night to try to find a lorry to take them to England. During the day they stand around chewing the cud like cattle."

"It doesn't sound as if that interests you. Have you given up the idea of crossing the Channel?"

"I've tried twenty-six times and been arrested by the police on twenty-four occasions. On the twenty-fifth I was discovered by the customs dogs just before the lorry drove onto the ferry. On the twenty-sixth, I saw my cousin dragged fifty metres under the wheels of a truck. He died in my arms. As you see, it's far too dangerous. So I've asked for asylum in France. There's a legal centre here where two women lawyers come from Paris once a week to help us with our dossiers. I'll introduce you to them if you like."

Then, as if he had told Adam nothing more than a simple anecdote, Ousmane turned away. He called out to a fellow Sudanese and whispered a few words in his ear. Less than a minute later, the man reappeared with a wrapped bar of soap, a tube of toothpaste and a toothbrush, together with a razor and a small water bottle half-filled with shampoo.

"You'll also need a machete. Everybody has one, or a knife. For chopping wood or rope, and to defend yourself if need be."

"I'm not looking for trouble."

Adam went to shake hands. Ousmane stared at him with a smile on his lips, then took him in his arms and gave him a big hug. Adam was so surprised at this friendly treatment his body stiffened.

"Now you know where to find me. I've got some tea waiting.

If you want to join us, we eat at nine in the evening, Jungle time."

"Jungle time?"

"Between nine and whenever."

Since the migrants had nothing to do in the daytime, the notion of punctuality was redundant. Adam left with a feeling of gratitude towards Ousmane.

But since everything has its price, he also told himself he should remain wary of him.

PART THREE

RESISTING

18

Night quickly blanketed the Jungle, the dying light from the campfires creating a faint glow above the dunes. Adam gathered his things, stuffed them inside the tent and zipped up the flap. He cranked the handle of his LED flashlight a hundred times, giving him ten minutes or so of light, which he spent gazing into the eyes of his wife and daughter in the increasingly crumpled photograph. He had been tempted to pray for them, but then he recalled all the bodies of innocent civilians in the Damascus hangar, the torture, the war, the mass graves. Why would God pay him any special attention?

Then shouts filled the air. It was the same every evening, as soon as darkness fell. Adam had even given these unbearable moments a name.

The night of cowards.

And he was part of it.

Adam clenched his fists and waited for sleep to deliver him from shame. But just when silence had returned to the Jungle, a lengthy wail tore the night in two, piercing his heart. It was an almost animal howl. No words as such, nothing intelligible at any rate, like a strange language made up only of vowels . . . followed by a scream of pain. But there was no doubt about it: it was a child.

Concentrate on Nora and Maya. Avoid getting into trouble before they arrive: Adam kept repeating this to try to convince himself.

By the time the screams came again, louder, more heart-rending, more animal-like, Adam was out of his tent, unable to remain nothing but a witness. He pocketed his flashlight and let himself be guided by his hearing. His steps took him to a relatively organised part of the Afghan section of the Jungle. Two men were standing outside a canvas structure larger than the rest, a kind of ten-metre-square circus tent.

As Syrians and Afghans don't share the same tongue, what happened next unfolded in silence. When Adam approached the entrance, one of the men on guard punched him in the chest. He staggered back a couple of steps, then powered towards the entrance again, like a stubborn battering ram. The guard tried to punch him a second time, but before his fist could land, Adam caught him by the wrist, twisted it, and jerked it downwards. The bone snapped. The second man ran up and seized him from behind. Adam threw his head back as hard as he could, and his skull flattened his attacker's nose. The Afghan fell to the ground, clutching his bloody face. The blade of the machete at his side glinted in the firelight, not much longer than a knife, with a curved blade like a sickle. Adam grabbed it and entered the tent.

A young black kid, about ten years old, was stretched out on his stomach. A man was on top of him, holding his two hands behind his back, one knee pressed between his shoulder blades to completely immobilise him. Another man, trousers down round his ankles, was gripping the boy's hips.

Astonished, they turned to look at Adam, but before they could understand what was going on, he pressed the machete blade against the rapist's throat. His accomplice took two steps back, then ran for the exit without waiting to see more. Adam had only seconds to act. Sweeping the man to the floor with a kick, he took his head in both hands and started beating it on the ground until his body went as limp as a rag doll. He stopped before he killed him.

Adam kneeled down and helped the boy to his feet, pulling up his jogging bottoms. Seeing his aggressor unconscious on the floor, the boy's dark, tear-stained eyes turned to Adam. At that moment, something occurred between them. A kind of pact. An alliance. Adam slipped his arm under the boy's legs and picked up the machete. The boy responded by wrapping his arms round Adam's neck. All this had taken what seemed like an eternity, so why were they still alone inside the tent? Adam realised the Afghans were lurking outside. He took a deep breath to give himself courage, but remained rooted to the spot. The boy gripped him even tighter, as though certain he would protect him, and this galvanised Adam.

As soon as he set foot outside the tent he was confronted by eight furious Afghans. When one approached, Adam whirled the machete round his head to ward him off, like a shepherd surrounded by wolves. But he wouldn't be able to keep them at bay for long. He kicked at the embers of the fire, scattering hot charcoal onto the tent canvas, which immediately caught fire. Almost everything in the Jungle was made of flammable material, and so most of the group rushed to put out the flames before their camp was reduced to ashes. Only two of them remained to face Adam.

The machete blade whistled through the air as he swung it violently to and fro. He didn't hit anyone, but they didn't dare come any closer. With one arm still supporting the boy, his muscles began to quiver. Summoning the remains of his strength, Adam leaped over the fire, knocking one of the men to the ground. Then he ran and ran until he was out of breath, twisting and turning between tents and shacks until he was completely lost. At last he stopped, hearing no sound from his pursuers. The night was so dark he found it hard to get his bearings, until he recognised beneath his feet the asphalt of the road that went round the Jungle, bordered by stumpy trees marking the edge of the dunes and the forest. He hid among the trees, his lungs bringing up what seemed like molten lava as he tried to control his breathing. The boy's breaths came in rattling gasps, his throat raw from the screaming.

All at once, Adam felt a sticky liquid trickling down his arm. He reached into in his back pocket and lit his flashlight. Red. Everywhere. On his arm, but above all on the boy, all round his buttocks. His trousers were soaking. He was pissing blood.

19

The CRS company on night watch over the Jungle had lowered the volume on the radio linking them to their control centre. They were where everything happened anyway, and if anything kicked off, they would have ringside seats.

The men were dozing in the back of the van, while the driver and their commander smoked cigarettes and set the world to rights in the front.

"It's like in horror movies, you know, when the chick is running through the forest, tripping over every three metres, while the murderer is pursuing her calmly at walking pace."

"I don't see the connection."

"There is one, you'll see. So she manages to escape from the forest and arrives at a small cottage. She bangs on the door, says she's going to have her throat slit, that she's being followed by a madman and so on. And then, if the owner doesn't open up, the audience think he's a nasty piece of work. That's normal, isn't it?"

"Yeah. Refusing to help someone in danger. But I still don't get the connection."

"It's that we're doing exactly the same thing. All these migrants are running from a serial killer and they come knocking on our door, but we pretend we can't hear them."

"Okay, except that there's ten thousand of them knocking.

And if we open the door to them, another ten thousand will turn up, and another ten thousand after that."

"I know mathematically that's true, but in human terms, it's still hard . . ."

A movement outside attracted the officer's attention. He dropped his cigarette out of the window.

"Headlights!"

"What?"

"The headlights, for fuck's sake. Switch on the headlights!"

The two beams cut through the shadows to reveal, a metre away from their van, a man carrying an unconscious child in his bloodstained arms.

20

Calais Hospital Centre

Bastien Miller was sitting patiently in the waiting area of the surgical wing. He was perched on a chair losing its stuffing, hesitating over the magazines left on the low table, some of them dating from the last century. The one on top of the pile patriotically heralded *Les Bleus'* victory in the 1998 World Cup. A gurney banged into the swing doors and came hurtling through, guided by two paramedics. Its wheels creaked as it turned a corner and disappeared. On it lay a small black kid who was crying softly.

The gurney was followed by a man wearing an orange police armband, escorting an athletically built Arab dressed like a tramp. Bastien immediately recognised Capitaine Cotin, the night duty officer from Calais police station. They approached the waiting area and the cop tried to communicate in English with the other man.

"You. Sit here. Wait. Okay?"

It was only when he had freed himself from his charge that he noticed Bastien.

"Miller, what the fuck are you doing here at this time of night?"

"Evening, Cotin. A domestic violence case. I'm waiting for the surgeons to reset my victim's jaw so she can make a complaint against her guy."

"You should have left it for the night watch. I'd have looked after it."

"We got the call at a quarter to seven. I went with the responders to arrest the husband, then calmed his wife down and dropped their kids at their grandmother's. I figured I might as well see things through."

"Yeah, you mean you didn't feel like going home."

Bastien avoided replying.

"Are you with the kid on the gurney?"

"Yeah," said Cotin. "Little black kid raped in the Jungle. I don't know how this Arab guy was involved, but he brought the boy to the CRS. He could be the boy's pimp, or even the one who raped him – you never know with these people – but I'm betting he's not the father. In any case, he can be the responsible adult. As soon as the kid's patched up, he can cart him off."

Given the sheer quantity of horseshit Cotin had uttered in just a few sentences, Bastien refrained from saying anything. The Arab, meanwhile, had lowered his eyes and clenched his fists.

"What about the investigation?"

"The rape? That's a matter for the police judiciaire at Coquelles. But they're not likely to jump on it."

"I understand: that would be too much to ask," Bastien said sarcastically.

"What would you do, Supercop? Give everyone in the Jungle a DNA test? It would come to about two million euros, so that's a tidy hole blown in our budget. Or you could appeal for witnesses in the camp: I'm sure they'd be delighted to talk to you. They all really trust the cops. Do you think we didn't try at first? Do you have any idea how many identical cases I've been lumbered with this past year? Two or three operations on anal tears each week. Sometimes these kids only have their arses to bargain with when they're crossing Africa. The same to get across the Channel. So live with it."

With that, Cotin went off to look for a doctor he could speak to about the young boy, leaving the lieutenant with the Arab, a man Bastien knew nothing about, apart from his reaction to the captain's harsh words. Bastien got up, inserted a few coins in the drinks machine then came back and placed two plastic cups on the low table.

"Coffee?"

The man looked up, hesitated, and accepted.

"My name is Bastien. And I know you understand us."

The man simply blew on the hot coffee.

"Where did you learn French?"

Silence. Still no reaction.

"Where do you come from? Can you at least tell me your name?"

Bastien was beginning to doubt his intuition when the man finally replied in a deep voice.

"My name is Adam. I am Syrian. I learned your language thanks to my father, so yes, I do understand you. What I don't understand is why the police refused to follow me into the Jungle so I could point out the men who did this to the boy."

Recovering from his surprise at hearing such perfect, almost accentless French, and equally disgusted at the situation, Miller felt somehow responsible.

"It's complicated," he heard himself say weakly. "We can't investigate inside the camp."

"Then I won't expect anything from you. I just want to know if the boy is alright. Can you tell me that, at least?"

Bastien looked around to see if he could spot Cotin, but there was no sign of him.

"It's the other cop who's dealing with it. You'll have to ask him."

"Cop?"

"Policeman," Bastien corrected himself. "I thought you knew French."

"Only what I learned from books. I don't think your colleague has a very high opinion of me. I prefer to ask you."

As Adam had been hoping, Bastien stood up and went off to the nurses' station. He returned a few minutes later.

"The kid is torn, but not so badly it needs stitching up. You'll be able to leave with him in the morning. If he spends two days resting in bed it will heal. Will you look after him?"

"He's nothing to do with me. He's a kid from the Jungle. I'm not sure he has a family: I don't even know his name."

"The doctors say this isn't the first time. That's he's been raped before. Were you the one who saved him?"

"I may have saved him, or I may have brought him even more problems, I'm not sure," said Adam.

A nurse came to tell Bastien the woman's jaw had been reset. And that she was taking advantage of it to badmouth the police, her husband, the nurses and the doctors. The lieutenant was about to disappear, and Adam couldn't pass up this opportunity. So when Bastien got to his feet, he gripped his arm.

"I heard that no-one in the Jungle wants to talk to you. You don't have any contacts there. I'd be happy to help. Having eyes and ears inside the camp could help you some day, couldn't it?"

Bastien sat down again, wondering what this new informant would cost him.

"What do you want in exchange?"

Adam's replying came flooding out.

"I was meant to join my wife and daughter in the Jungle, but they're not there. Perhaps they've been detained somewhere in

France. Do you have a record of arrests, a list of missing people, or of border crossings? I'd like you to check for me."

Bastien was surprised at how much the other man knew.

"How do you know all that?"

"In Syria I was a cosp as well."

"It's 'cop'," Adam said. "That's what we say."

Impatient, the nurse called again for Bastien to accompany her.

"Have you got a mobile phone?" he asked his Syrian "colleague".

"Yes."

"Let me have it. I'll punch in my number and take yours."

Two hours later, after much shouting and many tears, Bastien succeeded in taking the young woman's deposition. He left the hospital to calm down and enjoy the fresh evening air, cigarette between his lips. He found the night captain sheltering under the front canopy and lent him his lighter.

"Do you want me to contact the juvenile division?" asked Bastien.

"What for?" Cotin said, as if he hadn't understood.

Miller only had to give a disappointed sigh for him to explain.

"The juveniles only deal with minors from Calais. They have no jurisdiction, and above all no solution, when it comes to the kids in the Jungle. As far as I'm concerned, this one's an adult, and I'll treat him as such."

"I can understand you've got a lot of work on tonight, but he's not going to be able to walk back. It's more than six kilometres to the Jungle."

"Obviously I'll drop them there, Miller. What do you take me for?"

Bastien couldn't decide if he was a despicable cretin or just an exhausted cop.

"I'm sorry. Everyone in Calais seems at the end of their tether. I can't tell the difference between exasperation and pigheadedness."

"I'd bet on exasperation if I were you. It's usually that. It's also less insulting."

Cotin ground out his cigarette on the floor next to an over-flowing ashtray, proof of the stress felt by those who waited beneath the emergency unit canopy.

"By the way," he went on, "have the nurses told you?"

"Told me what?"

"What they found on the kid. Or rather, what they didn't find."

21

Hôtel Bleu Azur, Calais
Room 309
The same night

As soon as he had unpacked, Commandant Paris had ordered room service, and now the leftovers were on a tray on the desk opposite the bed. He had the television on without really paying much attention to it, while at the same time flicking through the files on his informant, the Jungle and the target his service had been trailing for a year now: Shadow.

There was a knock at his door: the informant was only six hours late. Paris heaved himself up from a far too comfortable bed and waddled over to let him in.

"Merle! What on earth have you been up to?"

The young man pushed his way into the room without waiting to be invited. His red hair seemed to have exploded on his head, as if he were wearing a cat. The freckles dotted all over his face gave the impression of an innocent adolescent. Until he opened his mouth.

"Don't start, for fuck's sake! It took me ages to get away from the No Borders people without them noticing. Besides, I told you it was a bad idea to come here. This is where the Albanians meet. Didn't you notice the guys hanging out in the lobby? They're all people traffickers. They come to the Jungle every other day to pick up clients. One of them could easily have recognised me. Thanks for being so discreet."

"If you want to hide, stay in the crowd."

"I couldn't give a fuck for your all your undercover cop shit. You have to listen to me as well. I'm the one out there risking his neck."

Paris switched off the television, cutting off Bruno Kremer in full flow in the umpteenth Maigret repeat. He opened the minibar.

"First you listen to me, Merle. Pour yourself a glass and calm down."

The informant took off his woollen cardigan, stinking of wood smoke and damp, leaned over the small fridge and stuffed all the little bottles into his pocket. While Merle was rifling the minibar, Paris laid a series of photos out on the bed. Six portraits, not all of them particularly clear.

"We've called him 'Shadow'. He's one of these six. Well, I hope he is. He's been recruiting for Isis for eight years, and it's only now we're getting anywhere close to him. That tells you how good he is."

"And what are you hoping to do with him? Turn him so he'll work for you?"

"Impossible. He's not a young idealist like you. He's the kind of man who's willing to die for his cause. There's no chance he'll collaborate. Like I told you, he's good, maybe one of the best around. So it's the people he's going to recruit who interest us, the new ones, the ones who'll make mistakes. They all belong to jihadist groups, and with a bit of luck they'll allow us to identify active cells on French territory."

"So you're not going to touch Shadow?"

"No. Shadow is like the exploding ink they put in banknote

bags. He'll stain a jihadist, who'll in turn stain a cell, and all we'll have to do is follow the trail."

Paris pointed to the portraits on the bed.

"Take photos of them on your phone, memorise their faces, and if any of them turn up in the Jungle, contact me. Is that straightforward enough for you?"

"I've never said it was complicated, I said it was dangerous. There are two mosques in the Jungle. A moderate one, where anybody can go to pray. The other is Salafist, it's fundamentalist and brutal, with a guard checking faces at the entrance."

"Except that Shadow's not going to spend the whole day in the mosque. You don't have to convert, all you have to do is wait for him to be hungry or thirsty."

"Yeah. I just have to wait. And talking of waiting, what can I expect regarding the white supremacist Sal nearly killed? My blood is still on his shirt."

In all honesty, Paris loved the moments when he could come across like a secret agent in a film.

"The affair has been covered up. No more blood. No more Nazi. No more investigation. Archived: unknown assailant. It wasn't hard to persuade the Coquelles police judiciaire. You're clean. Good to go."

Reassured, Merle took photos of the six faces and cast a longing look at the soft bed. It was three o'clock in the morning and the Jungle was more than five kilometres away.

"Do you mind if I sleep a bit while you're watching TV? It's ages since I've been in a real bed."

Paris beamed at him.

"Fascinating. Can you even hear yourself?"

"So that's a no?"

"Get out of here, Merle."

22

At first light, the police van dropped Adam and the young boy near the entrance to the Jungle, and sped off. The little black kid could walk – slowly but with no obvious difficulty or pain. Perhaps he was simply used to it. God knows (even if He'd closed his eyes to them) the horrors he'd already had to suffer in his short life.

As they were approaching his chosen spot, Adam could see the dune and his tree, but no tent or backpack. During the night he had been wondering what reprisals there would be: this one was not the worst he'd come up with, but it left him without shelter or clothes.

"Hey! Military man!" he heard Ousmane shout behind him, so loudly that he made early risers in the camp turn and stare.

Adam looked at him warily. This didn't give Ousmane a moment's pause: he ran up to him and embraced him with a familiarity he still couldn't get used to.

"Ousmane, I told you not to call me that. It could cause me trouble."

"You seem to be able to handle yourself. And if you're looking for your things, they're in the Sudanese camp. After what you did last night, I thought it best to keep them with me."

"How do you know about that?"

Ousmane burst out laughing.

"It's a small village here. When someone attacks the Afghans, it's so rare that everybody soon gets to hear about it. Especially if he does it on his own. No one takes them on, least of all in their sex den."

"You mean it's official? Everyone knows about it?"

"Yes, everyone but you. The Secours Catholique volunteers helped them build it. They thought it was for a school. The charge is five euros an adult, ten for a child. You poked your nose into a very profitable business. Normally I'd say you had only one or two days to live, but right now, I'm more hopeful."

"And I suppose I have you to thank?"

"No, you can thank your lucky star. They've heard you speaking French with the aid workers: you're just about the only one in the camp who knows their language. But above all, last night with the boy you went straight to the police, whereas in here, nobody trusts them."

"So?"

"So they're suspicious. They're wondering who you are, if you're an agent from the intelligence services. That's why, even if you don't like it, I keep them guessing by calling you military man. As long as they're unsure, they'll leave you in peace. They'll close their sex den and hide the rapist for a couple of weeks. But any spark could start a fire, so stay as far away from them as possible."

"Is that all?"

"No, my friend. If you're hoping to get to England, you've shot yourself in the foot. The Afghans are the ones who deal with the traffickers. Them and the Albanians. That will make it harder, but I'm here to help you."

"Why are you doing all this for me?"

"We have to find something to do if we don't want to go

crazy. I'm helping you because I can see from the way you behave you're a brave man. God brought us together, so there must be a reason for it. And anyway, good deeds are only loans."

"I like proverbs too, and I know one from your country. 'When the storm breaks, everyone protects their own head.'"

"Like you last night, with the boy?"

It was Adam's turn to smile.

"It was too violent a storm: he would have drowned."

Ousmane put an arm round Adam's shoulders and invited him to go with him.

"Come, my friend, come and collect your things."

A few metres further on, Ousmane glanced behind them.

"You know your little friend is following us?"

"Yes. What do you want me to do about it? I'm not going to throw stones at him."

When they reached the Sudanese camp, Adam and Ousmane settled near the fire. Although the days could get unbearably hot, in the early mornings the warmth from the flames was welcome. The boy stood watching at a few metres distance.

As usual, the other Sudanese men greeted Adam by laying a hand on the back of his neck, his thigh, or hugging him. Contact, with skin, with another person, in the Jungle, far from loved ones. The pain of absence. The need for affection. After Jungle Time, Adam was beginning to understand Jungle Love.

His backpack and rolled-up tent were laid on the ground in front of him, while Ousmane searched for something in his pocket.

"I found this in the sand on your dune. You must have dropped it."

Adam was confronted by Maya's smile in the photo. How could he have forgotten it, even for a single night? For a moment, the little kid had become more important than everything else. His attention had wavered.

"Do you know the boy I helped?"

"Yes, I've seen him before. He's been here about a month. He's a wild animal. He belongs to the Afghans. He's always trying to escape them, but the Jungle is small. They always catch and punish him."

"I don't know what you mean by 'belongs to'."

"A defenceless youngster will always attract predators. Think how much your journey to France cost. Probably almost everything you had. How do you think a kid like him was able to cross Africa? As a sex slave, or maybe simply a slave. They did the same with him here. Perhaps they even promised to get him to *Youké*. And although he now understands they would never help him, the damage is done. He belongs to them."

"Have you tried to help him?"

"You know I have, Adam. You know me by now. But he doesn't trust us Sudanese either, or black people in general. I think his spirit has been crushed. You seem to be the only one who can get near him."

"Does he understand us?"

"I've no idea. How would I know? Watch this."

Ousmane stood up and approached the little boy with a bowl of tea. The youngster scuttled away between two tents like a rabbit.

"At least I've got rid of him for you," Ousmane said with a smile.

23

Throughout that day, Adam felt a discreet but constant presence. No danger, no threat, but the boy didn't stray an inch
from him.

He had only left his saviour once for a very short while,
disappearing into the forest to collect what was dearest to
him. Concealed under some branches was all he had managed
to salvage from his past life: a lurid blue backpack with a red
front pocket. Inside it were a scrap of printed fabric that had
belonged to his mother, his elder brother's leather wristband
and a few other treasures that were valuable only to him. He
strapped on the backpack and ran to join his protector, while
still keeping his distance.

Adam was back on his dune. He had paid another visit
to Antoine, the old hippy volunteer. No news. The Djalfari
centre where food was officially handed out was nearby, and he
took advantage to go up, clutching his photo, to those in the
endless queue and ask for a moment of their attention, like a
down-and-out begging for coins. When he saw the sign outside
saying JULES FERRY CENTRE, he realised that "Djalfari" was
another appropriation from French. He spent three hours there,
gaining nothing more than a touch of sunstroke for his pains.

He had also been to see Julie from Care4Calais, in what
served as their "offices": a secondhand white prefab installed on

the sand behind the Belgian Kitchen. This was in the western part of the Jungle, where *Médécins sans Frontières* had its tents and the free legal aid centre its caravan. The latter was crammed with migrants clutching dossiers, hoping to have their request to join family members authorised by the UK authorities.

For two weeks now all Adam had met with were polite assurances, sympathetic smiles or distressed shakes of the head. And yet every day, from morning to night, he continued to show his photo to anyone who would look at it. He aroused the empathy of the aid workers, but he also reminded the migrants of what they themselves had lost, and as a result some of them had started to avoid him.

Worn out, he lay down in his tent, but it took him a long time to get to sleep. He understood the looks that told him not to wait any longer, not to keep on hoping, to be sensible before he was driven mad, to surrender and give up the fight. He understood them, and now saw them flickering beneath his closed eyelids. His stomach was heavy as lead, his intestines tied in knots: it was as though a hand were squeezing his innards until tears of pain welled in his eyes. For three weeks now, ever since Maya had drawn a heart in the condensation on the taxi window, he had been afraid for his wife and daughter. No-one can withstand three weeks of constant, lacerating fear. After a ghastly night, Adam emerged from his tent to face another day.

The little black boy sat wide awake on the dune watching over him, head resting on his knees. He had the bright blue backpack in front of him, and was holding a machete, using the blade to trace shapes in the sand. First an arrow, then a circle, finally a line like a spear. When he saw his protector, he quickly rubbed them out.

Adam recognised the curved blade as the one he had wrenched from the guard at the Afghan sex den and dropped at the edge of the forest where they had hidden. Somehow, after a night of suffering, the sight of this child in the early morning brought something to a head. He sat down beside him, allowing the first rays of sun to softly relax his features. Looking around for the first time, he saw how badly he had let things go. He had refused to properly install himself as if to convince fate he was only passing through. But morning catches people unprepared, without shield or barrier. It was no longer possible for Adam to lie to himself. He might be in the Jungle far longer than he had been willing to admit.

He had to make a fire and put stones round it. To buy coffee, tea and biscuits. Find a length of material to hang between the tree and his tent to protect himself from the afternoon sun. Plunging his hands into the still cool sand, he turned to the boy.

"Do you understand my Arabic?"

The boy waggled his head in a hesitant "yes" that told Adam he needed to use the simplest words.

"Did you stay here all night?"

Another nod of the head.

"What's your name?"

No reply. Adam remembered the cries he had heard that night. Wordless cries, guttural moans. And the boy's silence since then. He took him by the arm and pulled him closer. He tried to struggle, but Adam held him tightly. Then he grasped his jaw and forced his mouth open. The tongue was nothing but a stump. Cut or torn out. A useless scrap of flesh. The boy flailed his fists and legs until Adam let go of him. But even though he was now free, he stayed sitting alongside the Syrian.

"Can you write?"

Arms folded, mouth fixed in a pout, the boy shook his head.

"Okay. I'm going to have to find a name for you then."

Adam stood up. The boy imitated him.

142

"A tent as well. Even dogs have a kennel."

Annoyed at this, the boy frowned.

"Okay, I see you really do understand me," Adam said with a smile.

They made an odd couple. An unheard-of combination. The big Syrian, who looked tough enough that nobody would want to bother him, and the kid, his gaze as dark as his skin, walking together along the Jungle's Champs-Élysées. The other migrants stared at them incredulously.

On the way, Adam showed his photo whenever he passed someone he hadn't seen before. Intrigued, the boy watched as he did so, backing off a few steps if a stranger got too close. When they reached the entrance to the Sudanese camp, the boy sat on a flat stone and let Adam continue on his own.

"My friend," Ousmane greeted him, "I see you two have become inseparable."

"I don't mind. He's not much trouble. I'm trying to think of a name for him."

"Call him Kilani," Ousmane said, as though it were obvious.

"Why not? It sounds good."

"It was my son's name."

"I didn't know you had a son, much less that you lost him."

"You don't know much about me, Adam, and that's as it should be. I used to be a soldier. I killed men, and some who weren't yet worthy of the name. I had no choice. But they too had fathers who must hate me, or want to come looking for me. There's no end to it. We are so many different people in one life. Father, killer, friend."

A Sudanese man placed two ill-assorted cups in front of them, filled to the brim with tea as sweet as a beehive. Adam took a sip and pulled a face.

"When Nora is here, she'll make you a much better cup. You won't be able to drink anything else."

Nora and Maya. Ousmane had heard their names a hundred times a day, but had never told Adam what he really thought – he preferred to let him cherish his illusions. He pointed to the plastic tarpaulin erected round the fire to keep off the wind. On it, written in Arabic in black felt-tip pen, were a series of family and first names.

"Those are the names of all those who have succeeded in getting to *Youké*. We're sad to lose our brothers' company, but they give us hope. They tell us it is possible. One day, you, your wife and your daughter will be on that list. I'll write your names myself and it will be a great day."

Ousmane immediately regretted consoling his new friend with white lies. Adam would understand soon enough he would have to travel to England alone. But that moment had not yet arrived.

They finished their tea and Adam said farewell. All that day, as soon as he stood up the kid copied him, just like the mime artists Adam had seen as a boy on the streets of Paris.

"Kilani. Would you like that as a name?"

The youngster shrugged.

"Well, you'll get used to it."

24

A plastic table and four chairs set out on the sand under the baking sun served as Julie's office when the heat inside the Care4Calais Association prefab became unbearable. She had just finished an angry telephone conversation, and for the first time Adam saw her customary reassuring smile slip.

"Good morning, Julie. Maybe this isn't a good moment?"

She took a deep breath, as though turning a page and starting a new chapter. The smile reappeared.

"I'm sorry, Adam. That was an English aid agency asking for the list of unaccompanied children. They're promising to come and collect about fifty of them, but we've got almost a thousand. How am I supposed to choose? Why one rather than another? It's dangling a lot of hope for the kids. This is the third time I've brought the list up to date, but none of these so-called aid workers has ever set foot inside the Jungle. So who has to see the faces of the children who were hoping to get out of here only to be told it's not going to happen? Yours truly."

"Yours truly?" Adam echoed.

"Oh, I'm sorry: that means me. The children are the most frustrating part of my job, but also what gives me most hope. And they're in danger, more than you might think. A few days ago one was raped, and I've no idea who he is or where he is.

All I know is that he was saved by another migrant and was able to get to hospital."

Another deep breath, another new chapter.

"Tell me what I can do for you, Adam."

"I need another tent."

"You're asking too much."

"It's not for me, it's for him."

He jerked his chin in the direction of Kilani, who was hiding behind a caravan. Julie crouched down and gestured for him to come closer. Faced with her irresistible smile, which gave the impression she could embrace the entire planet and still have love to spare, the boy let himself be coaxed out of his hiding place.

Julie studied him. Trainers with holes in them, a long blue pullover with sleeves down over his wrists. Kilani cautiously stretched out a hand towards Julie's blonde curls and stroked them with his fingertips, as if they might bite at any moment.

"He also needs new clothes," said Adam.

The aid worker's eyes rested on the faded jogging bottoms, still covered in bloodstains. She turned towards the Syrian, then back at the boy, and the penny finally dropped.

"The boy who was assaulted and the migrant – don't tell me that was you two?"

Adam said nothing.

"Was it also you who set fire to the Afghans' tent?"

"What would you have done in my place?"

Julie straightened up and, although she was the first to discourage the gesture when any female volunteer entered the Jungle, she took Adam in her arms.

"You're crazy. You acted without thinking and put yourself in harm's way."

"I'd do the same again if I had to."

146

Her green eyes looked deep into Adam's, and his determined, resolute look momentarily knocked her off balance.

"I can only see one way of protecting you two, but you'll have to trust me. I'm taking you to the CAP, the Temporary Reception Centre."

They walked to the road bordering the north of the camp and followed it round to the women's huts. A hundred metres before they reached them, Julie pointed to a line of forty white shipping containers. Brand-new, three metres wide by fourteen metres long, they were surrounded by a tall fence preventing access. She headed for the entrance.

"I've been here before," said Adam. "It's so clean I thought this must be where you aid workers lived."

"No. Most of the volunteers are from Calais, the *Kalissi* as the Sudanese call them. They have their own homes. Others stay in hotels, or with local families. And some, like me, stay every other night in the Jungle. What you see behind the wire is the CAP. Unfortunately, the migrants don't trust it. They think the people in the centre take their fingerprints and open a file on them."

"I understand everything you're saying, but I've no idea what it means."

"Take a good look then," Julie said, showing him the entrance guarded by a canvas checkpoint with CAP written in red letters on the side.

A youngster, about twenty years old, passed them on his way to the checkpoint. Adam followed him with his eyes. A T-shirt with a big rip in the back, a black leather shoe on his right foot, a green plastic sandal on his left, and a grubby pair of underpants in place of trousers. He said hello to the two guards, then stood in front of a Digicode screwed to a support. He tapped in six numbers and was given access to the screening machine. He passed through the first sliding door, placed his hand on the scanner and waited for it to recognise him. The second door slid open, and he was finally admitted to the centre.

Adam was struck by the mismatch between the youngster in rags and the level of cutting-edge security technology he had navigated.

"The code they tap in gives access to the screening machine," Julie explained. "Inside there's a control panel. It's called a palm print access key. We had to find a key they couldn't lose, so we decided to use the palm of their hands. The laser scanner analyses the shape, separation and length of their fingers. But we didn't realise how suspicious the migrants would be. The Somalis, for example, are convinced we use it to take their fingerprints, and as soon as there are enough people from the same country, their container is closed in the dead of night and loaded onto a ship to take them back home."

"I doubt France would behave that way."

"That's because you're rational. Others who are less enlightened or more damaged believe all the rumours they hear. You know, there are almost ten thousand people in here who have nothing to do but wait for a chance to try to board a lorry for England. And very few of them make it. So boredom and frustration get added to their conflict trauma. If you like to read, draw or write, make sure you do it an hour every day – it's essential. Find something to do before you blow a fuse."

Adam looked puzzled at this expression: he had never encountered it in his father's books.

"Blow a fuse: go crazy," said Julie. "Some migrants have been here for months; others more than a year, and three-quarters of them have psychological problems, often acute ones. I know some who have completely lost it. They can't bear other people;

in fact, they can't bear themselves. They live like hermits in the forest bordering the Jungle, simply waiting for death."

"To prefer to live like an animal in a forest to being registered in the CAP is pretty extreme," Adam said.

"It's all down to the rumours. If they're repeated often enough, they become reality. A Kurdish man told me he refused to stay in the Centre because he thought we passed on his details directly to his government so they could persecute his family members back home. Thanks to stupid gossip like this the Centre is only two-thirds full, while in the rest of the Jungle they're piled on top of one another. But the main thing is, you'll be safe from the Afghans in here."

She saw Adam hesitate. She could imagine everything he had been told over the previous few days and understood perfectly that he had no idea who he could trust. But above all she could tell from his expression that he would never leave the entrance to the Jungle. His dune was his vantage point, and the CAP was buried too far inside the camp. He would risk missing his Nora.

For a brief moment she was foolishly jealous of this woman for whom Adam had journeyed across the planet. His suffering, anger and an ill-defined fear surfaced in each of his gestures and decisions, even in his breathing. Infinite hope was what drove him on. She found him both touching and seductive.

So Adam wasn't going to settle in the CAP. But for Kilani, it seemed like the perfect solution. Adam looked round to talk to him, but yet again the boy had slipped through his fingers. What myth had he believed in to be so terrified of this place?

"A pair of children's trousers and a new tent, please."

Julie shot him a look worthy of an exasperated schoolmistress, but quickly reinstated her smile. She walked to the checkpoint, tapped in the code, had her palm scanned, and disappeared into the first white container, where clothes and other essential goods were stored.

A few minutes later she emerged with a bag containing clean clothes and a tent. As she was handing them to Adam, the radio attached to her belt crackled. It was Antoine, the guard at the entrance to the women's camp. Julie unhooked the walkie-talkie and turned up the volume.

"I'm listening, Antoine."

"Peace to the world, Julie. I've just been told there are new arrivals. Sixty of them, at the Jungle entrance."

She could see how Adam clung to this news like a diver to his oxygen cylinder.

"Antoine, are there any women and children among them?"

"I've just been asked for two places. So, two women, two children or one of each. That's all I know. Don't tell Adam anything yet; better if you check first. I can't bear the look on his face."

Embarrassed, Julie cut the communication as quickly as she could, but Adam had only heard the first part of what Antoine had said. Nora and Maya had arrived: their calvary was at an end, and he had lived to see it through. Soon he would be able to show everyone the loves of his life, then together they would flee this purgatory between two worlds, the hell of Syria and the paradise of England.

He had never run so fast, pushing his way through and apologising as he parted the crowd of migrants, his heart about to explode, his lips trembling, forming the words he would say to his wife and daughter the moment they were in his arms.

25

Antoine borrowed Care4Calais's old white car and went to meet the new arrivals. He pulled up in a cloud of dust, got out, disappeared into the middle of the group, and reappeared accompanied by a woman and a boy. That's what Adam saw first, and the two newcomers immediately consigned Nora and Maya elsewhere – which could be anywhere on the planet, for all he knew.

It was like receiving an uppercut to the solar plexus. Adam's legs gave way; his knees buckled and he couldn't walk any further. He let himself sink to the ground, the photo in his clenched fist digging into the sand. He hated the woman and her kid. He struggled to control his breathing as his strength ebbed away. From the highest hopes to complete collapse.

Kilani had kept his eyes on him the entire time. When Adam looked up, the boy was standing in front of him, scowling, hand extended. It took Adam a while to react, but then he handed him his photo. Kilani had been watching what he did with it. He smiled confidently at Adam and rushed over to the new arrivals.

Adam was filled with gratitude when he saw him tugging at their coats and shirts, grunting to attract attention as he held out the photo, being jostled and almost trampled on. Kilani was as keen and determined as if he were looking for his own family.

One of the men pushed past him, and his heavy pack knocked the boy to the ground, making him let go of the snapshot. A gust of wind snatched it up. Throwing himself after it, Kilani managed to catch it before it blew away completely. It was then that he looked closely at the two faces for the first time. Nora and Maya. The woman looked wonderful, and the girl looked like her father.

Antoine drove towards Adam and pulled up alongside him. Catching sight of the woman and her child on the back seat, Adam wondered what right they had to be there. The boy smiled at Adam, who turned his head so as not to have to see how happy he looked.

"Your wife and daughter passed through Libya, didn't they?" Antoine asked through the open car window.

Adam nodded without a word.

"Then you should go and see that man over there, the one in the black T-shirt. Don't ask me what he's doing here, but he's a Libyan people smuggler who accompanied his group all through Europe."

To fight, then give in. Start again. Over and over. Adam felt like a dying man on borrowed time being injected with adrenalin to force him on a few more steps. He rose from the ground, clutching the photograph.

Julie and a nurse from *Médecins sans Frontières* were receiving the newcomers. Julie was telling them about the regulations, codes, and how the Jungle was organised. The nurse was assessing if they needed urgent medical attention after their ordeal.

As Salam Alaykom.

The Libyan looked round at Adam and returned his greeting.

Wa Alaykom Salam.

Adam should have shown him his photo there and then, but he already knew what the reply would be. It was always the same: the man would look at the two faces and say how sorry he was.

"I thought that traffickers who arrived in Italy turned round and went back to Libya."

Taken aback by this, the man stared at Adam. The two aid workers were overwhelmed by all the newcomers' questions, so he had nothing better to do than answer the Syrian.

"You're right. But more than anything, I'm a businessman. Crossing the Mediterranean is too dangerous. It's swallowed up tens of thousands of migrants, as well as a good number of my brothers. And in Libya, first the Islamists seize power, then they lose it, and then they take it again. It's too unstable. Bad for business. Nothing but hassle. Here, though, there's a new market that's far safer. People pay twice as much to get to England, and France is not only a democracy, it's at peace. So I've come to see what's on offer. When I have enough money, I'll buy a house in Cannes, where they hold the film festival, with all the movie stars."

Everyone arrived in the Jungle to follow their dreams. Adam decided it was time to reveal his own.

"I know it's a long journey and you must be exhausted, but I need to know whether you've seen my family."

He took out the photo, smoothing it with the palm of his hand on his dirty trousers.

"They left Libya for Italy, but I haven't had any news of them. You've done that crossing many times, so maybe . . ."

The Libyan scrutinised the faces. He recognised them immediately, but pretended to be thinking it over.

It was the woman who'd been pushed into the sea. And he himself had thrown the little girl overboard. He raised his eyes from the photo, looking sad and sympathetic.

"I'm really sorry, my friend. Thanks to me, thousands of people have been able to leave Africa and join their relatives, but you must understand I can't remember all their faces. Especially as the journeys are made at night."

And since the greater the hope the more fatal it becomes, he injected a huge dose of it straight into Adam's heart.

"More Libyans should be joining me soon. You can't open up a new market on your own. I'll tell you when they arrive, and you can show them your photo. You mustn't give up."

These words touched Adam, and so, just as Ousmane had done with him, he offered help.

"The Jungle is a complicated place. If you have a problem or any question, I'm always up there, on my dune. Don't hesitate to come and see me."

The Libyan held out his hand, and Adam shook it warmly. With that the two men parted.

After nightfall, their two tents pitched side by side, Adam and Kilani both succumbed to sleep. A sudden vibration roused Adam from his slumber. It was a message from the young police officer he had met at the hospital. *Police-Miller* appeared on the screen.

No info in France about Nora or Maya Sarkis. I'd have liked to be more helpful. Really sorry. Miller.

Adam's phone dropped from his hand. He wondered where he would get the strength to carry on in the coming days. He thought of his weapon, in its holster with his uniform, and was glad he didn't have it with him. A neat hole in the head, from which his suffering could trickle out, drop by drop. It would be so easy.

Lost in these sombre thoughts, he heard Kilani in the tent only a few centimetres from him, crying out and moaning in a dream Adam wouldn't have liked to share. Happy children have to imagine monsters hiding under their bed. Kilani had been forced to more than his fair share in his short life, and they were not the sort that hid.

26

"My name isn't Kilani," Adam's young friend kept telling himself.

If only I could tell him, he would know everything about me. I'd tell him about the nightmares I've had every night since arriving in the Jungle. But I keep the scrap of fabric from my mother's dress with me, so I can ask her to ward off the evil spirits. I know she's watching over me and that I'm in her prayers, but sometimes the spirits are stronger. They're like demons that wait for night to come to show me images I'd rather forget. I know they attack Adam too. I can hear him in his tent begging them to leave him in peace, beating his head on the ground. He calls out Nora. Maya. One night I even saw him punching the trunk of a tree until his hands bled, then collapsing to the ground and bursting into tears. Some memories burn, and no-one can escape their nightmares.

The one that haunts me most often takes me back two years to my home on the banks of my lake. Close to my loved ones.

Lake No, South Sudan. 2014
On the border of the states of Upper Nile and Unity

I'm stretched out in the grass of the endless plains that border the White Nile. I call them "endless" because there's really no other word for it. Whichever way I look, there's a green ocean.

When the wind blows it flattens the grass, as if a giant were caressing it. It's always here that the dream begins. Just before the blood starts to flow.

Then I hear the cries and see the army vehicles in the distance. My father says our land is torn apart by a president and another man who wants to take his place. That's all I know, and that this brings out the military.

The sound of gunfire. I run towards the lake, towards my village. I leave the cows behind, even though they are my family's only riches. My big brother has taught me all I know about being a cowherd; he warned me above all else never to abandon the cattle. But now even the animals are uneasy: they can sense the danger.

The closer I get to the lake, the more the grassy plains give way to marshy ground. I sink in up to my ankles, and then halfway up my legs. It's harder and more painful to run. It seems as though the distance is growing.

Smoke claws at my throat. A hut is burning right beside me. The men and boys have been forced out into the open. They are lined up, with the women sitting a few metres from them. Brothers are looking at their sisters; women at their husbands. They swear to one another that they'll get out of this.

A soldier lays the barrel of his rifle on my mother's stomach, then slowly moves it up to her chin, making her raise her head to look at him. My mother is the most beautiful woman I've ever seen. The soldier has noticed that too. Tugging at her arm, he makes her stand up and drags her towards a hut.

My brother is still young, but he is big and strong. He stands up in front of the soldier, blocking his way. My father left a week ago, to buy a new motor for our generator. He told my brother that while he was away, he was the man in the family. So my brother does what has to be done. He acts the man.

Without hesitating, the soldier shoots him in the head. His body is flung backwards. His blood sinks into the earth.

It's the end of my childhood.

I can see myself running as fast as I can to fling myself on the soldier. His fist smashes into my face and I hear him laugh as I'm knocked unconscious.

When I come round, he opens my mouth and pulls out my tongue. It's wet, and slips between his fingers. He unrolls his white scarf stained with sweat and brown dirt and wraps it round my tongue. Pulling a hunting knife from his belt, he shows the blade to anybody else who might be thinking of rebelling. He slices through my tongue almost at its base. Red liquid pours out. At first it doesn't hurt: fear blots out everything else. Then the pain overwhelms me, and I taste my own blood.

At this point, I always wake up, crying out, tears in my eyes and fists clenched, revolted, terrified. It takes me a long time to realise where I am, in this Jungle, far from my loved ones.

But now, when I howl in the dark to shake off the nightmare, two strong arms grasp me gently but firmly, and a voice I would follow to the ends of the earth offers reassuring words.

"Calm now, little one, stay calm. I'm here," Adam whispers.

27

Bastien Miller slipped the bulletproof vest on over his T-shirt and adjusted the straps. It was eleven at night and the meeting with the BAC wasn't for another hour. He checked his magazine, slipped it into the pistol, clicked a bullet into the chamber, then engaged the safety catch. Engrossed in his preparations, he didn't notice the look of alarm on Jade's pretty face.

"Are you going on a migrant hunt?"

Bastien put on his black jacket and leather gloves.

"Where did you get that expression?"

"From school. They say that's what the police do."

"And you think that's what I do? Do you believe that of me?"

"I don't know. I have to guess at everything in this house. About you, maman, your work. It's as though I'm living with strangers."

Bastien realised he had been so convinced his daughter was an adult by now, he had over-estimated her. Jade was still a child. She needed stability above all, and they had made her move house and leave her friends and habits for a town and a school she didn't know – not to mention being stuck with a couple in crisis, her mother profoundly depressed and her father parachuted into a job that was far more complex than he had anticipated.

"I don't really know what colleagues get up to in a town

that's completely different at night and which no-one wants to tell me about. It's time for that to change," Bastien said, as though to justify himself. "But that shouldn't make me forget what's most important."

"Me?" said Jade.

"Yes, you, obviously."

Bastien took his daughter by the waist and sat her on the corner of the bed. He kneeled down in front of her on the thick carpet.

"I've been to the Jungle and I can tell you I didn't like what I saw. I can't get the images out of my mind, as if I was somehow responsible."

Seeing that her father was talking about his job for once, Jade didn't dare interrupt him.

"I've also met someone. A Syrian migrant. He's a cop like me, but from another country. He's had no news of his wife and daughter. He's waiting for them, searching everywhere, but when he told me about them I was so selfish all I could think about was you. I know our family isn't in a good place; I know I ought to sort things out rather than wait for everything to explode before I step in. But at least I have you here with me, and we can resolve things. He has nothing anymore."

"What's his name?" asked Jade.

"Adam."

"And you want to help him?"

"I've been trying to."

"Okay, so if I've understood properly, on the one hand you give the migrants a helping hand, and on the other you hunt them down. It's great having a schizophrenic father and a depressive mother."

"We're doing what we can to give you a solid grounding," Bastien joked. "With a bit of luck you'll be taking drugs before

160

you're fifteen. Meanwhile, you should have been in bed ages ago."

"Can I read for just half an hour?"

"To learn to be even more sly and cheeky? Well, I guess so . . ."

Manon was curled up on the living-room sofa, watching a thriller in which a girl was being methodically beaten up.

"You shouldn't watch that," Bastien told her. "Besides, we've already seen it. It was the cop who did it."

Manon looked up at her husband, ready for action with his bulletproof vest and his gun.

"Where are you going?"

"On patrol with the BAC. I told you just now. This morning as well."

"I'm sorry, I'm a bit tired."

Bastien glanced at the strip of anti-depressants by a glass of water on the coffee table. They had been part of the décor for almost three months now, long enough for him to ask himself how effective they were. Sometimes he could be patient; at others he wanted to give his wife a good shaking. Now he kissed her on the forehead, pocketed his keys and bounded down the front steps.

Parked in the street outside, engine running, was the BAC's Nissan. Passaro was leaning on the bonnet.

"Good evening, Lieutenant. We're going to meet the Dog Unit at Junction 47. That's where the migrants try to board the trucks. We can check all our equipment. Do you want to sit in front?"

"Don't worry, Passaro. It's your team, you're still in charge."

Bastien climbed in the back. Cortex was driving, but Sprinter was missing.

"We're taking advantage of having you with us, lieutenant. We've sent Sprinter up in the chopper, to give us air support."

"What's that? You have a helicopter?" Bastien asked, surprised.

"Yeah, on loan from the traffic cops," said Cortex.

Passaro buckled his seat belt and turned to Miller.

"Tell-tale signs, lieutenant. When the BAC in your town needs a chopper, it means there's something rotten afoot."

A cluster of police vehicles had drawn up round the 24-hour service station, a few kilometres from the motorway junction. Only too pleased to have free protection, the manager doled out coffee and sandwiches every night. The Dog Unit was there, as well as some CRS vans, a roadsweeper truck on standby, ready to clean the road after any clashes, and a fire engine. It was as if it had become a habit to expect the worst.

Passaro was listing the equipment in the BAC's open boot.

"Helmet, shield, knee and elbow pads, gauntlets, body armour. The full Robocop."

"I don't have any of that," Bastien said anxiously.

"If things kick off, you can stay in the car. It's safer."

"And does it often kick off?"

"Their aim is to distract us. One group of smugglers attacks us at point A, while another group slips their clients up onto the trucks. Stones, bricks, scaffolding bolts: when it rains in Calais, it's a hailstorm. They sometimes make giant catapults from bike inner tubes to increase the impact. Do you know that game Angry Birds? It's the same principle."

Kneeling on the ground, Cortex was counting the team's tear-gas grenades. Although Bastien had used this kind of ammunition, he had never seen so much of it in one place.

There must have been two hundred canisters neatly lined up, like a swarm of wasps ready to attack.

"Are you sure all this is necessary? Or is it just to impress me?"

"You've understood by now that we don't really have the right to arrest the migrants," said Passaro. "Or rather, that it doesn't suit anybody. Our only task is to keep them away from the motorway, so they don't climb aboard the lorries or attack the drivers."

"We spend our nights catching them in our headlights like rabbits," Cortex continued. "It's a hunt, nothing more, nothing less, except we don't bring home the game. We fire so many gas grenades we get through pallet-loads every week. There are more in Calais than in the central riot police warehouse. The chief tells us we've spent almost two million euros on them in one year. And not a single arrest. Simply to secure the road to the ferries or the Channel Tunnel. And if the migrants don't get the message, we let the dogs loose on them. Or the CRS – there's not much difference."

Amid the hubbub of men talking and laughing loudly to gee themselves up, Sprinter's voice was heard over their radio.

"BAC 400 chopper to BAC."

"BAC receiving, over," Passaro said.

"We've just flown over La Rocade, two kilometres from your position. The thermal camera shows Walking Deads on the move. Several hundred on either side of the motorway. They're starting to build barricades. You need to slow the lorries down, disperse the migrants with tear gas, then send in the roadsweeper to clean up."

"Message received."

"Happy zombie hunt to all of you. Over and out."

"Hunt". The word had already been used twice, and Bastien wondered how he was going to tell Jade about all this, or if he dared tell her anything at all.

Behind them, a man with stubbly cheeks burst out laughing. He stank of alcohol and his clothes were crumpled. He kept his dog on a short leash against his thigh.

"Shit, I'm as excited as Wolf here."

Bastien stepped forward to greet Max, but the Dog Unit officer raised a hand to stop him.

"Don't get too close, lieutenant. Wolf doesn't distinguish between anyone these days. Cops, migrants, a female dog: he charges the lot of them."

Max kneeled down in front of his dog, and Wolf, already over-excited, narrowly missed him with a swipe of his muzzle.

"Hey, you really are a stupid dog, aren't you?" laughed Max. "It's only normal. He attacks almost a hundred times a night. If I did that, I'd need a muzzle and cage too."

He patted the dog's head, then stroked him. They both looked as if they could go off the rails at any moment.

"This dog has been set on black and brown guys for a year now. There's no way he can return to normal duties or even change departments. The last time I stepped into his cage he almost took a chunk out of me. I had to smash his snout to get him to calm down. When he's finished here, he'll have to be put down."

He kissed the dog's head.

"That's right, isn't it, stupid dog? You know that, don't you? I'll make sure you get the best dope, you won't feel a thing. And I'll go with you if need be, stupid dog."

The animal responded with a growl and a thrust of his muzzle.

His head reeling from all this offensive chatter, Bastien

walked off behind the service station. Cortex and Passaro soon joined him.

"Everything alright, lieutenant?"

And, as everything was not alright, Bastien gave vent to his anger.

"Are you crazy? You know who these migrants are, you told me so yourselves. People fleeing countries at war, trying to meet up with their families in England. We'd all do the same in their situation. How can you call them rabbits, game, Walking Deads or zombies? How can you joke about hunting them?"

Cortex lowered his head, and Passaro spoke up.

"Leave us, Cortex. The lieutenant needs a cigarette break."

When Passaro was alone with Bastien, he was more direct. He drew himself up to his full height:

"You're the one who's out of order, Lieutenant, with your three weeks on the job under your belt. Let me put you straight. Cortex, who's always playing the fool, is going through his second bout of depression. Sprinter, up in the chopper, tried to commit suicide last year. We're all at the end of our tether. We do and say what we need to not to crack. We'd like to get the hell out of here, but the Calais police service is a prison: nobody can move on."

"So you think it's normal to go out every night with men on the verge of a breakdown? Can't you replace them?"

"I don't want to replace them! Can you imagine what would happen if I ended up with cops who like this sort of thing? Gassing innocent people? My men are horrified by what they're doing, and that's my guarantee the job will be done without abuses or sordid pleasure. If we call them zombies, it's to dehumanise them, because our only role here is to attack men, women and kids who we'd normally protect."

"Why go on doing it then? Shouldn't you refuse to carry out immoral orders?"

"Because we want to. These lorries, the transport companies, are the lifeblood of Calais' economy. If they get hijacked every night on the motorway, they'll go somewhere else, to another port. My ex-wife had to shut her clothes shop in the town centre, and it's the same for your team. Erika's sister drives a hundred and fifty kilometres to work every day; Corval's cousin was forced to sell his restaurant for half what it's worth. And the tourists are staying away. It's our families' jobs we're protecting. And our town we're trying to keep afloat. We're the bogeymen: I never said it was proper police work."

"What about Max and his black and brown people?"

"Max is different. He's a slimeball."

"That's really reassuring."

For the second time that night, Sprinter's voice sounded over their radio.

"BAC 400 chopper to BAC. We have a problem. More than three hundred thermal images, and the barricades are already alight. They've moved quicker than expected. The lorries are heading straight for them. You've got five minutes to stop them."

Passaro turned to Miller.

"Are you ready? The time for words is over."

Near Junction 47, known as Point Romeo

Bumper to bumper in a solid line, the police vehicles and fire engines sped through the night. For several kilometres, this section of the A16 motorway was protected by wire fences more than ten metres high. Bastien watched the vehicles go by in a daze. He was familiar with ordinary barbed wire with its sharp points, meant to keep animals penned into their fields. But these fences were different, topped with butterfly-shaped razor blades. They were there to cut the skin, to cause a deep wound rather than simply to repel. Designed specifically for people.

A light drizzle began to fall. In the glow around the street lamps the rain resembled static on an old VHS cassette.

Bastien caught sight of a child's sneaker caught on the wire, then a torn scrap of fabric, flickering past like subliminal images: evidence of the nightly attempts to get over, testament to the migrants' desperate struggle.

Cortex put his foot down and raced to the head of a line of thirty stationary lorries, whose drivers had been warned by radio that there was a barricade up ahead. Some of them stayed fearfully in their cabins; others had jumped down and were walking round their trailers, torches in hand, worried about possible clandestine passengers and the damage they might do to their loads.

Less than twenty metres ahead of them, a huge bonfire was blocking the road, lighting the scene up much more effectively than the flashing police lights. Old furniture, mouldy mattresses, dustbins stolen in Calais, tyres, pallets, tree trunks and branches – it made for a spectacular display.

Lorry drivers, cops and firemen waited on one side of this blazing barricade. A longer and longer tailback. Unseen migrants about to launch an attack. Tension at breaking point. And yet nothing was happening.

Passaro had stayed in his car with the rest of his team.

"BAC 400 to chopper. What can you see?"

"We're flying over Junctions 43 to 46 to make sure this isn't a diversionary tactic. We'll be above you in a minute."

"Should we wait?" asked Cortex.

"Negative. We'll go and check."

Cortex walked round their car and got a massive flashlight

out of the boot. A Polarion Abyss dive light, known as "the Sun". So powerful it couldn't be used in towns, so bright it could blind and immobilise. Cortex strode over to the side ladder on the first lorry and climbed on to the roof. He switched on the Polarion. A beam of pure light banished the dark and revealed the waiting silhouettes.

They had climbed over the razor wire. Hundreds of them, crouching in the ditches on both sides of the motorway – the only place to hide now the town authorities had chopped down all the trees. They were lying still, just a few metres from the police vehicles. Cortex clambered down and got back inside their car.

"Shit, there's hundreds of them. And they're everywhere. If we use tear gas, we're going to asphyxiate everyone, cops and truckers as well."

"They succeed through sheer force of numbers," Passarro explained to Bastien. "They'll climb aboard the lorries and hide. We might not spot a few of them and they'll get as far as the customs controls a few kilometres down the road. It's a different story there. For now, the best we can do is work out which lorries they're heading for. Then we'll know where to concentrate."

At the back of the line of trucks, they heard the first lorry sound its horn, like a cry for help. Then a second one. Bastien turned to try to make out what was going on through the rear window, the dark night and the rain. Passaro loaded a tear-gas grenade into his Cougar launcher.

Then they were overrun. Literally.

Dark shapes emerged from the ditches and began to sprint in every direction. A human tidal wave crashing on to the lorries with no thought for the vehicles in their way, whether they were fire engines or police cars. They swarmed all over the

BAC's Nissan, climbing over the bonnet and the car's glass roof, smashing the rear-view mirrors and cracking the windscreen under their weight. Bastien and the others couldn't get out.

To prevent the convoy moving, two migrants punctured the first lorry's tyres. The driver's side window was smashed in with an iron bar; the headlights were kicked out. The trucker lay flat in his cab, hands protecting his head. One of the side doors was opened, and he was dragged out feet first, wrestled to the ground and beaten. By immobilising the first lorry, the migrants were giving the others time to climb into the ones behind.

Tarps were torn apart, rear doors forced open and the trucks invaded. One of the migrants ran up brandishing a burning branch to throw into the cab of the first lorry, but he was catapulted backwards by the impact of first one and then a second plastic bullet. Five metres away, Cortex reloaded his Flashball. Wolf, the half-crazed police dog, shot like an arrow from side to side, tirelessly charging everyone who wasn't white-skinned. Unaffected by tear gas, like all dogs, he seemed to be almost enjoying himself.

Given the unusually large number of assailants, Passaro and the CRS company had no choice but to try to clear the area. Dozens of tear-gas grenades arced like fireworks into the sky and fell onto what had turned into a battlefield. A cloud of choking gas formed all around them. The police too were blinded, their throats and nostrils on fire, as close to suffocating as the mob of migrants.

When the driver of the second lorry saw what had happened to his colleague, fear got the better of him. He decided that his best bet was to charge through the burning barricade. Slamming his vehicle into reverse, he hit the vehicle behind him, found first gear, and, engine racing, swung round the immobilised front lorry.

The noise was deafening: shouts, smashing glass and roaring engines created a terrifying din. Ignoring Passaro's protests, Bastien climbed out of the car, trying to find his own people in this seething hellscape where nothing was visible beyond the first five metres.

Cortex fired two more rounds almost blindly, then reloaded his Flashball. Every cop was attempting to deal with about twenty migrants, which meant none of them noticed the rig hurtling towards the barricade. Cortex was standing right in its path. Just as it was about to crash into him, Bastien leaped across the radiator grille, pushed Cortex as hard as he could, and held him pressed against the car bonnet. Eyes tight shut, face contorted, he felt the whoosh of the lorry as it almost brushed against his back. Danger averted, the two men could only exchange a brief glance before turning their attention to the lorry driver's crazed charge.

Without slowing down, the lorry careered into the bonfire, which exploded in a shower of sparks, sending burning fragments of wood in all directions. An iron bar pierced one of the truck's front tyres, and a metal box spring was jammed into the axle. The driver braked desperately, the rig swayed to the left, then to the right, before it toppled over, ploughing a deep furrow in the ground before coming to a halt on its side in the ditch.

This spectacular accident seemed to calm everybody down. In a fog of tear gas that even the police's flashing lights struggled to penetrate, one of the burning wheels of the upended lorry went on spinning in the darkness. The chaos created meant the road would be out of action for the rest of the night. The tension eased, like in one of those playground games when someone shouts "pax".

The silhouettes drifted calmly away, in no great hurry.

The migrants who had succeeded in hiding aboard the lorries climbed down and filed past the CRS to join the others. One bewildered kid fell to the ground and a cop, anonymous in his Robocop armour, picked him up gingerly.

The migrants would try again the following night. The cops would be there to meet them. A merry-go round that had been spinning for a year now.

The driver crawled out of his cab through the smashed windscreen, half of which lay in a lump against the bonnet. Cortex, whom he had so nearly run over, grabbed him by the collar and threw him to the ground.

The dark shadows moved off, but one fifteen-year-old Pakistani boy stayed close to the overturned lorry, as though it were physically impossible for him to leave, his eyes fixed on the vehicle's rear doors.

With the driver safely out of his cab, Bastien and Passaro climbed up into the back of his trailer. If somebody had got in there, he could be wounded. They clambered to the front, scrambling over tall boxes of electrical goods, or what was left of them after having been so violently thrown together.

Bastien's torch swept the enclosed space, coming to rest on a lifeless body, the head crushed under a huge refrigerator. The two men stared at it without exchanging a word.

When the firemen removed the body a few minutes later, Bastien caught the eye of the young Pakistani. When he saw what had happened, the adolescent fell to his knees as if all his strength had deserted him. Had he lost a father, a brother or a friend? When Bastien went over to him, he jumped to his feet and ran off to join the rest of the retreating crowd.

Some of the officers were still firing tear gas from both sides of the CRS vehicles, while others were spraying their eyes with a decontamination spray. Ignoring his own streaming eyes,

Bastien strode over to the trucker, who was still sitting on the ground, closely watched by Cortex. Bastien glanced at his watch and said to him:

"It's one thirty-two in the morning. I'm arresting you on charges of manslaughter and putting another person's life at risk. Cortex, cuff him and put him in the car."

"At your orders, lieutenant."

The helicopter flew low over them to disperse the tear gas and the smoke from the barricade in concentric spirals. Springer trained the searchlight on his colleagues thirty metres below him.

"BAC400 chopper to BAC. Everything okay?"

Passaro picked up his handset.

"There's one dead among the . . ."

The word "zombies" didn't pass his lips.

"There's one deceased migrant," he corrected himself.

This news was followed by a few seconds' respectful silence as the wind from the helicopter blades made the unzipped body bag flap.

"Anyone wounded on our side?"

"Cortex almost got cut in half, but the lieutenant was on hand."

"Well then, thank you, lieutenant."

Passaro threw his bloodstained, tear gas-soaked clothes into the washing machine and spent half an hour under the shower, scrubbing his body as hard as he could. He was washing off the shame as desperately as if it were a stain. When he passed the bathroom mirror, he kept his eyes to the floor.

That evening he had perceived his accustomed routine through Miller's eyes, and all his excuses, justifications and convictions had come tumbling down.

Crossing his dark, silent apartment, he stretched out on top of the sheets on his bed. Erika was sound asleep. A car's head-lights lit the room for a moment through the closed shutters. A lump rose in his throat. As so often, he tried to control it. His job was just his job, and someone had to do it. But this time there had been too much sound and fury. The tears began to fall, and Erika opened her eyes. Everybody thought Passaro was indestructible, but she knew his weak points. To see him weeping, fists clenched as if he had the whole weight of the world on his shoulders, was unbearable. She sat up and took him in her arms. Her man.

"I'm here . . ."

It was his turn to cling to her as tightly as he could, face buried in the crook of her neck.

"In the end, we're going to have to face up to everything we've agreed to do," he murmured. "And when that day comes, I'm afraid I'll be utterly disgusted with myself."

Erika bit her lip to avoid crying as well.

28

Calais police headquarters
BSU office

The accident was registered as manslaughter, and the duty magistrate decided that, before the police judiciaire was brought in, there was no reason why Lieutenant Miller should not hear the depositions. And so Bastien didn't go home that night.

The trucker was English, so an interpreter had to be found in the middle of the night so they could get an explanation for his crazy behaviour. He had, of course, been scared out of his wits when he saw his colleague being lynched. But other concerns, which now appeared completely ridiculous, had also induced him to speed towards a blazing barricade. According to the translation the interpreter gave Bastien, for every migrant discovered in a lorry on UK territory, the driver, who was responsible for what he was carrying, faced a fine of two thousand pounds. On top of that, any damaged goods could be refused and charged to the haulage company.

When added to the violence of the attacks they had to contend with, the financial pressure these drivers faced had just led to a man's death. A man who, lacking any proof of identity or nationality, would end up in a common grave, far from the leafy avenues of a cemetery.

At seven in the morning, just as Bastien was sorting out the statements, Erika appeared in the doorway, coffee in one hand and a bag of croissants in the other.

"That's the twelfth fatality this year. Always at the same place, Junction 47."

Miller was surprised to see her in the office two hours before her day was due to start.

"Unless you sleep with a police radio under your pillow, I wonder how you come to know so much."

Erika put the coffee down on his desk.

"Passaro told me about your night when he got in. Well done with Cortex – he owes you one."

The two of them had naturally begun to address each other more informally, and Bastien couldn't help a sly smile as he blew on his scalding drink.

"First that journalist Lizon and now Passaro. Have you scored with Corval as well?"

The hard stare Erika gave him left him in no doubt as to what she thought of this remark.

"I'm not a whore, Bastien. Just a single woman. And with Ludovic it's getting serious. I'll put your insult down to fatigue."

Realising his gaffe, Miller wrinkled his nose and screwed up his eyes. Besides, he knew he wasn't exactly one to give advice on life as a couple. Luckily for him, the appearance of Cotin the night duty officer saved him from any further embarrassment.

"Did you know we have a fatality?"

"Yes, I told you so myself, Cotin – four hours ago," said Bastien.

"No, not your one. Another one, in the Jungle. We got a call from the CRS, but I didn't really understand it. They say you need to come with a dog handler."

"A dog handler? What is this crap?" said Erika.

"Since you're both awake, you'd better come with me."

Calais Jungle

Shortly before eight that morning, Ousmane, already holding a spliff, arrived at the bottom of Adam's dune and called his name several times. The zips on the two tents opened simultaneously, and Kilani and Adam's faces appeared.

"You could at least have brought a bowl of tea," Adam grumbled.

"I'm sorry, my friend. No tea, and no good news either. You need to come with me."

Picking up a water bottle, Adam emptied half of it over his head, then passed it to Kilani, who copied him. Then they took the asphalted road bordering the Jungle until they reached the first CRS trucks, parked in the noman's-land between the refugee camp and the Calais industrial estate. About a hundred migrants stood facing a squad of police. Between them a dead body lay stretched out on the ground. About fifteen stray dogs were sniffing round it.

Among the police Adam recognised Bastien Miller, the young lieutenant he had met in the hospital almost a week before.

"As soon as there's a dead body," Ousmane explained, "it's dragged to the edge of the Jungle by the No Borders. The police have no wish to enter the camp anyway, and the migrants have no wish to see them, so like this everybody's happy."

Some of the dogs were bent over the body, while others circled it, growling, as if to show it was their property. To judge by the ravaged face, human flesh seemed to be to their liking.

"Why are you showing me this?" a disgusted Adam asked.

"Because it's your Libyan, Adam," Ousmane replied. "The one you've been talking about for days. The businessman who wanted to become a smuggler in place of the Afghans."

"How can you be sure, seeing what's left of him?"

"*Jungle news!* It travels fast here, you know. It seems he was killed last night and brought here around three this morning. We're all meat anyway, and the dogs can't see any difference. But if I wanted you to see this, it's to make you understand you shouldn't mess with the Afghans. Even if days have gone by, I'm sure they haven't forgotten, and this is the fate they have in store for you. I know you're not frightened, but think of Kilani. As soon as your back's turned, they'll seize the chance for revenge. That's why I'm asking you to come and join us."

One of the dogs picked through the torn pullover to gnaw at Libyan's entrails, then raised his bloodstained white muzzle.

A dog unit van pulled up next to the CRS vehicles. Two men got out and took their equipment from the boot. They quickly put on padded suits, thick gloves and helmets. Lowering their visors, they moved cautiously towards the pack of dogs, one with a taser in hand, the other pepper spray. Cops and migrants looked on.

The first dog that dared intercept them received a dose of liquid pepper straight in the face. It rolled on the ground and ran off howling pitifully. Unwilling to abandon the corpse, two other mongrels growled at the men, but soon decided to follow the rest of the pack.

Still wearing their protective suits, the dog handlers escorted a team of firemen to pick up the partially eaten body and deposit it on a stretcher. Thirty hours without sleep for Bastien, and this was the second time this same scene had played out. It was hard to take, even for a cop.

Ousmane's words echoed in Adam's mind. The Afghans haven't forgotten you or Kilani, he had warned him. He turned to the boy, and kneeled down level with him.

"You're to go with Ousmane and wait for me in the Sudanese camp. Do you understand me? You're not to stay on your own; don't leave our friends."

Kilani looked first at Ousmane, then at Adam, but a shake of the head showed he had no intention of going. Grasping him by the shoulders, Adam looked him in the eye.

"It's an order, understand?"

The word "order" had an immediate effect, as if something had clicked in Kilani's brain. He nodded, looking down at the ground.

"What are you going to do?" Ousmane asked Adam.

"I'm going to show I'm in good company."

Adam crossed the no-man's-land and reached the group of three plainclothes police, Bastien among them. When he saw the Syrian getting closer and closer, Captain Cotin grasped his baton and took a step forward, intending to suggest he go back where he had come from. At that moment, Bastien recognised Adam.

"It's okay, Cotin. I know him. So do you, in fact. It's the man who came to the emergency unit with the boy."

Cotin pulled a dubious face. To him, one Arab was just like any other, but in the end he walked away without comment.

"Good morning, Adam."

"Good morning, Bastoin."

Miller smiled, but didn't correct him.

"It would be a better one if you could tell me you've found your wife and daughter," he said in all sincerity.

"Unfortunately not. When they do arrive, I'll send you a message. I'll introduce you to them, and you'll lay eyes on the two most beautiful beings in the world."

Miller didn't have the heart to tell him he also had two treasures he would die for, and how lucky he was to have them with him.

178

"That would be an honour, Adam."

Then he noticed Kilani's dark, sullen look. Despite Ousmane's efforts to get him to follow him to the Sudanese camp, the boy hadn't left Adam's side.

"How's the little kid doing?"

"He's tough. He's surviving. But I get the impression he hasn't been a little kid for a long time now. Whatever, he's become my shadow."

Adam gestured brusquely for Kilani to clear off. The boy frowned but reluctantly turned on his heel. Rather than diminishing, the group of migrants gathered at a respectful distance from the two men had grown larger. Adam could sense them all staring at him: among them, as everywhere in the Jungle, a good third must be Afghans.

"Don't you wear a police armband?" he asked Bastien.

"It's in my pocket. It didn't occur to me to put it on."

"Could you do so now?"

It took Bastien several seconds to catch on. Then he searched in his pocket, took out his orange police armband and slipped it over his upper arm.

"You wouldn't be using me would you, Adam?"

"Yes, of course," the Syrian admitted openly. "When I helped the boy, I've made a few enemies. They're scared of the police, so I wanted to be seen with you."

"Well, while we're at it, you can help me too. Do you have any inside info?"

"Some. I know the dead man is Libyan. He arrived a few days ago. He wanted to set up as a people smuggler, but the Afghans control the market. He probably ran into one of them last night. I heard he was killed at about three in the morning and dumped here at the entrance to the Jungle so the police wouldn't have to come in to collect him."

"You mean it was murder? It wasn't the dogs who attacked him?"

"I couldn't swear to it, but we both saw those mongrels are too fearful to attack a man. They took advantage of a free meal."

"It seems to me you're getting your cop reflexes back, but you're a long way outside your jurisdiction," said Miller.

"I've been a cop all my life. It's all I know how to do. I'll try to find out more and keep you informed."

Bastien seemed troubled by this offer of collaboration.

"You know I've already searched for your family, and there's nothing more I can do for you."

"I'm not asking for anything. I knew the victim."

Adam looked round to check he was still the migrants' centre of attention.

"I know I don't look particularly clean, but if you would . . ."

The Syrian held out his hand and the two men exchanged a long, firm handshake that everyone around them noticed.

Maybe Adam had just won himself a few days' reprieve.

Erika had left Bastien to talk to the Syrian on his own. But just because she was polite, didn't mean she wasn't curious. She walked over to the lieutenant.

"Who was that guy?"

"I'm not sure yet."

"Problems in the future?"

"Possibly."

29

Even though they were supposed to wait for him there, Adam couldn't find either Ousmane or Kilani in the Sudanese camp. He looked round all the tents, went past a corrugated iron hut stinking of food that had perished in the hot sun, then peered inside their prayer room. He twice refused the tea offered him before Wassim, a young black man, no more than twenty years old, came up to him.

"Are you looking for the boss?"

"No, I'm looking for Ousmane."

The young Sudanese burst out laughing.

"Ousmane *is* the boss. You'll find him on the beach."

Although the Jungle only covered one square kilometre, Adam was constantly discovering fresh secrets about it. He asked Wassim to repeat what he had said.

"First there's the dunes. Then the forest. Beyond that there's the beach. I'll take you there if you like."

Adam followed his guide along the asphalted road bordering the dunes, then a dirt track that took them to the edge of the forest, parallel to the women's camp. It was guarded by a wall topped with barbed wire, but low enough to give him a view of an impeccable lawn the size of a football pitch and twenty or so white canvas marquees, fifteen metres long by five across. It all looked clean, calm, and as well-tended as a four-star camping site. The track continued past the women's camp, the wood and more dunes and wound its way between some ruined Second World War bunkers covered in moss, before petering out at the foot of a huge sandhill. With every stride their feet sank deep into the sand, and so it took a great effort finally to reach the top and discover a beach so vast it extended to the horizon in both directions. Not a single bather or walker in sight: the proximity of the Jungle meant neither tourists nor Calais locals ever ventured there. An abandoned paradise.

Sitting on the shore, Ousmane was watching a bare-legged Kilani jumping in the water, face wreathed in smiles. A gust of wind drew waves in the sand, and the Sudanese man shielded his tobacco and hashish cigarette in the hollow of his hand.

"I wonder how you manage to get your supply of hashish, and above all, how you pay for it," Adam said as he approached.

"I'm a man of many talents. I've got a few things going for me in the Jungle that bring in a bit of money. But I confess I was worried this morning, when I learned my Pakistani friend had died. He was my supplier."

"Another murder?" asked an astonished Adam.

"No, an accident on the motorway. He tried to board a lorry with his son. Since this morning, the son's taken on the business. The Pakistanis have a tent that serves as a café, and that's where I get my dope. A euro for cannabis, five for a gram of hashish, with a cup of coffee thrown in."

"So where do they get it from?"

"The high-rise buildings on the outskirts of Calais. There are gangs of kids waiting around all day with nothing else to do. But I tell myself I'm a fool, because with all the time I've been here, and with all this land around us, I should have grown my own stuff. I would have been rich!"

A ferry passed by in the distance, as slow as a drifting continent, its lifeboats clearly visible on the side. Written in huge letters, its name seemed to mock the migrants imprisoned in the Jungle: SPIRIT OF BRITAIN. Beyond the ferry, the English coast was clearly visible on this cloudless morning, its cliffs only eighty kilometres away, so tempting and so inaccessible.

"You didn't tell me you were the boss in your camp," Adam said.

"And you didn't tell me you were so friendly with the police," Ousmane retorted, lighting his joint.

"Is that a problem?"

"The police? That depends. Bad outside, good inside. Outside the Jungle, we run whenever we see them. But inside, I must confess that if they weren't there, keeping watch day and night, it would be war in less than twenty-four hours. Ethnic, religious, or simply because some of these people only know how to fight. So, what were you talking to him about?"

"The Libyan. I'd like to know what happened. How one can die in a country at peace without anyone batting an eyelid."

"He's not the first. Violence is everywhere because the poverty is so extreme. You can't all but incarcerate ten thousand men from the most dangerous countries in the world, leaving them to depend on the generosity of the people of Calais and aid workers, giving them no hope except an illegal crossing, and expect everything to go well. People die every week. The No Borders drag them to the entrance near the CRS, but sometimes they're simply buried in the dunes or the forest. If they ever demolish the Jungle, they'll have to avoid digging too deeply."

"Yes, but this particular death interests me," the Syrian said.

"I don't understand you anymore, Adam. You're investigating a murder, protecting a dumb boy, you want to be friends with the local police – are you still looking for Nora and Maya? I get the impression you're becoming settled in the Jungle, just like me. I don't see you showing your photo these days."

"I think everyone has already seen it. And I can read what's in their eyes. They're telling me not to wait any longer."

The ferry disappeared into the port, and Ousmane realised he had upset his friend. He changed the topic of conversation.

"Look at Wassim," he said, pointing to the Sudanese youngster who had guided Adam to the beach. "He's going to insult the English again!"

Feet in the water, staring out to sea, Wassim cupped his hands over his mouth and started to shout in English.

"*Look at me*, Youké! *You see me, now! You know I am for real and I am coming for you!*"

This first outburst was almost ironic, theatrical. But when Wassim shouted again, his voice had taken on a very different tone.

"*Look at me*, Youké! *I am coming for you!*"

Now it sounded as if he were imploring, and soon there was nothing funny about seeing this young man yelling his desperate desire at an island so scornful of him – no doubt fearing he might invade it – this youngster in his ill-fitting shorts and worn-out T-shirt, tears in his eyes, his dreams in tatters. Even Kilani stopped playing to watch, and then went over to him. Wassim stroked his head, as though reassuring a worried younger brother. They stood there, staring out towards England, until Ousmane finished his joint, buried it in the sand, and decided it was time to go and drink some sweet tea.

All four of them headed away from the beach's sandy paradise. As they walked along, Adam returned to the subject he couldn't get out of his mind, at the expense of almost everything else.

"Just now you told me the Libyan was killed at three in the morning. How do you know that?"

"There you go again!" said Ousmane. "Am I talking to my friend or to a police officer?"

"We're all several people at the same time – you told me that yourself. So? The Libyan?"

Adam's voice was harsher, almost authoritarian. Ousmane had never heard him speak like that before, and he didn't find it pleasant. He decided to give him the information he was seeking.

"I don't know if that was when he died. I only know that the dogs hadn't come by yet. I saw the time on the photo the No Borders guy took with his phone. The body was left as a warning where the Libyan had his tent. He stayed there for a good hour until the No Borders were called to take him out of the camp. They're always the ones who do that: the migrants are too scared they'll be arrested for murder. That was when the guy took the photo."

"Can you introduce me to him?"

"The kid with orange hair? At your orders, my friend," Ousmane said, deadpan.

30

No Borders. Against the law. Against order. Against the concept of a nation. Against the idea of frontiers. And coincidentally against the cops as well. That meant a lot of struggles, a lot of ideas to defend, even from their own. And yet Alexandre Merle had reason to feel proud, because it was No Borders who had raised the problem of security for women migrants by establishing squats in Calais to receive them. Faced with these illegal occupations, the state had decided to create the camp for women at the far end of the Jungle.

Another exploit Merle could be proud of: he was one of those who had welcomed the nine Iranians who had sewn up their mouths in protest at the dismantling of the southern part of the Jungle and the destruction of their shelters. To no avail: the bulldozers had soon reduced the size of the camp by half.

He was also proud of having blocked the Channel Tunnel and of storming a ferry to publicise the plight of the migrants held prisoner in Calais.

Then he was caught by the police. The ones that operate under the radar. The counter-terrorist team, who pressure people, lean on them, promise and threaten. Ever since, Merle had a leash round his neck, one that, if he didn't keep his masters happy, could become a noose. So he found himself working for the police, while at the same time denouncing them. A contradictory situation he found hard to handle, especially now that he had six photographs of strangers on his phone, one of whom was apparently an Isis recruiting agent.

When he was introduced to Adam, he told himself it was time for him to manipulate someone on his own behalf.

Ousmane asked the Syrian to wait for him at the entrance to the No Borders area, close to the Info Center tent, where they gave migrants legal advice if they had been arrested anywhere in Europe.

"Morning, guys! I'm looking for Alex," he said in basic but comprehensible English.

Several hands were raised in friendly greeting. Most of the No Borders were little older than kids – the oldest was thirty at most. World music, roll-ups and brightly coloured African clothes: you had to know how radical their actions and protests were not to assume they were just a group of hippies seeking communion with nature as part of their personal development on the path to tranquil karma.

"Ousmane, my friend!"

Merle appeared out of a spacious red tent for six people that even allowed itself the luxury of continuing into a small room covered by a tarpaulin. He gave Ousmane a hug and offered him a fruit juice. Salvador, the person in charge of the Calais No Borders group – even though the position of "person in charge" or "leader" was not recognised in the movement – poked his head out of the tent, saw it was Ousmane, and ducked back inside again, reassured.

Sitting next to their fire, Merle listened carefully to the Sudanese man and saw no problem with meeting his friend, someone called Adam. He followed Ousmane out of their camp and met a tall Syrian accompanied by a boy of about ten, as black as night.

"I hear you understand French?"

"Yes, if you speak slowly."

Keeping his eyes on them, Kilani accepted a can of Coca Cola from a terribly pretty No Borders girl, as well as a kiss on the cheek that set his stomach tingling. Usually so sensitive he was almost unapproachable, he made no move to shy away from this stranger. He went off to enjoy his drink on a grassy bank between two dunes a few metres away from the two men. Ousmane had already left, heading for the little Pakistani café.

"It's a strange thing you're asking. Haven't you seen enough dead bodies in your country already?" Merle said straight out.

"This one is different. I want to see him with my own eyes. To know if it was an accident or murder."

"I can confirm that straightaway. It wasn't an accident. When we arrived, there was blood everywhere. We had to wear refuse sacks to avoid getting stained."

Adam gestured impatiently.

"I'm pleased you have no doubts, but I'd like to see for myself."

"Why?" said Merle. "Are you a cop?"

Adam said nothing, and his eyes were cold. But Merle still did not produce his phone.

"Ousmane says you fled Syria to save your family."

"I think I put them in danger, but yes, I fled Syria."

"And you're Muslim?"

"No, I used to be Christian," said an irritated Adam. "Listen, I know everything here has a price, and you obviously have something to ask of me, so please get on with it."

Despite himself, he had raised his voice; it was obvious he

was annoyed. So much so that Kilani put down his drink and got to his feet, ready to join his friend. Adam gave him a look to reassure him everything was alright, and the boy sat down again.

"Okay, okay. Stay cool," Merle said. "I'll show you the photo, but you're right, I do need you."

By now Merle was certain Adam wasn't a believer, still less a fanatic. He had fled Assad, but also Isis, which made him the perfect candidate for the proposal he was about to make. Besides, No Borders were petrified of being caught snooping round the mosque, especially since that morning when he had once again seen how violent some migrants could be.

"I want you to go and pray in the mosque. It's a Salafist mosque, so they're not playing games. You'll have to do all five prayers."

"I told you, I'm not a Muslim."

"And I'm not a photographer. But we'll have to strike a deal because each of us has something the other wants."

"But I still don't know what that is."

Merle launched into the story he'd invented in two minutes just before they met.

"Right in the centre of the Jungle there's this radical mosque, run by Afghans. As you'll see, it's not hard to get into. They do a lot to convert people: they give out prayer mats, copies of the Koran, even offer their protection if you want it. They don't get on well with the Sudanese, but there's no problem with Syrians. I've heard rumours that one of the imams is encouraging the migrants to stay in France and not to try to cross to England. As you know, we think differently. The idea of borders is obsolete: the world belongs to mankind, not to states. I'd like to show you a series of photos, and I need you to come and tell me if one of these imams is in there and if he's telling people what

I described to you. In return, I'll show the photo of the dead man. Deal?"

Adam recognised the lie as easily as a mother recognises her children. He wasn't going to set foot inside the mosque or go anywhere near it.

"Deal," he said.

Merle copied the Syrian's mobile number and pinged him the seven photos.

"Do you think you could go today?"

"Tomorrow perhaps. More likely the day after."

"I need it to be sooner."

"Then you should learn to be a better negotiator. You've got nothing left to offer, so I'm the one who decides."

Merle was beginning to understand that manipulation is a sport you need to train for. Angry with himself, he watched Adam walk away, followed by his shadow, who had just finished his Coke.

As they made their way back to his dune, Adam scrolled through the seven photos on his phone. Of the supposedly radical imams, two were clean-shaven, another was wearing jeans and sneakers, and the last was smoking a cigarette on a café terrace with what looked suspiciously like a bottle of beer near to hand. If these were Salafist Muslims, they allowed themselves some surprising liberties. Finally, he came to the seventh photo.

A tent with the flaps open. The Libyan's body stretched out on its back, with two deep stab wounds. One horizontal at heart level, the other vertical in the stomach. The camera flash made the red of the blood all over his chest and clothing look almost vulgar. All in all, it looked like the work of a professional, or someone who was accustomed to killing.

Adam tapped to close the folder. Then he searched in Google for "Calais police headquarters".

PART FOUR

SURVIVING

31

Julie was reviewing the day's events with her team. Seated round a plastic table on the sand outside their cabin, the volunteers were listening closely to her briefing about the latest administrative efforts to ensure the Jungle remained a provisional camp rather than a lawless town.

"The Prefecture has once again refused access to hot water in the showers. It's the height of summer, so that's manageable, but as soon as winter's on the horizon, everyone's going to fall ill. And as we're more or less in a confined space, it'll only take one person to catch a cold for the whole camp to be sneezing the next day."

"If we add the cases of malaria, scabies, ringworm and all the other nasties spread by the rats and stray dogs, it's a real research lab for medical students in here," said one of the Care4Calais volunteers.

"And it's not getting any better," added another. "The cleaning company is refusing to come and clear out the portable toilets. They say it's inhuman. There are eighty loos, one for every hundred and twenty-five people on average, which means they ought to come twice a day rather than twice a week. In the meantime, the migrants are using part of the forest as a toilet. The part nearest the CRS, obviously. But that's only a temporary solution."

"Unfortunately, that's not the most urgent problem," said Julie. "The Prefecture has again demanded the demolition of all the shops in the Jungle, arguing they contravene food hygiene regulations. With hot water and functioning shops, the camp might almost be habitable! Can't have that, can we?"

"Yeah," the volunteer added, "they're happy to let them kill one another, but heaven forbid anyone gets gastroenteritis. It's ridiculous."

"It's not just ridiculous, it's desperate. They refuse to understand that however bad things are in the Jungle, new people will keep arriving."

As she was about the end the meeting, Julie noticed Adam waiting politely at the entrance to the women's camp. She gave her team the latest instructions for the cases they had to deal with and closed her file. Swiftly tidying her hair, she went to join the Syrian, beaming as usual. Adam extended his hand as she went to kiss him on the cheek, and the confusion left them both embarrassed.

Night was already falling, and here and there thick tree branches and logs were ablaze on campfires. Chopping wood and burning it was one of the main activities in the Jungle.

"I have to meet someone in town tomorrow," Adam said.

"That's good. Have you found something to do outside the camp?"

"More or less."

"I see you're following my advice. Keeping busy so you don't get bored. Do you want me to drop you off?"

"If that's alright with you. But above all I don't want to embarrass the person I'm going to see. To have clean clothes. To look like something other than a migrant. If I met myself the way I am now, I wouldn't even speak to me."

"Well, I think you're . . ."

Choosing not to finish her sentence, Julie disappeared inside her caravan to rummage in the most recent bag of clothes left by Secours Catholique. She reappeared with a white shirt, a pair of jeans and blue sneakers.

"I'm not sure they'll fit, but it's the best I can do."

Adam thanked her and they agreed where they would meet the next morning at the camp entrance. Julie agreed to everything, but peered over his shoulder with a knowing look.

"And will the little one be coming with us?"

Adam turned round to see Kilani, who was sitting cross-legged on the ground drawing shapes and signs with his finger in the sand. First an arrow, then a circle or a nought, which he quickly rubbed out.

"Yes, I can't leave him on his own," Adam confirmed.

Adam spent a good part of the night in the hut for charging phones. He waited three hours for a point to become free, then a further two for his battery to be fully charged. The boy had sat with him at first and then fell asleep, propped up against him. When the Syrian had finished, he picked Kilani up and carried him back to his tent.

The next morning, safely installed on the back seat of Julie's old car, Kilani spent the whole journey with his nose pressed against the window. Adam realised he had probably only left the Jungle to go to hospital. As the car went past the imposing belfry at the centre of Calais, the boy craned his neck to see the top of the tower. They passed a *frites* stand by the roundabout, and the smell of frying wafting in through the open windows made Kilani's mouth water. This was turning out to be an incredible day out for him.

Julie followed Adam's directions and finally pulled up outside the red-brick police headquarters.

"I wasn't expecting this kind of a meeting. Are you sure this is the right address?" she asked in astonishment.

Adam said nothing, but looked closely at the dingy three-storey building. He would have thought a French police headquarters would be more imposing.

"You can drop us here, Julie. We'll walk back."

"The Jungle is more than five kilometres away, you know."

"And I travelled six thousand to get here," Adam joked, placing his hand on hers.

Julie blushed. She waited for them to leave the car before lighting a cigarette and driving back to the camp.

Adam tapped a message on his phone and waited anxiously for Miller's reply. The lieutenant might be uncomfortable at having a migrant right outside his office: perhaps Adam would embarrass him in front of his colleagues. Maybe Bastien wouldn't even reply. The lieutenant's arrival, hand outstretched and a broad smile on his face, eased Adam's worries.

"Adam! Good to see you! What brings you into town?"

"Seeing you is what brings me here. Would you like us to move a bit further away from your building?"

"Why on earth would I want that? Come on in. There's a waiting room with a few chairs – we can talk more easily there. Tell the boy to follow us."

That was unnecessary, as Kilani would never stray an inch from his protector. When they entered the lobby, the receptionist, a buxom woman in her fifties, glanced casually at them, until she caught sight of Kilani's delighted face. Standing in front of a vending machine twice his height, it was as if he had discovered a new planet. The lights and brightly coloured wrappers made him put both hands on the glass, staring in disbelief at the chewing gum, cakes and chocolate bars, unable to decide which he would like most. He was so close to the treats that his breath made little circles of vapour on the glass. The receptionist melted at once.

"Who is this little angel? Is he with you, lieutenant?"

"He's a friend, Clarisse," Bastien replied with a smile. "Could you keep an eye on him while we're talking?"

Knowing how suspicious Kilani was of strangers, Adam bent down to him.

"Are you happy to stay here with the lady?"

The boy looked at the lady, then at the sweets, at the lady once more, and nodded, smiling broadly. Adam understood that in the boy's life, white people were not a threat.

"Okay, so what would you like, little man? You only have to point," said "the lady".

Adam sat opposite Lieutenant Miller on one of the waiting-room chairs. He held out his phone with the photograph of the Libyan with the two stab wounds.

"I told you it was murder."

"Looking at this photo, it's hard to refute that," Bastien confirmed. "Judging by the other dead bodies I've seen, it's the work of a pro. Two stabbings, both of them lethal. The guy didn't stand a chance."

"That's what the Afghan mafia has in store for anyone who gets in their way."

"Despite the dog bites sustained post-mortem, I imagine the forensic pathologist will have reached the same conclusion. But that doesn't change a thing. I've already told you, we don't investigate inside the Jungle."

"If you're not bothered that there's a place in France where a person can kill without any repercussions, maybe you'll be more interested in the other photos. You can scroll through the next six."

Bastien's finger sped across the screen.

"Tell me what I'm looking at."

"A No Borders member in the Jungle asked me to start going to the Salafist mosque. He wants me to find a fundamentalist imam who apparently encourages migrants not to travel to England but to stay in France. It appears he's one of these six men."

Bastien scrolled back to the start of the file and studied each photo more closely. His increasingly doubtful expression didn't escape Adam.

"Do you see what I see?" he asked.

"Yes. I see they don't fit my idea of an Islamic fundamentalist."

"Exactly. So there's a kid in the Jungle who has nothing of a cop about him but is passing me information about imams who are cleanshaven, drink alcohol and don't wear religious clothing."

"It looks as if they're doing all they can to disguise what they really are."

"So what do you conclude?"

"That I'm not one of the counter-terrorism guys, and that all this is way beyond my pay grade. Yours too, by the way. The question I ask myself is: why are you so interested in this?"

"It's annoying," Adam protested. "You're not the first person I've to explain myself to. I spent sixteen years in a local crime fighting unit, what you call a criminal investigation brigade. And you wonder why I'm investigating a murder?"

Bastien didn't know what to say to this.

"Also, I've spent the last four years putting myself in harm's way by fighting religious terrorists and a murderous president, and yet you ask me why I get worried when I see these men entering the Jungle, apparently expected by the members of a Salafist mosque? Do you think I regard a terrorist attack outside Syria as less disgusting? Or see a murder outside my own city as less dramatic? I'm only doing what's right, and you'd do the same, wouldn't you?"

"I've no wish to disappoint you, but I haven't the faintest idea."

"Well then, that's because you don't yet know yourself properly. The fact is, you need to contact your counter-terrorism people. Either this No Borders person is already with them and making a mess of it, or he's been recruited by someone else, and that's worrying too."

It took Bastien a good minute to reflect on this. Then he took his phone out of his jacket pocket.

"Can you send me the photo?"

"You see, you can't close your eyes to it either."

When they emerged from the waiting room, they found Kilani sitting behind the reception desk alongside Clarisse, pockets crammed with chocolate bars. Seeing Adam, he jumped off his chair and came to join him. Clarisse nodded at the little fellow, who seemed to think Christmas had come in July.

"Well, he doesn't say much, does he? Cat got his tongue?"

Adam took this to be a genuine question and replied quite naturally.

"No, someone cut it off."

Unaware of what was being discussed, Kilani held up the chocolate bars with an excited smile, as if he could scarcely contain his joy. Captain Cotin had told Bastien what had happened to Kilani that night in the hospital, but Clarisse could only stare at the boy in disbelief. Before he left, she slipped a five-euro note into his shorts pocket and gave him a smacking kiss on the cheek. By the looks of it, she would happily have taken him home with her.

As Bastien watched Adam leave the building, he realised the Syrian hadn't once mentioned his wife and daughter, whereas he himself had been searching once more through the police alerts that very morning.

"Is he a friend too?" asked Clarisse.

"No. A colleague. But I think he got lost somewhere along the way."

As they walked back to the Jungle, Kilani dug into his pocket, took out the five-euro note, and handed it quite naturally to Adam. It was as if it was impossible for him to keep any riches for himself.

When there was only one meal a day in the Jungle or, after standing in line for hours in the sun, Kilani and Adam arrived to find the canteens had run out of food, the Syrian often bought provisions in the different stores. Bread, rice with tomato sauce, fruit juice. He had never hidden his money from Kilani. It was his; theirs. Now Adam pulled up his T-shirt, unzipped the money belt, and slipped the note inside.

32

Some information is simply too hot to handle, and Bastien knew he had to pass what Adam had shown him on to Dorsay, the head of the Calais force. They had met when he took up his post and occasionally passed each other in the corridors, from which Bastien concluded he was probably still on probation.

He printed off the images and knocked on his superior's door.

Dorsay's grim face clearly showed that the six photos that had just crash-landed like a blazing aeroplane on his desk ran a serious risk of ruining his day. Bastien let his boss mull things over, watching him squirm on his chair.

"Tell me again who this friend of yours is?"

"He's not a friend. A contact inside the Jungle. A Syrian cop who ended up in the refugee camp."

"Uh-huh. Personally, all I can see here is six Arabs," said Dorsay, trying to convince himself.

"With connections to a Salafist mosque, and their photos were in the hands of a No Borders. If there's an attack in the next few days and it's discovered it was planned in your town, we can always say we didn't know about it, but our guilty consciences are going to give us sleepless nights."

"What were you doing becoming so pally with a migrant anyway?"

"As I said, we're not friends and that's not the question. I'm asking if we follow this up."

Hot under the collar, Dorsay realised he was trapped.

"Of course we follow it up, now I know about it. I'll call the public prosecutor's office, and they'll pass me on to the counter-terrorism people. Then we'll see. As if we didn't have enough shit to deal with from the Jungle, you have to go looking for more."

"I assure you I wasn't looking for it. Besides, if I'm not mistaken, that's our job."

"Oh, that'll do, Miller. No need to get on your high horse. Let me make a few phone calls, and from now on, keep your mouth shut. Not a word of this outside my office, is that clear?"

"Crystal clear."

Bastien leaned against the wall in the sun in the police station's tiny inner courtyard, having left his team to snatch a few minutes to himself. The case they had in hand, a supermarket robbery by a gang, didn't really require his presence.

Erika came up to him as he was staring blankly up at two seagulls wheeling in the sky above. She leaned back next to him and took her sunglasses out of one of the pockets of her green combat jacket.

"You'll get fed up with them, I promise."

"No chance. They always remind me of being at the beach or on holiday."

"I lived in Paris for two years," said Erika. "I had my windows double-glazed because of the traffic noise. Here in Calais, I did the same to block out those filthy flying rats screeching from sunup to sundown. They rummage in dustbins like dogs, and they can split your skull. As long as you find them picturesque, you're a tourist. The day you want to take a shotgun to them you'll be able to consider yourself a true citizen of Calais."

Bastien tore his eyes away from the two birds.

"Did you come to talk to me about seagulls, or is something about the case bothering you?"

"No. Even Corval can manage it on his own. But you've had a phone call. Someone who says he's a colleague of yours. He's calling back in five minutes."

"Do you know what he wanted?"

"Yeah. To talk to you about a girl. Someone called Nora Sarkis. Do you know her?"

For a moment, Bastien was taken aback, but he tried to regain his composure as naturally as possible.

"Yeah. Something from when I worked in Bordeaux."

Erika smiled sympathetically.

"You're cute when you lie."

"I'll tell you about it. Give me time, but I will tell you. Meanwhile, I need you to get Corval out of my hair. You must have an old case that needs a new door-to-door, right?"

"Corval hates doing door-to-door."

"That'll be perfect then."

Alone in the office, Bastien turned the INTERVIEW IN PRO-GRESS sign round on the door and shut it so that nobody would disturb him. He scarcely had time to sit down in his chair when the desk telephone rang.

"Lieutenant Miller here."

"Commandant Paris, Counter-terrorism."

"So you've . . ."

Paris cut him short.

"Yes, I'd really like to talk to you as well. Let's meet."

Bastien realised his interlocutor didn't trust phone conversations, and suddenly felt like an amateur.

"Are you intending to come to Calais?" he asked.

"I'm already in Calais. Do you have something to write with?"

Mastering his surprise, Bastien picked up a pen and wrote down the address, room number and the late hour: eleven o'clock that night.

"Try not to look too much like a cop," Paris said. "The hotel is packed with Albanian traffickers."

33

Calais Jungle
Ten p.m.

As the car was leaving Calais, it had pulled up on Rue des Garennes. A man got out, put on an old rucksack and adjusted both shoulder straps. Dressed in ordinary well-worn clothes and a backwards baseball cap, he looked like any run-of-the-mill migrant. The driver spoke to him one last time out of the car window.

"I'll be five minutes from here. God be with you."

He said a quick farewell and sped off.

The man walked past the rows of warehouses and oil storage tanks on the industrial estate. Two hundred metres further on he saw the CRS vans that marked the edge of the camp. He passed them as well, and under cover of darkness, was able to enter the camp and disappear into the mass of refugees without a problem.

Shadow was in the Jungle.

He was expected, and two men came to meet him. They were obviously intimidated: even though no-one knew his real identity and only a few had seen his face before, his reputation preceded him. He was an Isis recruiting agent. One who, it was said, could read souls.

Finding candidates for jihad was not that difficult. You

could select from those who were too religious to accept a modern world, too formatted to accept any other laws but those of God, but also those who were rebelling, damaged or simply deranged. They were plucked from poverty-stricken tower blocks, countries at war, even psychiatric hospitals. But what required experience was the ability to pick out those who would not hesitate. To blow up a stadium or a concert hall, shoot customers on a café terrace, drive into a crowd on the 14th of July and, if necessary, be shot, gun in hand.

Shadow knew how to identify them. He could spot the fake man of courage, the one who's all talk, who would back out or tremble so much he can't press the plunger on his explosives vest. Every one of those Shadow had recruited had fulfilled their mission. And then, according to their beliefs, the jihadist became a martyr surrounded by virgins, or nothing more than a dead body in a hole, another victim of deadly obscurantism.

Shadow followed his guides to the Salafist mosque. He was no taller than anybody else, no more impressive; there was nothing striking about him. He was simply one more migrant among ten thousand, and no-one noticed him as he passed by.

34

Jade was already asleep, and Manon had collapsed at nine that evening. Bastien worked as much overtime as he could, deliberately immersing himself in his work. Every time he saw the ghost of Manon, he was reminded how impossible it was for him to make her happy. He left Jade, who like all children soaked up emotions like a sponge, all alone with her mother in the gloomy atmosphere of their apartment, playing a role that wasn't hers, making her virtually responsible for a woman lost in an endless cloud of depression. It would take an electric shock to save what remained of their family, but Bastien had no idea what the spark might be.

At a quarter to eleven he hesitated over whether to take his gun and decided he should. He closed the front door gently, so his nocturnal escapade could go unnoticed. After walking a kilometre, he found himself outside the Bleu Azur Hotel, which gave on to Place d'Armes.

Commandant Paris had asked him to avoid looking too much like a cop. That wasn't difficult for Bastien: he could pass for a young lawyer, a broker, or possibly even a writer. But definitely not a cop. He entered the lobby, greeted the receptionist, who didn't take his eyes off the television, and climbed the stairs. On the third floor he ran into a group of four Albanians the worse for wear from drink. One of them barged into him without an apology. Ignoring him, Bastien knocked twice on Room 309.

"Come in, please," Paris greeted him.

Bastien took the only chair in the room, while his host sat down on the edge of the bed, making the mattress springs groan. Intimidated, Miller asked what must have sounded like a child's awkward question:

"Is your name really Paris?"

"My boss is called Toulouse and my assistant is Marseille. Does that answer your question?"

As he had that morning on the phone, Bastien reproached himself for appearing so amateurish. He was more like a fan of cop series on television than a cop himself. To forestall another stupid question, Paris asked straight out:

"Have you got the photos?"

"Yes," said Bastien, opening his phone and placing it on the bed.

Paris looked at the first one, swiped the screen with his stubby finger, looked at the second and came to a halt.

"Apart from your commissaire, have you shown them to anyone else?"

"No."

"Sent copies?"

"No."

"Very good. So tell me everything."

Bastien collected his thoughts and sorted events into chronological order.

"I met a Syrian migrant at the hospital on one of my night shifts. He was accompanying a child. Not his own."

"Why?"

"I don't know. He's a former cop, that must have something

to do with it. Afterwards, I saw him again when there was a murder in the Jungle."

"I thought the police didn't investigate inside the Jungle?"

"That's right. We just went to recover the body. That's when I met Adam for the second time."

"Adam? You call him by his first name?"

"Sarkis, if you prefer. The next day he came to me with six photos of what he said were supposedly fundamentalist imams. But the photos don't fit the description."

"Who gave him the photos in the first place?"

"A No Borders guy. Have you any idea who he is?"

"I've got some idea, yes. Do you know his name?"

"I wasn't told. The guy asked him to find out if one of the six men had come to the Salafist mosque, and to warn him if he had."

"Do you know why this Sarkis is passing the info on to you?"

"I told you, he's a cop. He thinks, as I do, that these people are potentially dangerous. I imagine he's doing what he thinks is right. We reckoned that if this No Borders guy was with you, you needed to be informed, and that if the opposite were the case – if you've never heard of him – you definitely needed to know. So? Is he with you?"

All the time Bastien was speaking, Paris was trying to give away as little as possible while gleaning as much as he could. It was clear that Merle had stupidly taken it into his head to delegate part of his mission.

"How long have you known this Sarkis?"

"Ten days or so."

"And what do you owe him?"

"I don't understand."

Paris pulled a file out of his briefcase and extracted a sheet of paper.

"You've enquired about a Nora Sarkis several times over the past few days. So I repeat: what do you owe him?"

Bastien cursed himself for not being completely open from the start.

"There's no deal between us. He's looking for his wife and daughter. He's worried they may have been arrested somewhere in France and sent back to Syria. Wouldn't you have done the same thing?"

"Absolutely not," Paris snorted. "You don't know a thing about him. He came into your life out of nowhere, with this sob story of a kid in hospital or I don't know what other tear-jerking bullshit, then he asks you to search our files, and you do. It has all the hallmarks of a sting."

Bastien didn't dare say a word.

"Luckily for you, according to my sources, Adam Sarkis is a member of the Free Syrian army, wanted for treason in his home country."

"And?"

"And it's possible you've landed on a genuinely good guy. And good guys interest me. Do you think he'd agree to help us?"

"Now it's your turn to explain."

"You know most of it already. Among those six photos there's an Isis recruiting agent. We've been trying to identify him for years. Our info tells us he's going to be in the Jungle. And the No Borders guy is one of our informants."

"Is he an agent?"

"No, he's doing it voluntarily, for the grandeur of France. But he's obviously running scared. Now, how can we tempt your Syrian? If he's aiming to get to England we could promise him a safe conduct. A crossing under our protection. We could drop him right in Piccadilly Circus, if that appeals to him."

"He'll refuse. Until his wife and daughter show up, he's staying put in Calais."

Placing both hands on his knees, Paris pushed down hard to raise himself off the bed. He opened the minibar door, took out a bottle, and poured himself a drink.

"Lieutenant Miller, you've got caught up in a sticky situation, and I'm sorry about that. But I really do need you. Your job is to find out how we turn this Adam Sarkis – what's important to him, what does he want most of all? And when you know, make him an offer. We'll make sure you can keep your promises."

Bastien turned down the vodka.

"If I've understood correctly, you're asking him to get inside the mosque to verify that one of your six targets is recruiting there."

But Sarkis wasn't Merle, and Paris could see an unexpected opportunity.

"Not exactly. We need him to make contact. In fact, ideally, we want him to be recruited."

Taken aback by the scope and the danger of what Paris was proposing, Bastien changed his mind and poured himself a vodka. There was a high chance the mission could end up with Adam being killed, a fact Bastien wasted no time in pointing out.

"Which would you prefer, Miller? For a Syrian no-one knows to be chalked up as collateral damage, or for fifty or so decent French citizens to die in a bomb attack on an airport?"

"That's an impossible choice."

"And it's my job to make them."

35

It would take a really foul smell to cover the already unbearable one given off by the refuse containers and portable toilets,
blocked and overflowing for more than a week, but as day
dawned, such a stench tore Adam from sleep.

When he unzipped his tent, a cloud of big bluebottles
momentarily abandoned the carcass of a stray dog deposited
right outside, its body slit from haunch to gullet, its guts emptied out and strewn alongside it. Adam waved off the insects,
but a swarm of them entered the tent regardless.

Since the dog had not come to Adam's dune to commit
suicide, it was obvious that this was a stark message. Kilani
was still asleep, and Adam decided to spare him the spectacle.
Grabbing hold of one of the dog's paws, he dragged it to the
asphalted road, then about fifty metres into the forest, before
dropping the stinking corpse at the foot of a tree.

Returning to the dune, he saw that Kilani had woken up.
He had found an old plastic bowl and was crouching down
to fill it with the dog's entrails. Years earlier he had scooped
out the guts of one of his cows whose milk had dried up,
and this didn't disgust him any more than that. Finally, with
bloodstained hands, he covered the sticky mess with several
fistfuls of sand.

The threat from the Afghans could not have been clearer,

and so Adam decided it was time to heed Ousmane's repeated invitations. It was time move to the Sudanese camp, but first things first.

"Follow me," he told Kilani. "We'll throw all that away in the forest. Then wash ourselves in the sea."

Holding the bowl of scarlet innards in his bloody hands, Kilani smiled at the idea of a stroll on the beach.

After a good clean-up in sea water, Kilani was now busy hammering in his tent pegs. He had already put up Adam's tent without being asked. Ousmane was sitting by the campfire, balancing a saucepan of water on the embers.

"In Afghanistan they call that *Bacha Bazi*. Playing with boys. It's a tradition. You stole their 'boy', and they're telling you they haven't forgotten. You're right to come and settle in our camp, but after this, I'll have to talk to the others. I may be in charge here, but to antagonise the Afghans is a decision we have to take together."

"I understand," said Adam. "So tell me how I can get Kilani to England. You said you tried more than twenty times. Even if you failed, you must know the ropes. If Nora and Maya make it here, I won't be able to keep him with us. We'll leave and he'll be left on his own."

For the first time, Adam had used the word "if". Ousmane had warned him about the kind of hope that can lead to madness if you cling to it. And yet hearing him surrender with this one word, this single syllable, brought him no pleasure.

"It will cost you a lot of money, you know."

Adam instinctively felt for the bulge under his T-shirt.

"I have money. What I want to know is what experience has taught you. How to go about things – the mistakes to avoid."

Ousmane removed the pan from the fire and poured them

two teas while Kilani spread a length of fabric between the tents to offer some shade.

"A razor, a refuse sack, a condom and a thermal blanket. Those are the basics," said Ousmane. "You need to burn the plastic off round the blade so you can use it to slice open the tarp and climb up into the lorry. The refuse sack is to put over your head when the customs officials appear. They can detect the carbon dioxide people breathe out. You have to hold your breath as much as possible, and only breathe in short gulps. The thermal blanket keeps in heat, so the helicopter cameras won't spot you. The aid agencies still have some."

"And the condom?"

"That's for stress. Fear upsets the stomach, twists your intestines. If you prefer, you can call them portable toilets."

Adam imagined Kilani sitting there with a refuse bag over his head wearing a thermal blanket.

"Even with all that, there are still two major obstacles. First, you have to pay a trafficker, and given your relations with the Afghans, you're going to have to use the Albanians. Don't ask me which of the two is worse, I've no idea."

"I can understand a trafficker for the Mediterranean," Adam said. "They find you a boat, make the crossing with you, share the dangers the same as you. But here in France it's not the Afghans who find you a lorry, or who drive it . . ."

"In Libya or Egypt, traffickers with boats are a necessary evil. They're the only ones who can get you across the sea. But here, apart from building and setting fire to barricades to slow down the lorries, the smugglers do nothing. They're nothing more than thieves. They control the rest areas, the motorway junctions, and if you're caught trying to climb aboard a lorry without paying them, they throw you off. You're lucky if you get away with a beating. Some migrants have been killed. As

I've told you, the Afghans are the most numerous here, so they act as a mafia. They take their cut from everything that makes a profit in the Jungle. Wherever you are in the world, however great the poverty or distress, you'll always find a heartless man trying to take advantage. Afghan or otherwise."

"And the second obstacle?" asked Adam.

"The police, my friend. They're better than dogs at searching the lorries, and you never know how many of them there'll be. Sometimes the Afghans set fire to several barricades at different junctions to confuse them, but that's rare. It takes a lot of organising and quite frankly the traffickers couldn't give a damn if you get across or not, because they already have your money."

"And you accept all that?" asked an astonished Adam. "You don't look to me like someone who suffers without a response."

"We've fought back many times, but you weren't here in the Jungle to help us. Afghans against Sudanese. Machetes and iron bars. Some even had guns. Battles between hundreds of men that lasted all night. We burn their camp, they burn ours. We kill one of them, they wound ten of ours. In the end, there's always more of them. You have to know when the odds are stacked against you. Since then, as leader of our camp, I've come to an arrangement with them."

"The little deals you were telling me about?"

"Nothing I'm proud of, I assure you. When someone from Sudan arrives with enough money to attempt a crossing – usually collected from his entire family back home – he contacts me. I introduce him to the Afghans, they offer a special price, and I get a hundred euros or so from it."

"And if the crossing fails?"

"Well then, he's left with no money. And he belongs to the Jungle."

Adam kept his eyes on the ground.

"Like I just said, wherever you go you'll always find someone who profits from others' misery. Do I disappoint you?" asked Ousmane.

"You survive. I don't judge."

Though it would be complicated for Adam to contact the Albanian traffickers who had established themselves in the centre of Calais, he could perhaps, thanks to the police, find a way to gather the information needed to help Kilani cross the Channel. He wondered whether "Bastoin" would agree to help him again. He walked out of the Sudanese camp, sat on a rock on the far side of the asphalted road and tapped a number into his phone.

When the name ADAM flashed up, Bastien hesitated, though he had almost called the Syrian several times that day. He let the phone ring until Erika looked up from her work, surprised he didn't pick up. At last, it stopped buzzing.

"Someone you're avoiding?" Corval asked.

"No, it's nothing," Miller said, getting up. "I'm going to get a coffee, I'll be back."

Erika frowned as she watched him leave. Bastien noticed her expression as he shut the door. He was hiding things more and more often, and she was offended by his lack of confidence in her.

"What's Miller doing?" Corval asked, not as stupid as he looked.

"Whatever he wants. He's the lieutenant," Erika snapped.

In the inner courtyard, Bastien wedged the phone between his head and shoulder and lit a cigarette. He only smoked a couple a day, but he needed one right now. In the Jungle, Adam picked up almost immediately, and the two men exchanged greetings.

"I'll be honest with you, Adam. Your photos have made a big impact. I need to see you."

"I need your help as well. For Kilani, the young boy. Can I come and see you at headquarters?"

Bastien was a good student and learned from experience. He tried to be more discreet than usual on the telephone.

"I think we need to talk in private. Adam, would you do me the honour of having dinner at my home?"

This proposal was followed by an awkward silence.

"I realise I don't even know if you have a family," said the Syrian.

"Yes, I do. A daughter, Jade. She's fourteen. I've already told her about you. And, of course, I have a wife as well. She's called Manon."

The similarity between their two families struck Adam like a slap in the face.

"I'm not really presentable, you know. And I can't come on my own."

"Kilani is very welcome, and I'll be offended if you refuse."

Invited to dinner. By a family. Adam's thoughts went back to his apartment in the Muhajirin neighbourhood of Damascus.

"Put 'Calais belfry' in your phone. It's right next to police headquarters. I'll come and pick you up there. You can't go wrong: the clockface almost touches the sky."

"Yes, Kilani stood staring at it for ten minutes. I think he believes somebody lives there."

"He might be disappointed when he sees my apartment. It's much smaller."

"I doubt it. We both live in tents, Bastoin."

36

Bastien and Manon were travelling in the same direction, like two parallel railway tracks. And just like them, they never touched or met.

Which is why, when Jade came home from school, opened the front door and heard her parents arguing, she felt a flicker of hope.

Anything was better than the violence of their silent breakfasts, when the sound of spoons against bowls and knives on toast was deafening. She walked towards the kitchen, without going in.

"What were you thinking, Bastien? Of course I'm really sorry about his family, but we don't even know him. A migrant, with an orphan. In our home! Couldn't you meet him somewhere else?"

"What is it that bothers you? The fact that he's a migrant? Or an Arab? If I'd invited a colleague, would you have asked so many questions?"

"Whoa! That's got nothing to do with it! I'm not racist, I'm thinking of our daughter."

Bastien's voice grew louder.

"You see! You're making it sound dangerous. Do you think they're out to get her? Don't worry, I still have my gun. If they're rude, I'll shoot them in the living room. Seriously Manon, I don't get you."

Jade's small silhouette stepped forward.

"Are you talking about Adam?"

When she heard the name, Manon flopped into the nearest chair.

"Incredible! So she knows! You've already talked about him? I can just shut my mouth, can I? I can even eat out and leave you two in peace if you like!"

"Shit!" Bastien exploded. "You'll stay, because we're a family. That still means something, doesn't it?"

Manon rushed to the bathroom and took out the box of Lexomil tablets. She shook it over her open hand until one came out, cut it in two and chewed one half without bothering with water. Returning to the kitchen, she was as conciliatory as ever.

"So what am I supposed to cook for them?"

"I've bought some pizzas," said a livid Bastien.

"Ah, French cuisine at its finest."

"Why? Do you remember how to cook?"

"Go screw yourself."

Bastien had barely slammed the front door before Manon went back to the bathroom to take the other half of the Lexomil tablet.

"I'll lay the table and light the oven, Maman. You've got time to change if you want."

Manon didn't turn round, but studied her daughter in the bathroom mirror.

"Why, are you ashamed of me?"

"I dunno, but you're in your jogging bottoms. We're used to it, but we have guests. We don't know them, but that's no reason for us to look like tramps."

Jade's tone was exactly like her father's. Her eyes as well.

And her temperament. For a split second, Manon hated her daughter. A moment later, it was herself she despised. She left the room to put on a baggy sweater and a pair of jeans.

Opening the front door, Bastien invited Adam and Kilani to follow him into the living room. As expected, there was a moment of embarrassment all round. Adam, with the disturbing scar beneath his eye and his imposing stature, felt grubbier than ever. Kilani stayed hidden behind the Syrian, staring wide-eyed at everything. Jade hesitated over the thousand questions she would have liked to ask. And Manon, who had been polite enough to greet them with a half-smile as well as more appropriate clothing, was still wary, as if the mere presence of these intruders might ruin her carpet.

"Adam, this is my wife, Manon."

"How do you do, madame?"

"And Jade, my daughter."

"It's a pleasure, mademoiselle."

Adam stepped to one side to reveal their other little guest.

"My turn to introduce you to Kilani."

Manon and Jade looked at the young boy, who instinctively smiled happily at them.

"I'm sorry, if he doesn't say anything, it's because—'

Before the atmosphere was completely ruined, Bastien butted in:

" . . .because he's dumb."

Adam sat on the sofa and Bastien did the same. Jade collapsed into one of the bean bags opposite them. Kilani watched as she was engulfed by this strange object, and Jade pointed to the other one. He stood in front of it, then leaped into it and was swallowed up. He burst into such marvellous clear laughter that all at once everything seemed completely normal. A family dinner. Only Manon remained on the defensive.

"Okay, I'll go and get the refreshments," she announced rather coldly.

The Syrian leaned over to Bastien and whispered confidentially:

"Are you sure everything is alright, my friend? We don't have to stay long, you know."

"Don't worry. It's not against you. Manon lost her father a few months ago. She's been unhappy ever since."

"I can understand that."

None of them had noticed Kilani extricate himself from the gluttonous seat and follow the smell of cooking into the kitchen. Manon turned round carrying a tray full of glasses, a jug of orange juice and another of sparkling soda. When she saw Kilani she was so startled she almost dropped the lot.

"Sorry. You took me by surprise."

The boy took a step into the kitchen, looking all round him and glancing every now and then at Manon to check he was allowed in there.

"I don't even know why I bother speaking to you. You don't understand me, do you?"

A disarming smile from Kilani. Laying the tray down, she served him a big glass of soda.

"Is this what you came looking for?"

The youngster seized the glass in both hands and gulped almost all of it down in one. The bubbles exploded in his mouth and nose, bringing tears to his eyes without altering the happy upward tilt of his lips.

Manon watched as he drained the last drops.

"You really don't smell too good," she said disconsolately, taking the glass from him.

Kilani continued his inspection of the kitchen and came to a halt in front of a framed photograph hanging on the wall. One of those rescued from the hat box in her mother's loft. A foggy morning on a bridge in Prague.

"Do you like it?" she asked softly. "I took it. When I was a lot younger."

She walked over to the photograph. Kilani grasped her hand.

Surprise at first. An instinctive flinch away from him. Then she looked at his skin, so young and yet so rough. His filthy clothes. How dark the back of his neck was. His slender wrists. His slightly laboured breathing. A child. Nothing more than a child. She felt a lump rise in her throat.

"I've got lots more. I'll show you if you like."

Back at the dining room table it was the huge pizzas with melted cheese that Kilani couldn't take his eyes off. He stared at them so imploringly he was the first to be served.

"They have chicken on them," Manon said. "I mean, there's no pork."

"I'm not Muslim," replied Adam. "I'm not Christian either. I think God is a myth."

"So we can open a bottle of wine?" said Bastien gaily.

"Finally! I was beginning to wonder if we were really in France."

Bastien got up and went into the kitchen. Jade didn't waste a second in claiming their guest's attention.

"Now you mention France, how come you speak our language so well?"

Wiping his mouth, Adam turned to her.

"All the migrants speak French. Do you know what the first three words they learn are? 'Oui', 'Non' and 'Dégage'. Well, they pronounce it 'Dougaj'. Go away – it's what they hear most often."

Jade didn't find this joke funny. Feeling uncomfortable, Adam coughed a couple of times and gave a proper answer.

"My father was a French teacher at Damascus University. There was a civil war in the Lebanon, a neighbouring country, and in 1981 the French ambassador was assassinated. The Lebanese thought our country was responsible, and relations became strained. Everybody wanted to know what the others were saying: France, Syria, Lebanon. So my government was looking for French translators and contacted my father to ask him to work for them. We never really discovered who had killed your ambassador, but my father stayed in the job, then later worked for a number of years at the Syrian embassy in France."

"So you know Paris?"

"Well, I was taken there in my parents' luggage many times. My earliest memories are of the corridors of the Hôtel de Crillon on an official trip. My father says it was there I took my first steps. He was madly in love with your country and would read me a story in French every night. Ever since, I've read books in your language or in Arabic without distinction. Do you know *Fantômas*?"

"Not very well, I must say. He was a superhero, wasn't he?"

"More or less. He was my childhood hero anyway."

Manon served everyone a second helping of pizza. Kilani wolfed down half of his in an instant. Adam finished his glass of wine and accepted another. His gaze met that of Manon, whose attitude had subtly changed as the conversation went on.

"I'm so sorry, Manon. It was insensitive of me to talk so much about my father. Bastien told me about yours. Please accept my apologies."

Manon shrugged as if it wasn't important. The fact was, it hadn't even crossed her mind.

"I also know about your daughter and wife, Adam," she replied. "I hope you'll be reunited with them soon."

The Syrian thanked her with a slight nod of the head. Then, for the first time that evening, Manon took the initiative with Adam.

"Bastien tells me you were a policeman too?"

"Yes, for sixteen years. Captain Sarkis, of the Damascus crime investigation unit, at your service."

"Captain?" said Jade. "My father is a lieutenant. That means you're his superior. Like, you could give him orders?"

Adam and Bastien exchanged amused glances.

"When it comes down to it, I suppose so," he said.

"And does Kilani come from Syria as well?" Jade asked.

"No. I think he's Sudanese. But I don't know much more than that."

"So how did you two meet?"

"He was a boy 'to play with'. Adults took advantage of him sexually in the Jungle. I helped him, and now I protect him."

Adam was obviously not on the same wavelength as Bastien, who had managed to avoid a moment's embarrassment by describing Kilani as dumb earlier, but who hadn't seen this admission coming. Jade stared at the little boy, finishing off his pizza with an innocence he ought to have lost long ago. Manon was so horrified she simply laid her knife and fork down on her plate.

Was it the effect of alcohol? The anti-depressants? Or had she finally taken in their situation? For whatever reason, tears welled in her eyes. Kilani immediately lost all interest in his plate. He took two small steps to go and stand beside her, peering at her, trying to understand.

224

"Everything's alright, little one," she reassured him. "It's not your fault."

She turned to Jade.

"Will you clear the table? We'll leave the men to talk in the living room, and I'll serve dessert later. And you can come with me, my boy. I'll show you some more photos."

This time it was Manon's turn to take the boy's hand.

When they were back sitting together on the sofa, Bastien lit a cigarette and offered one to his guest. Adam lit his, then slipped Bastien's lighter into his pocket.

"I've got problems," he said. "In helping Kilani I've antagonised some dangerous people. This morning they killed a dog and left it outside my tent as a warning. I don't know how much longer I'll be able to protect the kid. I'd like to get him out of the Jungle."

"Does he know anyone in France?"

"Probably not. My friend Ousmane reckons he's seen him in the camp for more than a month. He wouldn't have stayed so long if he had somewhere else to go. Like everybody in the Jungle, he wants to get to England."

"And what can I do?" Bastien replied with a shrug.

"I'd like you to tell me how people get on the ferries. How to avoid the police or customs."

Bastien took a deep drag on his cigarette.

"As you must know, it's almost impossible. There are barbed-wire fences all along the route, helicopters, thermal cameras, dogs, police units, and that's before you reach customs. He could fall from the lorry, or be crushed by a load, or be run over trying to climb aboard. And if I tried to take him in my car boot, I'd risk five years in jail."

"There must be a solution," said a frustrated Adam.

"I don't get it. There are a thousand kids in the Jungle. Why choose to help this one in particular?"

"Because he's the one who crossed my path. I didn't choose anything."

"You know that as well as the risk of failure, this is going to cost you a huge amount of money. What will you do if your pockets are empty when you finally find Nora and Maya?"

"I agree that, taken as a whole, the obstacles are daunting. But if you look at them individually, none of it's impossible. I'll see when the time comes."

Adam spoke of all this as though it was no more than a series of logistical problems. There was no suggestion that it was his wife and daughter he was talking about. Bastien massaged his temples and hesitated a few seconds before taking the plunge.

"Perhaps there's another solution. But you'd be the one in danger."

"Tell me, my friend."

"It's not the friend talking, but the police officer. It's about the photos you brought to my office. Let's just say they interested people in high places. People who would have no difficulty getting the boy safe passage to England."

"And what do these people want from me?"

"As you suspected, the people in those photos are not imams. One of them is an Isis recruiting agent. They would like you to join the Salafist mosque and, if possible, become a recruit."

"You want to know what he's planning, is that it?"

"That's the idea."

"And in return I can be certain that Kilani will be taken to England?"

"Yes. But you know that—"

"No," Adam interrupted him. "I'll do it. For the kid. Who do I have to pass the info on to?"

He had become the professional police officer once more. He wasn't Adam now, he was Captain Sarkis.

"Er . . . To me for now, I guess."

Bastien and Adam came to a halt in the bedroom doorway. On the sofa opposite the bed, Manon was turning the pages of a photo album and talking to her daughter, who was sitting next to her. A moment of intimacy of the kind Bastien hadn't seen for a long time. Kilani was flat out, his head in Manon's lap and legs on top of Jade's.

"I'm sorry. He was sick and then went out like a light."

"It's okay," Adam reassured her. "He also threw up the chocolate bars he was given at the police station. I think we're going to skip dessert."

The Syrian shook the boy's shoulder. Kilani slowly woke up, looked round at the three adults and pretty young Jade and understood it was time to leave. He stood up and, still drowsy, took up his position alongside his protector's leg.

"I'll drop you outside the Jungle," Bastien said.

"No, we'll walk. It'll do him good."

Once the front door to their apartment had closed, the Miller family found themselves in the living room. Although for once they were together, they all felt terribly on their own.

"You can read in your bedroom if you like, Jade," Bastien said.

"I'd rather go on my tablet for a while. There's lots of things I want to look up."

Jade left the other two even more bewildered. They said nothing for a minute, then Manon leaned her head on Bastien's shoulder.

"I was insufferable. I feel so stupid," she whispered.

"I thought you were wonderful."

"That's because you love me too much."

Turning towards him, she pressed her lips on his in an unusually warm kiss.

Adam was still on the landing outside their apartment. He had taken out the lighter he had filched from his host, kneeled down and was now scorching the bottom of the front door, leaving a small trace of soot.

"Come on. Back to the Jungle," Adam said, standing up again. "And keep your eyes open on the way."

37

In the Sudanese camp the next morning, nobody greeted Adam.
That wouldn't have been so worrying if everyone hadn't also
avoided meeting his eye. Even the usually tactile Wassim stayed
away. Obviously Jungle Love was in short supply.

A few metres further on at the entrance to their prayer room,
Ousmane, who had been up since dawn, was engaged in an
intense discussion with a group of five men who were regularly
glancing in the Syrian's direction.

Realising he was the object of their conversation, Adam settled calmly beside the bonfire and waited for them to approach
him. Close by, Kilani's tent opened, and he poked his nose out.
Adam shook his head with a serious expression. Kilani frowned
and stayed inside.

Ousman left the group, shaking hands with some of the
men, slapping others on the back, before finally coming to sit
down with Adam. He poured two teas without a word.

"When do you want us to leave?" Adam asked point blank.

"You have to understand," Ousmane said. "The Afghans
came last night. They asked us to choose. If we keep Kilani
and you in our camp, we lose the right to cross to England."

"And that would be the end of your little deals."

Angered by this, Ousmane exhaled heavily.

"Be careful what you say, Adam. I'm probably your only

friend here. This has nothing to do with money. You know I've given up on the idea of getting to England, but for the others that's the only thing keeping them from losing heart. Like you, playing at being a policeman in the Jungle and adopting a kid, instead of looking for your family. You do everything you can to avoid thinking of them. Soon you'll forget them completely."

Adam's jaw clenched.

"Now it's your turn to watch what you're saying, Ousmane."

The Sudanese man gently placed his mug on the ground.

"Without really knowing one another, we both know who we're faced with, and that we would lose a lot by becoming enemies. I'm the leader in this camp, and the others expect me to protect them."

"So I ask you again: when do you want us to leave?"

"You have all day, but not the night. Unless you accept the second proposal the Afghans made."

There was no doubt in Adam's mind what this would be. He turned towards the tent where Kilani was staring at him, close enough for nothing of what they had said to have escaped him.

"Kilani is with me. Tell them that. Tell them that if they come anywhere near him, I'll kill them all."

There was no threat in his calm voice. Simply a promise.

"You react like someone who fights back instinctively, blow for blow, without any proper strategy. I get the impression you're already certain you're not going to make it," Ousmane concluded.

The two men stood up, facing one another in silence. Adam held out his hand and Ousmane took him in his arms. Without realising it, they were repeating the gestures they had made when they first met, when the Sudanese had called him "military man".

Adam started along the path out of the camp, and Kilani

rushed from his tent to follow him. Still within earshot, Ousmane tried one last time to reason with a man who appeared to be walking headlong into a storm.

"Even if you do manage to get him to England, what will that change? You don't even know if he has family over there. You don't think anything through! He was alone here, he'll be alone there too!"

As he vanished round an overflowing refuse container, Kilani looked back one last time. Ousmane said farewell with a sad smile.

Realising what Ousmane had been obliged to do for the others in their camp, Wassim came up to him and laid a hand on his shoulder. Ousmane impatiently brushed it off.

Julie put two cups of coffee on Care4Calais's plastic table. Kilani was sitting on sand still damp from the dew, watching the Jungle wake up.

"Your friend isn't wrong, Adam. Sending the boy to England without knowing what he can expect there is a big gamble."

"Don't you have any contacts in *Youké*?"

"Yes, with official associations run by the state, but they only get involved when the migrants' asylum visas have been validated or if they have family connections. But we know nothing about this boy. We can't even be a hundred per cent sure he's Sudanese. If we can't prove his nationality, he doesn't exist. He's a ghost. Do you know if he has identity papers, at least?"

She leaned down to Kilani and asked him in English:
"*You, papers? I.D. Card? Family in* Youké?"

Although he didn't speak English, the word *Youké* made Kilani open his eyes wide.

"He can barely follow my Arabic," said a frustrated Adam.

Yet Kilani, as well as understanding the warning Ousmane had issued when they were leaving the Sudanese camp, had long since learned to decipher situations, facial expressions and tones of voice. The two adults were looking at him and kept on saying *Youké*. He understood it was time for him to recite his magic formula for them. The one he had learned as he travelled from the White Nile to Egypt and from Egypt to Libya. The one he was always repeating in his head and drew in the sand at least once a day.

Separated from his family, he had managed to escape Sudan on an overloaded truck. Close to sixty people crammed in like a stack of logs. Squashed at the bottom of this pile, a man and a boy had suffocated, and they had to stop at the Egyptian border to dump their bodies. On the road out of Bentiu, the capital of Unity State in south Sudan, Kilani got to know a woman and her two sons. Seeing this lost, terrified little boy, the mother had simply made him part of her family. As the kilometres went by amid dust and sand, threats, insults and beatings, through official army checkpoints and those run by armed militias, they had supported and aided one another. Her name was Nosiba, and before the war she had been a schoolteacher. She taught him a rhyme that was so powerful it was like a magic charm. A charm that would open the door to *Youké*, one he should only use at the right moment and with the right people, she told him.

Their paths diverged in Libya, and Kilani had never again seen the ephemeral surrogate family that left him only this magic rhyme as a souvenir.

Kilani tugged at Adam's T-shirt to attract his attention, and then traced a first sign in the damp sand with his finger. It

232

looked like a 7 or a walking stick. The Syrian remembered he had often seen the boy doing this, and came to sit, with Julie joining him.

Kilani had never forgotten the rhyme Nosiba had chanted, nor the signs that she had drawn on the earth or on sand, so he could learn by heart something that might one day change his life.

You're going to need a strong stick to help you go round the circle of the planet.

After the 7 for the stick, Kilani drew a 0 to represent the circle of the planet. Then he repeated the rest of the rhyme to himself and drew the symbols illustrating it.

Two spears to protect your cows. Their udders full of nourishing milk. Two stones one on top of the other to crush the snake threatening them. A tear for when you leave your loved ones. Another for when you find them again.

And slowly, despite some imperfections, the series of ten signs became a telephone number: 70 11 33 85 66.

The magic charm opening the way to *Youké.*

Intrigued, Julie picked up her phone and punched in the digits. After a few rings, an automatic message informed her that the number was not available. She ended the call, then smiled at her mistake. She dialled again, this time adding the code for the UK. A soft voice crossed the Channel to Calais.

"*Sunchild Association. How may I help you?*"

Julie stood up and walked away from them to continue her conversation, notebook and pen in hand. Kilani watched her, stupefied.

The magic charm was working.

A few minutes later, Julie came back.

"It's quite incredible. This kid has travelled halfway round the Earth with the number of a child protection association engraved on his brain."

"How is that possible?" asked an astonished Adam.

"I can only guess, but I bet it's someone he met on his journey. Information travels all over the world and arrives, sometimes in a month, sometimes several years, in deepest Africa or the Middle East. A while ago, a young Syrian boy arrived with the number for a children's judge in Bobigny written on a scrap of paper! His big brother had arrived in France before him, and this man had helped him. Unfortunately, when we called the court, the judge had been transferred months before. As for Kilani, it's enough that this association once helped a Sudanese person, who then mentioned this to his family back home, for this telephone number to be known worldwide."

"So what did they tell you?"

"If I understood correctly, they're outside official channels. As soon as Kilani reaches England, all he needs to do is phone again and they'll come and pick him up at Dover."

"Kilani can't talk," Adam reminded her.

"Then he can ask an adult. I never said it would be easy."

Julie tore out the sheet of paper on which she had written the telephone number, the name of the association and some brief details about the boy.

"Slip that into his pocket: he'll be able to make himself understood. But before that he has to get on a ferry. That's the part that worries me most."

"That's exactly what I'm going to sort out today. Meanwhile, I have to find him somewhere safe."

Julie immediately saw this request was meant for her, and since the women's camp also welcomed children, she suggested it as a solution.

"But if children are accepted there," said Adam, "why are there so many in the Jungle?"

"They're scared of being shut in. As soon as there's a door or fence, they're terrified. You have to remember where they've come from and what they've lived through before they get here. And then there's the rumours, the myths. The scary ones are the most persistent. Some children think they'll be sold as slaves to French families. Others are convinced that one morning they'll wake up with a kidney or an eye missing, cut out by organ traffickers. They want to be able to run away when they want to, so a guarded camp isn't for them."

With that she picked up her walkie-talkie.

"Antoine, Julie here."

"Peace to the world, Julie."

"Yeah, whatever. I need a place for a kid. Is that doable?"

To see Ousmane again so soon would have been awkward, so Adam was relieved not to find him in the Sudanese camp. He quickly gathered up his things, mimicked by Kilani, who simply picked up his bright blue and red backpack. They left their tents where they were, because the boy was going to the women's camp. Mindful that he was under constant threat, Adam knew where he himself would hide.

The took the road round the Jungle until they came to the post manned by Antoine, the most Zen guard in the whole history of guards. Adam had a quick word with him to make sure Kilani would be safe. Antoine was certain he would, because apart from volunteers and children, no male migrant was allowed in this part of the Jungle.

"But it's entirely voluntary, you know. If the kid wants to leave, I can't keep him here."

"I'll take care of that," Adam told him.

He kneeled down next to Kilani, placing both hands on his shoulders.

"I have things to do today. Important things for you and your journey. Do you understand?"

Kilani nodded, but his sullen face implied the opposite.

"You're to stay inside and sleep here. I forbid you to leave, got it?"

And since the word had had its effect before, Adam used it again:

"I'm giving you an order," he said, leaving him with Antoine.

He strode off without looking back, because he could imagine the black looks Kilani must be giving him.

The day was just beginning, and there was the guy from No Borders to see.

38

Alexandre Merle was one step ahead of the game. Or so he imagined.

The Syrian, however, had overtaken him, having been rapidly snapped up by the counter-terrorism services. Since Merle was no longer much use to them, Commandant Paris had ordered him to take a step back. Released from his contract with them, he should have seized his chance and done as he was told. But, of course, that wasn't how things turned out.

For several days now there had been two huge guys he'd never seen before standing guard outside the entrance to the Salafist mosque, and during closed prayers you had to show credentials to enter. That was unusual. Then again, everybody who went past the mosque was scrutinised. So Merle had decided to install himself in the Pakistani café some ten metres away, just in case. And his lucky break came thanks to an addiction. A simple addiction to tobacco.

Every two hours a man came out, surrounded by four bodyguards. He lit a cigarette, drew on it as if it were his last ever, then went back inside the mosque, where smoking was strictly forbidden.

Merle slipped his phone into the pocket on the left strap of his backpack. Exactly two hours later, the man came out again, accompanied as before. Merle took advantage of a passing group of migrants, falling in step with them and walking by less than a metre from the smoker, secretly filming him with his phone.

He returned to the No Borders camp terrified that at any moment someone would seize him by the shoulder like a security guard laying hands on a thief. He ducked into his tent to watch the video several times. His hands began to tremble when he recognised the man smoking: it was No.4 on his list of six.

Shadow was in the Jungle, which meant Merle still had a role to play. But there was no way he was going to fight on two fronts. If he reported Shadow to the counter-terrorism people, he would be forced to leave the camp and his fellow No Borders. There was no way he could remain in the kingdom after causing its downfall. But neither did he have any intention of politely handing over the information to Commandant Paris after he had so clearly washed his hands of him. Nothing would be offered for free.

While Merle was going over all this in his head, he began to pack his bag, tossing his things in haphazardly. He wanted to be ready to slip out of the camp that night, taking advantage of the relative calm when the migrants were asleep. All of a sudden, one of the tent flaps opened, and Adam was standing there watching as he stuffed the last of his clothes into the bag. His phone was still on the plastic crate he used as a bedside table.

"Going somewhere?" the Syrian asked.

Merle's half-second hesitation was sufficient reply.

He went over to his phone and slipped it into his pocket. Adam didn't move: if it came to a fight, he would have the upper hand anyway.

"I've spoken to your No Borders friends. They say you've been spending your days in the Pakistani café. I went to look, and it gives a perfect view of the mosque. Have you discovered something?"

"Nothing interesting," Merle said, trying to remain calm. "Anyway, I get the impression you're their new agent. You can run the risks from now on, I'm out of here."

Adam's giant frame blocked the tent entrance.

"Show me what you have on your phone, please."

Merle took a step backwards, but in two strides Adam was upon him. Knowing threats would be a waste of time, he went directly into action, putting his hand over the youngster's mouth to silence him. He seized one of Merle's hands and bent the middle finger back to the wrist, then whispered into the whimpering youth's ear:

"Stay calm. It's nothing. You'll soon get used to the pain."

Merle was breathing heavily through his nose. Adam could feel his saliva on the palm of his hand.

"You still have nine fingers left. I can ask you the same question nine more times."

Merle wrenched himself free. Adam made no move to stop him.

"Bastard!" yelled Merle, like a young kid unfairly punished. "Can't you see they'll drop you when they no longer need you? What have they promised you? If you believe a word they say, you're not as smart as I thought you were."

"The phone," Adam repeated calmly.

Merle threw it in his direction and sat on the camp bed clutching his hand.

"If we play this right we could both make some dough," he said. "The info on my phone is worth its weight in gold – and you're going to give it to them just like that? Without asking anything in return?"

"I'm not interested in money."

Stooping to retrieve the phone, Adam went over to Merle, holding out a corner of his sleeping bag.

"Let me see your finger . . . and cover your mouth with this."

People who trip over try to soften their fall with their hands, and often break or dislocate their fingers . During his police career, Adam had seen this dozens of times, and he knew exactly what to do. He took hold of Merle's hand again, felt for the dislocated joint, and snapped it back into place.

Merle howled into his sleeping bag.

"You son of a bitch!"

"Sorry," Adam said coldly.

Kilani reluctantly followed Antoine as he took him down a dirt track, past the Djalfari Centre, then into a secure area the size of a football pitch with around twenty large tents pitched on a neat lawn.

Antoine checked his list and went to the ninth tent. Lifting one of the flaps, he pointed to a bed inside.

"You stay here," he said to the boy in broken English. *"I am go . . . er . . . toilette things for you, okay? Don't move."*

Amused by the old man's waving arms, Kilani stared at him, then looked left and right at his new surroundings, where thirty or so migrant women, plus fifteen male and female volunteers and some children, spent their days. Some were washing clothes in a tub; others were following a French class, sitting in a circle round a young woman with the air of a school ma'am. Further off, a volunteer was hammering in a tent peg.

As usual, Kilani did not move from where he'd been left, patiently waiting for Antoine to return. Then one of the flaps opened at the far end of the long marquee and he saw a silhouette enter and walk along the length of the tent, its features becoming clearer as it advanced. Kilani held his breath, as though it might somehow render him invisible. He clenched his teeth and bunched his fists. He had to get out of there as quickly as possible. If he had recognised the figure, the opposite could be also be true.

By the time Antoine returned, Kilani had vanished into thin air.

"Where's the kid got to?" he asked everyone in the tent, his arms laden with new clothes and toiletries.

Adam now had something he could use to barter with the counter-terrorism boss. Or at least show his willingness to co-operate. Knowing Kilani was safe, he found himself a calm spot far enough away from the Sudanese camp not to cause them problems, and remote enough that the Afghans might forget about him.

When Wassim had first taken him to the beach, Adam had noticed a row of Second World War bunkers. One of them had been blasted open, providing shelter from bad weather but also offering a clear view of all nearby comings and goings.

He moved some rubble aside to make room for himself. He could light a fire in the centre, and there was even enough space to put up his tent. Surrounded by these ruins, he felt as if he were drifting from war to war, as if that was all he knew, all he deserved.

He felt for the photo of Nora and Maya, smoothed it and placed it upright between two rocks. Opening the video app on Merle's phone, he too noted the strong resemblance between the man in the mosque and photo number four, before sending the footage to Bastien Miller, followed by the first in a chain of text messages:

Target confirmed in Jungle. I'll try to get near him today.

When Bastien received the text, he was with an old lady

whose house had been burgled. The most excitement he had had all day. He left Corval in the kitchen shouting questions at the deaf homeowner, and quickly tapped out:

Shadow is in Jungle. Sarkis requests permission to approach him.

Commandant Paris's phone roused him from the soporific effects of daytime TV. He read the message and passed on the information to his superior, Toulouse.

Shadow in Jungle. Phase Two?

It took a good hour for the reply to arrive, because the news had alerted an entire wing of counter-terrorism staff and led to an emergency meeting. Then the text messages cascaded down in reverse order.

Toulouse to Paris: *Let Shadow get installed. Renew contact in 24 hours.*

Paris to Miller: *Good work. Fresh instructions in 24 hours. Stand by until then.*

Miller to Sarkis: *Lay low for 24 hours. Take care, please. Tell me if you need anything.*

Adam stretched out on ground that felt hard despite the sleeping bag. He focused on his breathing, listened to the waves breaking on the beach and breathed in and out to their rhythm. After a while it was as if he were controlling the movements of the sea, when in reality he had been unable to control anything at all for almost two months now.

39

Hotel Bleu Azur, Calais
Room 309
Six p.m.

Paris had quickly tidied the bundled-up clothes and takeaway leftovers so his webcam would reveal a neat and tidy room. He checked how he looked in the bathroom mirror, pulled a disgruntled face at his reflection and straightened his tie.

An electronic chime told him that the video conference with headquarters was about to start. He sat down, clicked on the icon, and Paris's face appeared on screen.

"Just so that you know, Paris, I'm not alone in the room," he said by way of introduction.

"I can imagine," the commandant replied, not wishing to be indiscreet. "Sarkis is ready to go into action," he added.

Toulouse looked over his screen, as if seeking advice from the person or persons in front of him.

"Well yes, about that . . . Our priorities have changed. We're going to ask you to return to base."

"I don't understand."

"Then don't try. Simply answer our questions."

Paris was learning how unpleasant it was to be out of the loop.

"What would it take to make Shadow react?" asked Toulouse.

"What precisely do you mean by that, sir?"

"What would it take to get him to leave the Jungle?"

"Shadow survives thanks to his paranoia. At the slightest suspicion of anything untoward, he'll abandon his plans and do his best to drop off the radar once more."

Toulouse moved out of the picture for a moment. When he returned, it wasn't clear if his proposal was coming from him or had been suggested by someone else.

"Would disturbing phone reception all over the Jungle for a few minutes be enough?" he asked.

"Enough for him to make a move, yes," Paris confirmed. "But there's a strong possibility he'll slip through the net. You know that nine times out of ten when we tail someone it ends with the words 'Sorry, we lost him'. Especially with somebody like him."

"All we're concerned about," Toulouse said, drawing closer to the screen, "is getting him out of there and away from the CRS surrounding the place."

"What do you intend to do after that?"

"*Ad augusta per angusta.* Through trial to triumph. That's one of our mottoes."

"Has the president given his approval?"

"An hour ago. The DGSE* is taking over."

Dunes Industrial Estate, Calais
Ten-thirty p.m.
Four and a half hours later

Rue des Gravelines, the road leading to the Jungle from Calais, bordered a dense wood crisscrossed by forest tracks. A dark-blue

---

* Direction générale de la sécurité extérieure: Counter-terrorism force for outside France, equivalent to the British MI6.

saloon car crept down one of these paths, cushioned by broken branches and dead leaves, and advanced almost twenty metres until it was out of sight of passing traffic. The driver cut the engine, and the passenger on the back seat opened a carry-on-sized Innox case and awaited orders.

During his very first meeting with the counter-terrorism group, Merle had shown them the exact position of the Salafist mosque on a map of the Jungle. The driver used this information to verify their position via GPS.

"Objective is at four hundred and eighty metres."

"I'll adjust the range," said the technician.

A military-sounding voice in their earpieces told them the two SWAT teams were in place and gave them the green light. The technician fine-tuned the wavelength jammer and turned the key on his control panel to activate it.

"Wave jammer on," he confirmed. "Only our frequencies are active."

Shadow was interrupted by one of his bodyguards in the middle of Isha, the night prayer. There had to be a pressing reason for him to be disturbed at such a moment, and so instead of reacting angrily he listened, his face sombre. The man whispered in his ear:

"The phone network is down."

Shadow got to his feet, left the prayer room and went to the back of the tent.

"What about Internet?" he asked anxiously.

"No connection. I've sent for your driver – he's waiting for you at the Jungle entrance. You have to get out of here as quickly as possible. Your things are ready."

Shadow was escorted to the edge of the Jungle, not far from the CRS vans. He asked his bodyguard to let him go the rest of the way on his own. He walked down the road until he came to an old Ford waiting for him, engine running, headlights dimmed in the darkness.

"We're leaving. Don't put your lights on until we enter town," Shadow ordered.

The driver moved off slowly. He felt under his seat and handed a pistol to his passenger, who clicked the mechanism several times to make sure the magazine was full.

Just as they were about to leave the road leading out of the Jungle and turn left onto Rue des Gravelines heading for the centre of Calais, all four of the car's tyres burst, punctured by a spike strip. The driver swiftly controlled the resulting zigzag swerve, slammed on the brakes and came to a halt. An instant later, the two men had raised their weapons and were peering into the darkness around them, holding their breath.

On either side of the car, a dozen or so small flashes lit up the night. The gunfire, muffled by silencers, was no louder than a series of popping champagne corks. The car's front windows were shattered and the two men inside were killed on the spot.

A van pulled up alongside the Ford. Four men jumped out of the already open side door. One of them turned Shadow's face roughly towards him and took a photo that was immediately transferred to command centre. Less than ten seconds later, he received confirmation of facial recognition, more than ninety per cent certain.

The two bodies were pulled out of their vehicle and loaded onto a plastic sheet on the floor of the van. A breakdown truck appeared from one of the forest tracks and hitched up the old Ford in record time.

The operation had taken precisely three minutes and twenty seconds.

These events had been relayed live on a secure video link from the SWAT team's buttonhole cameras to the counter-terrorism crisis centre and Commandant Paris's Calais hotel room.

Their objective achieved, Paris's computer screen reverted to the crisis room and Toulouse's smiling face. The commandant was not so happy.

"Over a year's surveillance, ending up with a targeted assassination," Paris complained.

"We act in the best interests of the nation. It was the optimum solution. Or the least bad."

"They'll find a new recruiter, and we'll have to do it all over again," Paris objected.

"Not someone as good as him. It's not just an attack on French soil we've prevented, but all the potential atrocities he could have instigated."

"You realise my whole team was aware of our surveillance of Shadow? They're going to be astonished when it all suddenly comes to a end. There'll be quite a few people to keep quiet. I'm surprised the big Teddy Bear gave the go-ahead. However it came about, we'll have to tread carefully."

"What are you afraid of, Paris? That the president boasts about it in a book?"

40

Since daybreak, a light rain had been falling steadily on Calais. Raindrops trickled down the windows in Commissaire Dorsay's office, making it look as if the town outside were melting. Lieutenant Miller was still struggling to absorb his superior's news.

"Promises were made," he said, dumbfounded.

"To whom? To you?"

"Obviously not. To Sarkis."

"Your Syrian protégé? Whether you call them snitches or sources, the first rule is not to get involved with them. You came to us from the police judiciaire, you should know that. One day they could be the fall guy and if you're not willing to burn them, it'll be because you've become attached to them."

The image of Kilani fast asleep on Manon's lap flashed through Bastien's mind. Then Adam talking things over with Jade in their living room.

Yes, possibly too attached.

"The DGSI's target has left the Jungle. They're continuing their investigation. Somewhere else. The fact is, your famous Commandant Paris left Calais during the night, and you're being asked to cut all contact with Sarkis. Phoning counter-terrorism to ask them to explain is off limits as well. They'll want to debrief you soon, but I hope you've understood that none of this happened."

After this conclusion, something straight out of a spy film, Bastien was encouraged by his superior to continue his day as normally as possible, but instead found himself wandering the corridors of Calais police headquarters in a daze. At some point, he heard Erika calling out.

"Has anyone seen the lieutenant? Shit, but the guy's a ghost!"

She burst into the corridor, almost colliding with him.

"Where did you get to? The station's about the size of a matchbox, and I've been looking for you for ten minutes!"

"I was with the big boss," Bastien said.

"Is there a problem?"

"A hiccup. Nothing serious; it's been sorted."

As convincing as a kid pleading their innocence, fingers covered in chocolate. Erika softened her voice. To anyone who knew her, this was a telltale sign that she was getting increasingly exasperated.

"A hiccup. That's it? A hiccup? Well listen, from now on, I'll pretend everything is just fine. I'm no longer going to try to understand what you're going through or how I can help. And you know what? It's entirely my own fault. You're my superior, not my friend. I don't even know why I imagined you were anything else."

Bastien was at a loss for words. How could he tell her that he couldn't tell her anything? His lips parted as if he were finally about to say something, but no words emerged. Even more infuriated, Erika raised her eyes to the heavens. To stop herself from strangling him, she stepped back into her professional role.

"There was a call from the Jules Ferry centre. There's been another murder in the Jungle. In the women's camp. The fire brigade is on its way."

The colour drained from Bastien's face.

"Has the victim been identified?"

"You know as much as I do."

"Let's go then."

"Don't you want to call the police judiciaire at Coquelles? I know they don't usually investigate incidents in the Jungle, but the women's camp is a special case. The examining magistrate is going to want photos from the scene and at least a summary investigation."

"Tell Corval to call them. I'll meet you in the yard."

Erika clenched her fists as she watched him bound down the stairs, calling a number on his phone as he went. Dorsay had prohibited all contact with Adam, but there was no way Bastien was going to obey that order.

Adam's battery was dead. He told himself that with a bit of luck the morning's rain might have discouraged the other migrants from gathering round the few charge points in the Djalfari Centre. To get there he had to go past the women's camp, and on the way he found a dense crowd milling around outside the entrance. Among the clamour of voices and tongues, Adam made out the word "murder". It spread like poison through his veins.

At first, he tried to pick his way through carefully, but as he became increasingly anxious he began to use his hands to clear a path for himself, pushing people out of the way until he reached a fire engine parked by the control post. Peering inside the vehicle, he saw the stretcher was missing. If there had been a murder, he would have to wait, heart pounding, to see how big the body bag was. He felt a hand on his shoulder.

"Kilani is with me," Antoine said. "I put him in the cabin."

Adam could feel the tension and fear ebbing away.

"What happened?"

"A woman has been killed. During the night. An Afghan woman. Stabbed in the heart, the firemen say. They couldn't get here any sooner because there was a big fire in the town centre."

"Did the kid see anything?"

"I don't know. He doesn't speak French. In fact, he never says anything. I can't even be sure he spent the night here, because he slipped away from me ten minutes after you left. All I know is I found him sitting outside my office when I arrived this morning."

Adam ran to the camp entrance, flung open the door to Antoine's cabin and saw Kilani sitting in a corner, head resting on his knees. He stood up, and a relieved Adam took him in his arms without a word. Behind them, two firemen went by, pushing a trolley that jolted across the stony ground. It was carrying a black bag with a zip from top to bottom.

Above the hubbub of the restless Jungle came the sound of two blasts of a police siren. Kilani turned towards it.

Bastien parked between a refuse container and some portable toilets. Despite the siren, it was impossible to get any closer without risking running someone over. He abandoned the car in the midst of the crowd.

"Hey, Miller? You're not really going to leave it here, are you?"

When he didn't answer, Erika got out and followed him, swearing as she did so. Bastien was scanning the flood of people like a father who has lost his child in a shopping centre, neck craned and breathing hard. Amid a thousand silhouettes, a hand slipped into his own. Recognising Kilani, he picked the boy up and hugged him as if he were his son, oblivious to what Erika might think. As he did so, he saw Adam looking in his direction and sighed with relief. Erika meanwhile was staring at him, unable to believe her eyes.

"Listen, Bastien. I don't want to know. I'm going back to the car before we only have the wheels left. I'll wait for you outside with the CRS. I'm not worried, I'm sure you'll find your way there. From what I can see, you're pretty much at home here, right?'

Watching her stride away, Bastien realised her patience was running out, and he needed to do something about it.

Adam invited Bastien to follow him along the track that led to the bunkers between the Jungle and the shore. The two men climbed the ruined walls of the one that sheltered Adam's tent and sat looking out at the horizon.

"Were you afraid for us?" the Syrian asked, both grateful and amused.

Since there was no point stating the obvious, Bastien changed the subject.

"I didn't know this beach. It's wonderful. I can't get over what a desert it is."

"It isn't a desert, it's deserted," the Syrian corrected him. "The migrants are too close for the *Kalissi* and tourists."

The two men sat silently as the waves lapped at the sand.

"The victim is a woman," Adam said. "Stabbed with a knife, according to the rumours. I'll know more as the day goes on. But if we compare this to the killing of the Libyan guy, we could find out if the same weapon was used."

The Syrian had already launched headlong into an investigation no-one had asked for. Bastien didn't know how to reveal the DGSI's betrayal.

"Stop it, Adam. You're not a cop here."

"Don't you want to know if there's a killer in the Jungle?"

"I'm not with the police judiciaire. It's not my job."

"But there's nothing to stop you comparing the two autopsies, is there? You can read the reports, can't you?"

More waves. More wind raking the grass on the dunes. Bastien cut their pointless discussion short.

"The counter-terrorism people are no longer investigating the mosque," he admitted finally. "They left this morning."

Adam made no reply. He didn't even turn to look at Miller.

"I'm no longer authorised to contact them. Do you know what that means?"

Adam had shown Kilani their new home, and now the boy was returning with armfuls of twigs and branches to keep the fire going amid the wind and rain. He joined the two adults on the roof, sitting down next to his protector.

"That means," Bastien went on, "they won't do anything for the kid."

Adam didn't react. It was hard to tell if he'd understood. Beneath their feet, a gust of wind struck the bunker. It swirled round the rekindled fire, bounced off the walls, and dislodged the photo of Nora and Maya propped up between two stones. Carried through the air, the photo hung there for a moment, then dropped into the flames. Their faces shrivelled up; their smiles disappeared.

"The autopsy could show what kind of blade made the wounds," Adam went on, refusing to be sidetracked. "That could tell us if the same one was used in both cases."

His stubbornness was the last straw for Bastien. He flew into a rage on his own behalf, for the Syrian, for Kilani.

"Stop it, will you! I don't need you to tell me how to run an investigation! No-one needs Captain fucking Sarkis to investigate a murder! You'd do better to worry about . . ."

Just before he went too far, Bastien swallowed the end of his sentence.

"Please don't talk about the murders anymore."

But what else could Adam cling to? Nora and Maya were in his heart, but it was Kilani who kept him going. He was separated from his loved ones, and now the counter-terrorist services had betrayed him he felt incapable of helping the boy. The murder investigation was the only thing preventing him from going mad.

What if he just disconnected? It would be so restful to give in. To stop struggling, let go and sink right to the bottom of himself . . .

Miller stood up and held out his hand, but Adam made no attempt to return the gesture. He sat there, his mind on the horizon. Kilani saw this and looked from one adult to the other, feeling helpless. He didn't understand what had gone on, but could sense the tension in the atmosphere. After a few seconds, Bastien dropped his hand and jumped down off the bunker roof.

There were only four people in Kilani's life now. Adam, and the family who had welcomed him, if only for an evening. One of the most beautiful he could remember. Tears welled in his eyes as he too stood up, kicked out angrily at Adam, then slid down the side of the bunker and headed for the beach.

Bastien found Erika sitting on the bonnet of the police car, a cigarette between her lips. He climbed into the passenger seat. His colleague took her time, smoking her cigarette to the last drag. This was the second time she had seen Adam and could tell there was something between the two men. She felt slighted at being left out.

Bastien didn't open his mouth once during the journey,

letting Erika fume in silence. As they went past the docks, she turned the car sharply, accelerated, and drove into a disused warehouse where a few wrecked boats and tangled fishing nets lay rotting. She wrenched on the handbrake to bring the car to a halt, the echo of the squealing tyres amplified by the metal walls.

"Now you're going to talk, Miller! Who is that kid? Who is that guy?"

41

In the bathroom, Bastien splashed water on his face, without noticing it was going everywhere. Then again. And again.

That moment of introspection when you look yourself right in the eye in the mirror, peering deep into your soul as though weighing yourself up, challenging yourself.

Manon slipped behind him and wrapped her arms round his waist.

"I won't be in this evening," he said, perplexed.

"Should I be worried?"

"I think I'm about to do something stupid," he whispered.

"Something I'll be proud of?"

"I can't understand why I feel responsible."

"You didn't go looking for this. They crossed your path."

Conversations between Bastien and Manon could seem disjointed. They understood one another without the need for words. This bond had been submerged through a period of what seemed like endless mourning. And yet there it was again, surfacing timidly in the eye of the storm.

"You're not on your own," murmured Manon.

The same phrase, word for word, that Erika had uttered in the disused warehouse as they sat, car doors wide open, smoking cigarette after cigarette as he told her his long story. The meeting at the hospital. The Syrian and the boy. The dramas that had destroyed them and brought them together. Their families, scattered somewhere across the planet, everyone looking for everyone. The horrors they had seen. Their solitude and their hopes. Their strength, the courage needed to carry on. And the Jungle prison.

In spite of Dorsay's orders, Bastien had even told Erika about the promises the DGSI had made.

"Adam will never leave the Jungle without his wife and daughter. But then there's the kid. He's in danger every day. I could never forgive myself if I did nothing to help him."

"You're not on your own," Erika had reassured him. "If you're going to do something stupid, you've got a whole team behind you. Trust me – let us help you."

Just as Erika had, his wife listened to the story without interrupting.

"What should we tell Jade?" she asked, sitting on the edge of the bath.

"The truth. She's old enough. Besides, she's too smart, we can't hide anything from her."

"She's at her friend Dorothée's and she won't be back for another hour. I'll see to it."

She stood up and pulled off her T-shirt, crossing her arms and lifting it gently from the bottom, proffering her firm breasts, her no longer completely flat but still wonderful stomach, an awkward expression on her face that was disturbing and inviting at the same time.

"She won't be back for an hour . . ." she repeated, pressing her body against his.

Passaro had a small townhouse. One of those with a wrought iron gate, a front garden and Chinese lanterns hanging from the porch. Night fell at around nine, and after explaining in detail what he had already told Erika, Bastien stood in front of the BAC team and gave them a moment to digest everything.

"It could be a good thing for us," Passaro agreed.

"It could cost us our jobs. That would be almost worthwhile," Sprinter added.

Cortex once again felt the rush of wind from the lorry inches behind his back. The lorry that by all rights should have barrelled straight into him.

"You can count on me, lieutenant, I'll follow you anywhere."

The discussion continued, as technical and precise as if they were planning a hold-up.

"The more migrants there are, the less chance he'll have of succeeding," said Bastien. "He needs to be the only one climbing onto a lorry."

Accustomed to troubleshooting, Passaro, Cortex and Sprinter held a brief brainstorming session.

"To ensure there are no other clandestine stowaways, the driver has to avoid Junction 47 on the A16. That's where the traffickers build their barricades and bonfires to give the migrants time to climb aboard."

"Okay. So we set up a fake checkpoint before Calais. We escort the lorry into town as far as the Cité Europe retail park. While we're checking it, we smuggle the kid into the back and then escort them through the centre of town to the N216. That way we bypass the CRS and any barricades. After that, the driver can cover the seven kilometres to the port without a problem."

"We'll have to choose a lorry with a trailer and tarpaulin that lets air in. Otherwise the kid will be caught by the CO_2 detector."

"And it'll have to be a European haulier. If it's an international one, the lorry will be sealed and if we break it open, they'll spot it at customs."

"It's not the customs officers who worry me, it's their damned dogs."

"Dogs like Wolf?" asked a worried Bastien.

"No. Sniffer dogs. They're trained to detect something all the migrants carry with them. The smell of burnt wood. We'll have to get the boy new clothes and wash him thoroughly several times, otherwise all this will be for nothing."

"Five thousand lorries pass through every day, so we should be able to pull it off," Cortex reasoned. "And at last I'll have a decent story to tell my other half."

Bastien stood up solemnly and looked round at this team. His team.

"So we're all agreed?"

The few embers left of the fire gave off a feeble glow, casting shadows on the bunker walls. Among the ashes Adam didn't even notice the tiny intact corner of Nora and Maya's photo. He was busy guarding the sleeping Kilani.

That day, several migrants had visited the beach and noticed their refuge. By now the information had probably reached the Afghans. The boy slept with a threat hovering over him like the seagulls over Calais.

Adam's phone vibrated in his pocket. He spoke before Bastien could.

"I shouldn't have spoken the way I did. And I asked too much of you," he said.

"Too late, my friend. I've already forgiven you. Besides, I was the one who made you a promise, not the DGSI. So get Kilani ready. He's leaving the Jungle in twenty-four hours."

Adam turned to look at the child, curled up in his sleeping bag but tormented by nightmares.

"You don't have to do this," Adam told Bastien.

"You did your bit without having to either. Do you think you're better than me?"

"'In the end, we'll have to look back at everything we've agreed to do. And that day, I refuse to be ashamed of myself,'" said Miller. "A colleague told me that tonight. And his words are what stopped me going back on my promise."

"That's not just a good cop but a good person you have on your side, Bastoin."

"I know. And he's not the only one." A moment's hesitation, a necessary silence before a question that left so much unsaid . . .

"What if you left with Kilani? You're his only family, and perhaps he's yours too by now?"

"I'll think about it," replied Adam after a few seconds.

42

Bastien had spent the day on the phone, scheming with Manon, Adam and Passaro. For her part, Erika was put in charge of overloading Corval with work; it was too risky to include him in their plans. Since the day a cousin had shuttered his restaurant due to a lack of tourists, the Corval family hadn't exactly been fans of migrants.

Between two calls, copies of the autopsies Bastien had asked for landed on his desk, but he ignored them, his mind completely occupied by his efforts to minimise the risks Kilani might face.

That afternoon, Manon had visited a sports shop and bought a full ten-year-old's outfit in black. Backpack, sneakers, socks, T-shirt, jumper and jogging bottoms. The cashier scanned them one by one, raising an eyebrow at the monochrome look.

"Is your boy training as a ninja?"

"No, we're prepping for a family hold-up," Manon said.

It was a feeble joke, but Manon was pleased to discover her sense of humour was making a comeback.

Passaro, meanwhile, had concocted an alibi, and contacted the CRS to tell them his team would be staking out a dealer on one of the Calais estates. The BAC would have to stay there until eleven that night. Right after that, he reassured the CRS, they would join them at Point Romeo near Junction 47.

Inside the Jungle, Adam had told Kilani how the French police officer was going to help them cross the Channel that same evening, and that they would soon be in England. There was no need for a thermal blanket to conceal his body heat from the helicopter cameras because it was grounded at its base that night. Nor would they need a sharp blade to cut the tarps. All they had to buy was a condom for use as a portable toilet, and Adam was going to get that from one of the stores on the Champs-Elysées.

Scarcely able to contain his excitement, Kilani prepared his backpack. He wrapped his big brother's leather wristband in his mother's square of fabric and put them with all the other treasures he had accumulated during his journey and his time in the Jungle. Most important of all was the piece of paper from Julie, on which she had written the magic telephone number and some information about Kilani.

Proud he had got everything ready so quickly, he stood in front of Adam, impatient to be leaving the refugee camp.

"I'm sorry, you won't be able to take anything with you," the Syrian said. "I've already told you about the police dogs."

Kilani clutched the bag to his chest.

"Did you know a dog can smell ten thousand times better than a human? They'll find you because of the memories you're trying to take with you. I'm not saying you should throw them away. If you like, we'll bury your bag together, somewhere in the dunes. The only thing you can keep is Julie's piece of paper."

The boy took a step back, far from convinced.

"You can come and find your bag when you return one day," Adam lied.

Then he clinched it with a single sentence.

"Do you want to stay in the Jungle or leave with me?"

Sullen but persuaded, Kilani jumped down from the bunker, sat cross-legged on the sand and examined his possessions one last time.

Then he dug a hole with his hands. First in the sand, then in the soft earth. He hugged his bag one last time and slipped it into the hole, before covering it over and placing some stones on top so he'd be able to find it again one day, when he returned.

Before he left headquarters that evening, Bastien checked with the secretary that there was no news of any traffic police operation in the vicinity of their fake checkpoint. Reassured, he headed for the stairs to the exit, where he bumped into Ruben Corval.

"Good luck," the brigadier murmured.

Bastien was going so quickly he was already past Corval, so he turned and climbed back up two steps.

"Was there something you wanted to say, Ruben?"

"I was given two cases to handle on my own. Nobody's said a word to me all day, and even though I was doing all the work, you both seemed very busy. I imagine it's because you don't trust me, and given the way I've behaved, I can understand that. I also know you're on the level, so even though this looks like a pretty dubious operation, you must have your reasons. So . . . good luck."

Without waiting for a reply, he nodded at Bastien and walked off, leaving the lieutenant pleasantly surprised. Corval might be lazy, but he wasn't stupid.

At eight that evening, Adam and Kilani were waiting in the shadow of the Calais belfry, which still had the same hypnotic effect on the small boy. The Syrian was touched, imagining how the boy would react at the sight of Big Ben.

Right on time, Bastien gave two short blasts on his horn as he came into view. He bundled them into his car, then told Adam a story as brief as the drive to his home.

"Did you know that burglars in this country have a code?"

"To recognise each other?"

"No, to mark good targets. First they case the neighbourhood. Big houses, expensive cars – sometimes they look in through the windows to make sure the living room has all the latest equipment. And as they go, so that they don't forget, they mark the doors with a sign. One might mean 'poor', another 'on holiday', or 'guard dog', and even 'wall safe' if they saw one when they talked their way inside by posing as a cable TV engineer or a postman. So for cops, it's become a habit to examine one's front door occasionally, especially when you first move in. It's a kind of reflex."

Adam didn't have to wait for the end of the story to know Bastien wasn't just making small talk.

"You mean the scorch mark?'

"Which appeared just after your visit, yes."

"You think I'm going to burgle you?"

"Please, give me a little more credit than that. I think you marked the way from the belfry to my home for Kilani. In case anything happened to you. So as not to leave him on his own."

"Are you annoyed with me?"

"You've come from a country at war, so when you say the boy and you are being threatened, I believe you. I can understand your gesture, but what did you want us to do? Adopt him? Hide him forever?"

"I live day by day, Bastien. After four years, I never think beyond that."

*

No sooner had Kilani set foot in the apartment than he was literally swept off his feet. One hand in Jade's, the other in Manon's, he found himself in the main bedroom where they showed him his new clothes and backpack, a little less garish than the one he had recently buried. He reached out to touch everything, but since the aim was to make sure there was no smell of firewood on him, he was quickly whisked away to the bathroom, where a tub of hot water awaited him.

Manon lined up soap and shampoo on the edge of the bath, and was about to explain he would have to scrub hard, but when she turned round, Kilani was already stark naked. Tiny bottom, broad smile.

"Okay . . ." Manon giggled.

She had to make sure no inch of his body was left out.

"Here we go then. Let's make some bubbles."

Kilani kept his eyes closed as she washed him all over. He stayed calm, with a peaceful expression on his face. Manon wondered whether he was thinking of his mother doing the same. The wounds were not immediately visible on his skin, but when her glove slid across his shoulders, she found a burn mark. On one of his legs, a scar ran all the way up the calf. On his back, swollen ridges. His hands were as rough as if he had spent a lifetime working. Manon wasn't upset. Well, not just upset. She was also angry. An intense anger that swelled with each fresh discovery. Her fingers could read the child's life like it was marked in braille.

Once rinsed off, Kilani planted one foot out of the bath, but Manon shooed him back. She raised two fingers before dousing him a second time in liquid soap.

"We're starting again, little one. We can't run any risk of you being caught."

Kilani shut his eyes.

*

In the living room, Adam and Bastien went over the different stages of the crossing to England, while the boy devoured a huge plate of pasta with parmesan. Slow carbs, Jade had decided in the kitchen. To give him lasting strength.

"I bought him some energy bars," she said. "And maman has been to change three hundred euros into pounds at the bank. We'll put it in his new backpack."

Impressed by her maturity, the Syrian regarded the adolescent with respect.

"What do you make of all this, Jade? Do you agree with everything?"

Bastien realised he had taken her complicity for granted, and though he thought he knew his daughter's character, he was curious to hear her reply.

"The State is obliged to take responsibility for every minor on French soil," she recited. "We're not the ones who started acting outside the law."

As promised, she'd done her research.

Meanwhile, Manon had left the sitting room and was bent over the old hat box. She searched among the negatives and photographs until she laid hands on her old camera. A host of memories flooded her mind as she loaded a new film. She thought of her father and for the first time, instead of the pain of his absence, she felt his comforting presence.

In the kitchen, Bastien was kneeling in front of Kilani, pouring a handful of instant coffee into each of his trouser pockets. He did the same with his backpack, including the front pocket.

"It works for cocaine dealers," he told Jade, who was watching him in astonishment.

"They hide it in packets of coffee to put the dogs off the scent," Adam confirmed.

The two men turned round when they heard the click of the camera as Manon pointed it at them.

"Two cops moonlighting as traffickers. This has to be kept for posterity!" she scoffed. She went over to Kilani and showed him her camera to get his consent. He straightened up and raised his chin. She focused on his face. The texture of his skin, the depth of his gaze and the indefinable look of hope in his eyes, as if tomorrow might finally be a better day.

Bastien glanced at his watch and announced they should leave, half an hour before they really had to. Simply because he knew the goodbyes wouldn't be easy for his wife and daughter. There were lots of tears and kisses as Kilani went from one embrace to the next, smothered with love. His heart was beating so wildly he felt giddy, but he soon recovered.

The front door closed. After all the emotional farewells, the silence was unbearable.

"I'm going to need a pick-me-up."

Jade frowned, picturing her mother rushing to her personal pharmacy and rummaging among all the packets for what would work best, before collapsing on the sofa.

"A glass of wine should do the trick," said Manon. "Will you join me?"

"Try and stop me!"

43

Cité Europe shopping centre, Calais
Nine-thirty p.m.

In the service station cafeteria, lit up like an operating theatre, amid brightly coloured magazine covers, soft toys for parents who'd forgotten their children's favourite teddies, and cabinets of refrigerated sandwiches, Kilani was yet again hypnotised by a vending machine. A coffee machine this time. Unable to take his eyes off it.

The night cashier was half-asleep, lost in dreams, staring into the distance as she served one of the two customers in the bar. The other walked over to the machine, his way blocked by a boy dressed all in black, wearing a cap.

"Are you going to choose? I haven't got all night."

When his question had no effect on Kilani, he pushed him out of the way. The boy growled like a little animal.

"Hey, take it easy! Where are your parents?"

"We're his parents."

The customer turned to look at the two men. A serious-looking white man and an imposing Arab with a scar on his face. Taken aback, he withdrew his plastic cup before the coffee had finished pouring. He scalded his fingers but said nothing, tossing his head as he left as if to show it was all the same to him.

On a table surrounded by stools in the "quiet corner" of the cafeteria, Bastien's phone vibrated. A message appeared:

Lorry intercepted. Arriving 3 to 5 min.

The driver followed the BAC car to the service station car park, pulled up and waited for instructions. Cortex climbed the step to the cab and stuck his head through the open window. He adopted the expression of a conscientious officer doing his duty, the kind of cop you don't want to get into an argument with.

"Alcohol and drugs test. Bring your driving licence and the vehicle's papers, please," Cortex reeled off.

Miller kept a close watch through the cafeteria window as Cortex breathalysed the driver, an apparently docile sort, well aware that the quickest police checks are those where you do as you're told. The moment had arrived, and Bastien called Kilani over. Slipping on the straps of his backpack, he studied him one last time. The cop was the more nervous of the two, because for Kilani the knowledge that he wasn't going to make this journey alone seemed to give him heart. Out on the car park, it was Sprinter's turn to distract the lorry driver.

"Your tachograph disc, please."

No sooner had he finished blowing into the breathalyser than the driver had to climb back into his cab to collect the disc. As he was handing it over, Passaro arrived on the scene to make sure his head was turned the right way.

"What are you carrying?"

"IT equipment. And photocopiers."

"You stopped at a lay-by eighty kilometres back," Sprinter said. "You do know that's the best way to attract clandestine passengers, don't you?"

"Open your trailer, monsieur."

A cop either side of him, questions and instructions flying round. Even so, the driver had the courage to stand his ground.

"I pass through customs in a few kilometres anyway. They're going to check my load, aren't they?"

"As you wish." Passaro shrugged. "If we check now, it's free. If the English do it, it'll be two thousand pounds per migrant."

An irrefutable argument. The driver took the keys from his pocket, turned one twice in the lock, and the rear doors were wide open. The BAC team saw two rows of pallets loaded with boxes of various sizes all wrapped in plastic film, like mummies. Cortex climbed on board, pocket torch between his teeth, just as Adam and Kilani emerged from the cafeteria and headed towards Bastien's car.

"Your disc shows you exceeded the speed limit twice," Sprinter said, still up by the cab.

The driver had to leave the rear of his vehicle and go to the front to face the officer's allegations. Adam took advantage to lead Kilani over to Passaro. The BAC officer grasped the boy under his arms and lifted him into the trailer. Worried that Adam hadn't climbed in as well, Kilani turned to look back at him.

"Go right to the front," the Syrian ordered him. "I'll join you."

Kilani grabbed his arm and pulled it as hard as he could to get him to climb up. Adam had to wrench himself free, and his voice did not sound as reassuring as he would have liked.

"Trust me," he murmured.

Cortex was still inside the trailer. He pushed the boy forward, and Kilani did not resist. He advanced through the stacks of boxes, feeling his way or following the beam from the policeman's torch, and hid between two pallets. Crouching down, he leaned out to see if Adam was really following him, but all he saw was the doors closing like the lid on a coffin, plunging him into darkest night. Yet he still kept faith.

With the alcohol test negative and the load checked, the truck set off once again. Adam and Bastien were left behind in the car park. The BAC car led the way, escorting the driver back to the main road.

As the trailer jerked into motion, Kilani became desperate. Leaving his hiding place, he stumbled between the stacks of boxes until he reached the back doors. He tried in vain to open them: Adam had lied and abandoned him. He slid down the side until he was seated on the floor, his spirit crushed.

Adam had chosen between his family and him. But Kilani couldn't bring himself to hate the Syrian for it. It was partly his own fault. If he'd been able to confess everything he knew, perhaps his protector would have preferred to leave the Jungle. Maybe then he would have gone with him? The boy blamed himself for keeping his secrets to himself. But how could he have revealed them to Adam?

Redirected by the police, the truck was on the last leg of its mainland journey. The driver slipped between two other vehicles in the fast lane and put his foot down. The BAC car had disappeared from his rear-view mirror. At the end of the main road leading to the gates of the port, he approached the first checkpoint, looking just like a motorway toll. Six lanes, six booths, and fifty or so lorries on two square kilometres of asphalt, crisscrossing so often it left you giddy. Access lanes, exit lanes, private international lanes, French and UK customs, contractors, border police. Even for someone accustomed to it, the plaza gave the confusing impression of a labyrinth, made worse by the dark night. The driver pulled into the third lane and forced himself to remain patient. In the trailer behind him, all Kilani could hear was anonymous shouts – he had no idea what anyone was saying. Every few minutes, the lorry advanced a few metres. Then a voice sounded so close to him he jumped.

"Don't bother with the CO_2 detector. It won't work with the tarps. Go straight to the 'truffles'."

A few seconds later, the boy heard dogs panting as they strained at their leashes. Their claws dug into the asphalt, then scrabbled against the tyres to gain height so they could sniff the loads. His tyres?

A bark. Then another.

Kilani clung to his tiny backpack like a lifebuoy.

"Positive over here!"

The boy was expecting the rear doors of his lorry to swing open and for probing torches to sweep the interior. Yet he remained in complete darkness. Anxiously, he lifted the tarpaulin and saw, bathed in the white neon light, a couple climbing down from the next lorry less than a metre from him.

"Out! Out! Out!" one of the officials barked.

A father, a mother and their two girls, arms raised, their whole lives in two enormous sacks on the ground in front of them.

"Get out of here! Go away!" the customs official shouted again.

Kilani gently lowered the tarpaulin. He could breathe again. Then he felt a slight jerk. His lorry was moving. Then it stopped again. More voices outside.

"Checklist of your load, please. What are you carrying?"

"IT equipment and photocopiers."

The customs official ran his finger down the manifest then looked round wearily at the fifty other trucks approaching.

Since the searches were random, he decided to let this one go, and told the driver so.

"I've already been checked by the police anyway."

"The police and customs aren't the same thing," the uniformed official retorted.

The driver immediately regretted his words.

The official left his hand on the side of the lorry to keep it in the inspection area. Hesitating, he looked again at the line of waiting trucks and made a decision that almost seemed to amuse him.

"Pull over, monsieur."

Doing as he was told, the driver turned the wheel, cursing himself for opening his mouth just as he was about to be let through.

"We've finally got the same toy as the English," the customs man explained to a colleague. "It's our chance to test it!"

When the lorry had parked up, six small magnetic metal pads were placed on various parts of the bodywork. Each of them was connected by cable to a computer terminal the size of a supermarket trolley. The technician adjusted the frequency of the detectors so that they picked up only one sound. Heartbeats. The English called this new piece of kit the "heartbeat detector", and it was incredibly effective.

Kilani's heart was thumping so hard in his chest it almost hurt, and yet it made no audible sound. The computer monitor, however, showed an earthquake appearing at regular intervals, produced by the heart of a petrified child.

"I've found a pulse!" the technician announced proudly to the customs officials.

This phrase, normally uttered when someone is trying to save a life, now pointed to a far less uplifting outcome.

*

The rear doors were flung open and the customs officials waited for their prey to emerge. But when they saw a child, alone and afraid, they glanced at each other, more embarrassed than angry. Kilani sat on the lip of the trailer, jumped down, and found himself surrounded by adults. One of them shouted at him, waving his arms, as if to drive away a stray dog.

"Go away! Get lost! We're not going to adopt you. Go away!"

Kilani stood rooted to the spot, looking from one face to another. He had no idea if they were scolding him, ordering him to stay still, or on the contrary telling him to run off. One of the giants seized him by the arm. It was as though he'd received an electric shock. Without thinking, Kilani began to run, bewildered by the concrete labyrinth he had emerged into, past the first control booths, shrinking back at every barking dog, caught in the beams of the men's torches. He saw a fence in the distance and a line of lorries. To the drivers' astonishment, he sped down the line, zigzagging between the heavy trucks, slipping under a trailer. At last he found himself on the road out of Calais. Though his leg muscles were aching from sitting cramped in a corner for almost an hour, he ran without turning round or slowing up for even a second, until he was gasping for breath.

His blood was pounding in his temples, his breath coming in short, rasping gulps, as if the air was somehow toxic. His vision was blurred – he stumbled on almost blindly, and when the headlights of an enormous thirty-three-tonne monster dazzled him, it was as if everything around him caught fire. He heard shouting, the rattle of sub-machine guns, and the hut roofs of his home village were burning in a black cloud of ash. His lake: the White Nile. He heard his mother's voice calling to him from afar:

"Ayman!"

He collapsed unconscious by the roadside on yellowing grass poisoned by exhaust fumes.

44

My name isn't Kilani.

My parents named me Ayman. The lucky one, in Arabic. Even if I've been forced to forget it.

When the soldiers withdrew from my village, they took all the children of fighting age with them. To fight against whom? Why?

In exchange, they spared the women and the old people. That day, more than twenty of us were recruited.

All I could take with me was a scrap of fabric from my mother's dress. The wristband was torn from my brother's dead body and given to me, so I would never forget . . .

We marched for days, sleeping on the ground at night. Even though it was slowly healing, my tongue was still bleeding, so I spat blood so as not to have the taste in my mouth.

I was starved, raped, beaten. We all were. After a week, we came to a military camp and met our warlord. The man controlling our destinies.

My spirit was broken. I was no longer Ayman. I was a soldier. I no longer had a family. I was part of an army.

We were given weapons and taught how to use them. How to aim, take a breath, fire, and then start again. How to load and clean our rifle. Told not to waste a bullet on the wounded. To finish them off with a knife if necessary. A stab to the heart, to make sure. But that was just the training.

One morning we set out for Koch, a village a hundred kilometres south of mine. Our vehicles and marching feet raised a cloud of dust that announced our arrival from a distance.

A hundred metres from our target, one of the children refused to advance. He threw down his rifle. He began to beg, his sister was married to a man from Koch. My warlord told him he could go and find her and tell the village the President would spare their lives. The village was only a hundred metres away: two hundred steps for the boy. I counted ten before I heard the explosion and saw the back of his head blown off as he collapsed to the ground.

All the vehicles were ordered to drive over his body on their way into the village. By the time the last one had passed, it was almost buried.

When we entered the village, the cows had been taken some distance off, all the inhabitants had hidden in their homes. My warlord shouted that this was an insult to the President. Two child soldiers were stationed outside each house. One to open the door and fire a burst; the other to finish the wounded off with a knife. I had the knife.

Neelam, the boy who was paired with me, turned to stone. So paralysed he couldn't even grip the door handle. My warlord levelled his rifle and came over, ready to give a second lesson to anyone refusing to obey orders. That left me with no choice. Seizing the gun from Neelam's trembling hands, I kicked in the fragile door. I sprayed bullets inside without looking. Cries, the smell of gunpowder, of blood. The flames spurting from the gun barrel momentarily lit up faces and bodies. The rifle's recoil tore it from my grasp and it fell to the ground. The warlord picked it up and slipped the strap round my neck with a smile. I got the impression he was proud of me.

When I left the village, I had twin shadows. One from the sun; the other from the raging flames that seemed to scorch the sky. The warlord came over to me and told me to get into his pick-up with him. He had heard about the boy who had had his tongue cut out. A dumb soldier who would betray no secrets. And who had just killed five families.

From that day on, I became his dog, constantly at his side. I was treated well. I was given plenty of food, and I didn't have to exchange these favours for sex.

We left Koch and headed even further south to add to our forces. The villages of Leer and Adok were our next destinations. It was in Adok that my rifle jammed. I had already put one bullet into a shepherd's stomach. He looked at me as if I were cursed, as if my fate was far worse than his. He seemed to feel sorry for me. I obliterated that look with my rifle butt. Nothing was left of his face.

When I went to fetch water in our camp that evening, the men kept their distance out of respect. Or fear. I had become somebody.

By now our troop was big enough. It was made up mostly of adults, but with some adolescents and children. I was with the men, always no more than a step away from my master, ready to defend him.

There were enough of us to take on the rebels, and so we headed towards Bentiu, the capital of Unity, two hundred kilometres to the north, where the President's men were fighting their enemies. But some of the children began whispering at night about Bentiu and the refugee camp there that accepted everyone without asking questions. A place where even soldiers didn't dare enter. All you had to do was escape one night and hide in the camp. That meant you would be freed from the war. They had prepared their escape, and even taken a map of the region from a dead body. One of them could read and he had drawn their road to freedom in charcoal on the paper.

I don't know why I stole the map from them; still less why I showed it to my warlord. Out of loyalty, perhaps.

The next morning, seven of the whisperers were hanged from a tree.

We set off again, and came to a halt a day's march from Bentiu. We set up camp and waited for the return of the scouts we had sent out to spy on the rebel positions. The scouts went out at night to avoid being seen, so they were due to arrive back at dawn the next day.

I dozed off, only to be woken with a start by the clatter of sub-machine guns. The rebels had captured our scouts and made a surprise attack on our camp. It was carnage. I flung myself to the ground and played dead. I saw boots running past my eyes and the President's men falling one after the other. I was covered in blood.

At sunrise, the rebels piled up the dead bodies. Even if some of the men were only wounded, they were thrown on the heap and burned alive. My warlord was tied to his pick-up and dragged round the camp in circles while the rebels fired off their guns to celebrate their victory.

Only the children were spared.

We were herded together, our weapons taken from us. For a brief moment I thought it was all over. But they just checked the guns were working properly and handed them back to us.

*

We went from being the President's soldiers to part of the rebel army. Soon we were retracing our steps to pillage once more and to recruit anyone who hadn't already been forced to join us. We returned to the fighting round Bentiu with these new recruits: it felt to me as if all these horrors were taking place on a single day, first for one leader, then another.

But for me things were different. I was no longer my warlord's guard dog. I belonged to no-one, and no I longer had protection. Envious looks had turned to threatening ones. Whispers died away when I approached. My fate was sealed: they were just waiting for the right moment.

That night I ran away, heading for the Bentiu refugee camp. I walked all night and at first light I caught sight of the camp. Immense, endless, intimidating.

Bentiu is like the Jungle, only ten times bigger. I heard there were a hundred and twenty thousand refugees there, protected by European countries or America. The biggest town I had ever seen. A town of tents and wooden huts, all covered in dried mud and dust.

I saw starving children eating earth. Gnawing at roots. Hunting rats and praying to God, thanking him for His generosity.

That evening I crept into a tent belonging to a woman and her two children. I was searching their things for food when the woman woke up. I had kept my knife with me and for a moment wondered if I should kill her. She looked down at the blade, then held out a bottle of water and took some dry biscuits out of her pocket. I ate, then slept with them.

Her younger child died two days later. He was coughing so badly I think it was a relief for him to go. His mother gave me his blue and red backpack. After that I never left her, and she treated me exactly the same as her own children.

Her name was Nosiba. She talked about Europe as if it were a magical realm. Her older child told me that in France a plane took off from Paris to spray perfume over every town. That in Italy there was a place where people lived underwater. That in America people died from eating too much. But the most beautiful country, he was convinced, was England. The country his mother had been talking about ever since the conflict began.

The Bentiu camp wasn't Nosiba's final destination. She had been a schoolteacher in the capital. Her husband had been forced to take up arms and she had come to Bentiu to hide, because her sick son had made it impossible to undertake any long journey. Now that he had been buried on the outskirts of the camp, she could think of England once more. She had enough money for her two boys. Now I took the place of one of them.

We left the refugee camp one morning on board a very strange van, completely rebuilt from spare parts. We drove for several days: Nosiba paid for our journey, sometimes with money, at others offering her body. At night when we were going to sleep she sang me a magic rhyme. A rhyme she'd taught all her students, one she'd learned from an English aid worker. In the daytime, she drew it in the sand. I heard her sing and draw it a hundred times.

We crossed Egypt. We crossed Libya. We went from cars to trucks, but as our money ran out, more often than not we walked. At times as much as forty kilometres a day in more than forty-five-degree heat, with no shade except our own shadows.

In Tripoli we took advantage of the ruins of an abandoned building site. We stayed there for a week until Nosiba found a trustworthy smuggler to take us to Europe. That evening she held me in her arms and sang the magic rhyme again, making me promise never to forget it.

When I woke up, they had left without me.

For days I searched for them on the beach where the boats for Italy leave from. One afternoon, a man noticed me. A child on his own made an easy target. He was a people trafficker, and he offered to take me across the Mediterranean for free. In exchange I only had to agree to work for him for a while on the streets of Rome.

Thanks to him, three nights later, I boarded a boat with more than two hundred other people. I saw a woman and her daughter being pushed about, almost crushed. She reminded me of my mother and brother. And of Nosiba with the magic rhyme and her son. I still don't know why, but I sat in front of them to shield them, head on my knees.

Then the little girl began to cough.

My trafficker left the tiller and shoved his way through towards us. The woman pressed her hand over her daughter's little mouth to try to get her to be quiet.

"Your little girl. You have to push her overboard," he told her.

As he stepped towards them, I stood up, trying to defend them. He kicked me right on the chin, making me see stars.

When we reached Italy, the trafficker put me up for a few nights. I ate well and slept as much as I could. Then I had to repay him.

For a week I worked as a prostitute on the streets of Rome.

Every night, with men's sweat sticking to my skin, I escaped for a time by repeating the magic formula over and over to myself. My body was being abused and humiliated, but my spirit was hidden out of sight.

One evening, the child soldier in me woke up. I gouged out

a client's eye with my thumb. One of those men who like to beat you. I left in the middle of the night, before he was discovered. I signalled to the other kids to follow me, but none of them moved. They were all too broken, too cowed, their spirits crushed just as mine had been by my first warlord.

I set off again and, hiding in lorries or joining forced marches, followed other migrants so that I wouldn't lose my way in a world where everything was strange to me. Finally I arrived at the Jungle in Calais, the last town before *Youké*.

All alone and terrified, I stayed on the edges of the camp. I didn't trust anyone – not the Africans nor the Arabs. Yet every animal has its predator, and a group of Afghans chose me as their plaything. Since there were no women in the camp, the men went crazy over me.

But my new warlord saved me. Now he was the one I had to respect, the one I had to obey and protect.

Adam.

Except that Adam is much more than that to me.

More than a warlord.

A father.

PART FIVE

GOING UNDER

45

The screech of a lorry woke Kilani with a start. For a brief instant he found himself between two realities. Between Sudan and France.

Then behind him he saw the lights of the port of Calais and his dream dissolved.

He had missed his opportunity. He knew what the others had done for him, and he had missed his chance. He felt so ashamed he began to beat his face with the flat of his hands until his nose started bleeding. By the time he stopped punishing himself his palms were red, and his face was aching. Clenching his fists, he howled into the darkness.

Cars and trucks sped by, momentarily illuminating him in their headlights. He looked up, and in the distance, as reassuring as an old friend, he saw the Calais belfry, two kilometres away.

He got to his feet, adjusted the backpack, and set off, the vehicle engines roaring right next to him on a road that had witnessed so much hope and despair.

As they left the service station, Bastien suggested Adam come back to the apartment with him. Aware that the odds were stacked against the boy, the Syrian had refused, preferring to return to the Jungle, just in case.

When Bastien got home, Manon and Jade were waiting in the living room for him, worried sick. Unfortunately for them, all Bastien could tell them was that Kilani had managed to board the lorry. To their other questions, he could only reply "I've no idea". The three of them prepared to face a sleepless night.

Adam climbed up on the bunker roof and lit one of the cigarettes Bastien had given him. The hours went by, and the further they took him from the moment he had seen Kilani leave, the more confident he became that the boy had got through. By two in the morning, he was convinced of it. But just as he was about to enter his tent, he saw Kilani's staggering silhouette. Although it was only five kilometres from the port to the belfry, and from there to the Jungle, it had taken the boy more than three hours, with many wrong turns along the way. Adam ran towards him and Kilani fell into his arms, exhausted and wretched. He wept into the Syrian's shoulder in a mixture of rage and humiliation.

"It's nothing, my son. Nothing."

As the night wore on, hope spread to everyone involved. The three men in the BAC car had decided to leave Junction 47 to the CRS and patrolled the most remote side streets of Calais to avoid any trouble. Erika, a believer when need be, lit a candle on the windowsill of the small studio she refused to leave despite the lovelorn Passaro's incessant pleas. At the Millers' apartment, Manon folded and refolded Kilani's dirty things several times and then wandered from room to room as if she had forgotten where she was. Jade sought refuge under her duvet, listening to music. Bastien stayed glued to his phone. He received Adam's message at ten past two in the morning, and so was the first to learn their efforts had failed. With that, a fragile space filled with hope suddenly emptied, leaving only a black hole that swallowed time, light, emotion.

46

Out of bed at six the next morning, Bastien was at headquarters by seven, hoping to take advantage of a moment or two alone. But he found Erika was already there: like him, she had found it impossible to stay at home doing nothing. Two hours later, when he saw how miserable they looked, even Ruben Corval managed to refrain from making any comment.

Bastien opened first one file, then another, simply to give his hands something to do. But his mind was still at the roadside cafeteria, at the moment when everything still seemed possible. He had to glance twice at the folder to realise what he had in front of him: the comparisons between the two murders in the Jungle. The Libyan man's and the Afghan woman's. He read the forensic pathologist's reports, focusing on the sections concerning the weapon used and the conclusions regarding the angle and depth of the wounds.

If their failed attempt had left Bastien this deflated, he hardly dared imagine how Adam must be feeling. Still less Kilani. But now he had stumbled on something that might make the Syrian's day a little less depressing, and so he decided to call him.

That night, Adam had discovered a completely changed Kilani. Little more than a ghost. In the morning, he saw the boy sitting on the sand about a hundred metres off, staring out at the English coast that had once again mocked his hopes. Soon perhaps he would start shouting at them like Wassim. Adam's phone, perched on a rock, began to vibrate like a drum. The Syrian greeted Bastien in a dull, lifeless voice, and their conversation got off to a difficult start, like a piece of rusty machinery.

"How's the boy?"

"He's sitting facing the sea. I don't think he's slept. Neither have I."

"No-one has, I can assure you."

"What about Manon and Jade?"

"It'll take them a few days. But I know it's nothing compared with Kilani's frustration."

"There is no way of comparing the weight of sadness."

"We could try again. I'm sure everyone on my side would go for it."

Adam did not reply. Of course they could, but the despair of failing doesn't ease overnight; it would take time for desire and hope to be rekindled.

"Above all I need to find something for us to do in the coming days," was what he chose to say at last.

Bastien glanced at the open folder on his desk. He wasn't sure this would be the best way to distract Adam, but the Syrian had always insisted he was a cop, and that that was all he knew how to do.

"You were right about the murders," Bastien admitted. "It's the same weapon. And probably the same killer."

"You have the autopsy reports?"

"Yes, I had the two deaths compared. You see, I listened to you. But I don't think it will get you very far."

"I'd have difficulty getting less far right now. So tell me."

Bastien read the report word for word so as not to undermine the forensic pathologist's professionalism.

"The three wounds present the same characteristics as regards depth. Corpse 73/2016, that is the Libyan male, received stab wounds to the liver and heart. Corpse 85/2016, the Afghan woman, suffered a single stab wound to the heart. Both bodies were simply pierced, rather than run through, as they would have been if the blows had been more powerful. This lack of depth suggests a relatively weak assailant, possibly a woman, an adolescent or small man. Or a weary one."

Adam raised his eyes to the beach, where Kilani sat immobile.

"We're all weary," he said.

"I warned you it wouldn't get us far. Shall I continue?"

"Please do."

"What the report says about the weapon is more interesting. The three wounds are identical, defined as semi-circular with abrasions. So it was definitely a knife of some sort. A knife with a curved blade."

Bastien's words sent a shudder down Adam's spine. For a second time his gaze fell upon the immobile Kilani.

A weak assailant.

A curved blade.

The Libyan, killed in the Jungle.

The Afghan woman, in the women's camp.

"You see?" Bastien concluded. "This info isn't going to solve the case. Anyway, I'll inform the police judiciaire."

The silence that followed made him repeat himself. Again there was no answer.

"Adam? Are you still there? Adam . . ."

Adam jumped down from the ruined bunker. It felt as if red ants were crawling over his heart and his sight became hazy.

Kneeling down, he began to dig with trembling hands at the exact spot where he had seen Kilani bury his blue and red backpack. A sand-covered strap was the first thing to appear. Instead of continuing to dig, Adam tugged at it. His fingers felt suddenly so arthritic he had to try twice to undo the zip. There, in this child's bag, the curved blade of Kilani's machete reflected part of his face. A little machete shaped like a sickle, so unusual Adam had seen nothing like it after more than two months in the Jungle.

He knew the boy had seen the Libyan. And the Afghan woman had been in the women's camp with him for one night at least. The night she had lost her life.

But none of that made any sense. None at all.

Despite the weapon before his eyes, insisting the opposite, despite the victims and where they were killed, what could the motive have been? Adam could have sworn Kilani was not a monster. He was a . . .

He plunged his hand further into the bag. A square of patterned fabric, a leather wristband, and under them, hidden at the bottom, a purple ball with two big ears sticking out. Adam's heart skipped a beat; his breath caught in his throat. Gently, almost reluctantly, he tugged at one of the ears, terrified by what he was going to find. He heard Maya's voice. He saw her face, blurred by condensation on the window of the taxi carrying her away. His daughter, clutching her cuddly toy. Monsieur Bou.

Monsieur Bou, at the bottom of Kilani's bag, and now in Adam's hands. His eyes filled with tears. They trickled uncontrollably down his cheeks as the feel of her toy brought memories flooding into his mind. A dark rage clouded his brain. What did it mean? Betrayal: he had protected this boy like a son . . . If he had killed two people in the Jungle, what had he done to Nora and Maya?

Their paths must have crossed somewhere. Maya's toy was the proof. His daughter would never have parted with Monsieur Bou! Kilani must have killed them. At last Adam knew! It was almost a relief. As if finding the guilty person freed him from the anguish that over the weeks had become torture.

Dead. They were finally dead.

The fragile barrier that had kept Adam from sinking into complete madness gave way as easily as a dam made of matches swept away by a torrent.

He strode towards the beach, Monsieur Bou in his hand.

When he was ten metres from the boy, he shouted his name like a man denouncing a murderer.

"Kilani!"

The boy turned, and his gaze fell on the purple rabbit.

Nora and Maya.

How could he explain to Adam that he had tried to protect them? How could he tell him that all he had been able to save was the fluffy toy that had fallen from Maya's grasp when she was thrown overboard? How to explain there was nothing he could do when Nora herself was pushed into the raging sea . . .

47

Adam was consumed with hatred. Rage. Violence.

His eyes glinted with a promise of death.

Instead of stiffening with fear or running away, Kilani remained where he was on the sand, relaxing his muscles and kneeling in front of his master.

What other ending could he expect? Wasn't this exactly what he deserved?

The first blow was a slap that set him sprawling, face in the sand.

Adam shook Monsieur Bou in his face.

"You stole it from her!" he shouted. "Just as you stole their photo from me. I know you did!"

Kilani would not have dared to so much as crease the photograph. He sat up again, head bowed in submission. He wouldn't fight. Not with Adam.

"You killed the Libyan so he couldn't help me, didn't you?"

Adam was trying to make all the pieces of the puzzle fit, even if he had to force them.

He hit Kilani a second time, this time with his fist. Kilani was left groggy, lips bleeding. Adam grabbed his arm and dragged him towards the sea.

"Why that woman?" Adam insisted. "Why the Afghan

woman? Why her? And Nora? And Maya? What did you do to them? Are they dead? I know they are!"

Adam took a first step into the sea, still holding the boy's arm so tightly he was almost crushing the bone. The water came up to Kilani's calves, then his thighs, then his midriff. He let himself be dragged out into the water.

He glimpsed the English coast on the horizon. He had so nearly reached it!

"They're dead! You killed them! I know it!"

By now Kilani's head was submerged. His eyes were open though, as if he calmly accepted his sentence.

He had done so much killing. Perhaps more than a hundred people. Why should God care about him?

He began to run short of oxygen, and his fogged brain sent him a jumble of images. Possibly a reflex action, to tranquillise him before he died.

Adam scoops him up and leaves the tent, grasping the machete, ready to face death for a kid he doesn't know. The night their destinies collided.

The photo of Nora and Maya on the ground when Adam dropped it and Kilani saw their faces for the first time. And instantly recognised them.

Adam pulled the boy's head up and shrieked at him:

"Why them? How did you manage to hide the devil inside you? I should have seen it!"

He had once been his protector; now he was his executioner. Adam plunged the boy's head back underwater. For longer this time. More images flashed through the boy's mind.

Kilani had never forgotten the face of the Libyan who had thrown Maya overboard. When he saw him arrive in the Jungle and even talk to Adam, he knew what he had to do. That night he had scratched at the man's tent flap like a little wild animal, digging and searching. The Libyan had come out. He was big, very big, but Kilani had killed more powerful men. The first stab to the stomach had brought him to his knees. The second went straight to the heart. A near instantaneous death: almost too merciful. The Jungle dogs had done the rest.

Choking, gasping for air, the boy was shaken by uncontrollable spasms. The survival instinct. All Adam could see of Kilani was a blurred silhouette under the water, the waves washing over him, sand swirling round him as his body convulsed.

The Afghan woman in the women's camp. The one who had pushed Nora out. He recognised her from the first instant. Nothing then was more important than to avenge his warlord, his friend, his father.

Another convulsion. A blinding light. Kilani saw the sun through the waves.

One final image.

With Manon and Jade. With Bastien and Adam. All together in the same home. Enough love received to fill several lives. Enough to die happy today.

48

That afternoon, Manon had gone into town to get her negatives developed. She planned to set up a darkroom in their apartment and to teach Jade how to use it. He daughter had asked her countless times, and far too often her reply had been "tomorrow".

She put her scalding-hot cup of black tea on the living-room coffee table and spread the photos out in front of her. A patchwork of stolen moments.

Bastien and Adam, setting the world to rights . . .

Jade sitting on the beanbag next to them, eyes and ears wide open, listening intently . . .

Kilani and his indomitable smile . . .

Night crept in, and Jade came home from school, looking out of sorts. There was no way she could be allowed to tell anyone about the evening her father and his colleagues had chosen to do the right thing. She was forbidden to shout from the rooftops how proud she was of her parents. Despite the heart-wrenching outcome.

She hid in her bedroom and buried herself in her homework. An hour later, she came out, flung herself into her mother's arms and stayed there a long time. For no particular reason. Simply to be close to her.

All of a sudden, they heard someone knocking at the front door . . .

Manon looked at her watch, Jade her phone. It was too early for Bastien to be home, and besides, he hadn't forgotten his keys. They weren't expecting anyone.

When they opened the door they had to look down to find an exhausted Kilani in a heap on the floor. He was still in his soaking ninja outfit, clutching a small blue and red backpack.

Adam hadn't had the heart to go all the way.

Manon tugged at Bastien's arm to drag him into their bedroom. Jade followed on their heels. Bastien had just got in and was still wearing his jacket and his gun.

Manon pushed the door open gently, revealing Kilani fast asleep on their bed.

"I have no idea how he found our address," said Manon, "but he must have an incredible sense of direction."

"Oh shit!" murmured Bastien.

This wasn't the reaction Manon had been expecting, and she was taken aback. She tried to put a situation that didn't seem all that catastrophic to her into perspective.

"It's not that serious. When he wakes up, we'll give him something to eat and you can call Adam to tell him to come and get him. Or we can drop him at the Jungle."

"You don't understand," Bastien said, his face still grave.

He crossed the room and kneeled down level with the sleeping boy.

"Kilani, Kilani," he said, to wake him up.

The boy opened an eye, and when he saw Bastien was quickly wide awake.

"Adam?" Bastien asked straight out.

Kilani's chin began to tremble and he shook his head. Then

he flung himself into Bastien's arms, knocking him back so he was resting against the wall with a weeping child to comfort. Manon felt she didn't know the whole story.

"What's going on?"

Bastien's hand stroked the back of Kilani's neck until the boy gradually calmed down.

"Adam taught him the way from the Jungle that first night."

"Why did he do that?" asked Jade.

"Because he knew he was in danger. Kilani was only meant to come here if Adam was . . ."

There was no need for him to finish the sentence.

Jade was standing there holding the garishly coloured backpack; inside she found the rolled-up black one Manon had bought with all the other things. Feeling inside the front pocket, she discovered the crumpled but still legible telephone number of the Sunchild Association. She held it out in front of her.

"Hey, you two!"

Sometime after nine that evening, Jade took Kilani to her own room and tucked him into bed. Then she sat down on the thick pile carpet and sang him a song, holding his hand. Since she didn't know any nursery rhymes, the boy was offered *Mad World* on a loop, after Gary Jules's gentle version.

Manon was pacing up and down the living room.

"Stop twirling like a spinning top," Bastien begged her.

"I don't care. We'll do it. You said yourself it's easier and a lot less dangerous. Ordinary tourists in cars are inspected a hundred times less often than lorry drivers and their loads."

"I said it was less dangerous for the migrants. It's different where we're concerned. Do you know how many years in jail we're risking, with Jade at your mother's or with social services?

I'm not even sure it's a good idea to help the boy get across . . . or if we're just being cowards. Are we helping him or getting rid of him? We're not even sure if he has family in England."

"And in what language are you going to ask him? And how will he reply?" Manon raged. "What we are sure of is that there's nothing for him here!"

"Remember, it's France you're talking about!"

"Exactly! You know what that means better than anyone. Besides, did I invent that telephone number? There's someone on the other side of the Channel who wants to help him, isn't there?"

"But who are they? We don't know anything about this association."

"I don't care! I don't care! Adam trusted them, didn't he? Don't you understand that if we do nothing, we'll never forgive ourselves? Don't you see we have no choice? It's easy enough to forget when it's on the news, but what if the problem lands in your own living room?"

"Around half a million migrants turn up in Europe every year, and you want me to put my family in danger for just one of them? That's crazy. The impact would be so infinitesimal it's almost ridiculous."

"Infinitesimal? The boy sleeping in your daughter's bed is infinitesimal? Maybe we won't change anything on a grand scale, but it will change everything for him! And fate brought him to our door! This concerns us! So what do you want to do? Take him back to the Jungle?"

"What I don't want is for Jade to get a call from an English police officer informing her that her parents have been arrested as people smugglers!"

At this point Jade joined their discussion, with all the Miller family's legendary tact.

"You're joking, right? You can't be serious. Do you think I'll stay here waiting for you? If we do this, we do it together!"

Stunned but admiring, Bastien smiled as he looked at his two girls.

"Okay, you're off your heads."

Jade had the best command of English in the family, so she was given the task of phoning the Sunchild Association. Bastien meanwhile had shut himself in the kitchen, a glass of chilled vodka in one hand, his phone in the other, a cigarette between his lips.

"I'm really sorry about your friend," said Erika sincerely.

"I'm trying to put that to one side for now, but it's going to be hard to come to terms with it."

"You realise you'll be on your own this time? We won't be able to help you."

"And that's as it should be. I'm already putting enough people in danger. I just wanted to tell you that if things go wrong, I'll only be allowed one phone call. That'll be to you. I'll let you tell the whole story to Commissaire Dorsay."

"But that isn't going to happen, is it?"

"No, that isn't going to happen."

Erika's voice was choked with emotion.

"You know . . . The first time I met you . . ."

"Yes?"

"I immediately saw who you were. Passaro as well. Don't ask me to put that impression into words. I'm just happy to know you."

"Don't worry, I intend to come back and sort Corval out," Bastien joked. "And now, tell me what I can expect with the ferry."

*

The family gathered in the living room to discuss how to proceed. The last time Bastien had talked things over like this had been with the BAC, and for the same reason. Now he was getting his wife and daughter involved and the consequences could be much more serious.

Bastien relayed what Erika had told him, and Jade summarised her conversation with Sunchild.

"The association isn't based near the coast. They're further north, in Leicester, but they come down to Dover twice a week. Today's Saturday, and they'll be there at nine tomorrow evening and then next Friday at the same time."

"Tomorrow's a bit soon, isn't it?" said Manon.

This didn't fool Bastien. He smiled at his wife.

"I can understand you wanting him to stay a bit longer. I'd like that too, but we have to consider what he would make of it. If we keep him here for another six days, he's going to think it's forever. He'll be devastated to find himself moved on again. We need to act as quickly as possible, even if it's painful. Like tearing off a plaster. Tomorrow's perfect. We'll have the whole day to prepare him."

He turned to his daughter.

"Did you tell them he's mute?"

"Yes. That didn't seem to bother them. They just said they'd have to teach him sign language."

"And do you have a precise location for the rendezvous?"

"I wrote it all down."

A determined voice and a stubborn attitude. Bastien realised that whatever happened, Jade would emerge a different person. Practically an adult.

49

Port of Calais
Check-in area
Six p.m.

They had rejected the idea of taking Manon's car, an old red Renault 5 that had withstood the test of time and fashion. Instead they took the ugly but roomy Renault Espace belonging to her mother, who thought a quick trip to the realm of Queen Elizabeth was an excellent idea that would do them the world of good.

Or it could be little more than a string of calamities, Bastien thought.

So it was in this car that they joined the queues for P&O Ferries, exactly an hour before embarkation.

Bastien at the wheel. Manon beside him. Jade in the back.

And their luggage in the boot.

Ahead of them, beyond the ferry company's cabin, they saw the French customs post: their first obstacle.

Bastien showed their tickets to the P&O employee and thanked her. Then he drove at a snail's pace to the customs shed.

"How should we act?" asked an anxious Jade.

"The two of us will be a loving couple," Manon said. "And you're fourteen, so just look grumpy, staring at your phone, cap down over your ears."

"Yeah, so the same as usual."

Bastien winked at her in the rear-view mirror and moved up the queue. Two cars ahead of them. Then one. Then it was their turn.

"Anything to declare?" asked the customs official, peering in through the window.

"Yeah," said Bastien, pointing to the back seat. "A stroppy teenager. Does that count?"

"Unfortunately not, monsieur," laughed the man. "Could I see your passports, please?"

He checked them rapidly and even smiled as he ushered the car through. Bastien drove slowly to the second post: French border control.

A bored policeman. Passports barely glanced at. A quick look inside their vehicle. It was obvious he wasn't that interested, relying on the English to inspect them more thoroughly. They saw UKBF in big letters on the side of a metal shed twenty metres ahead of them. United Kingdom Border Force. The third and last hurdle before the boat.

The English official had plainly left his smile back at his country cottage, and his look brought a chill to the car interior. White shirt, blue bulletproof vest and regal crowns sewn on his epaulettes.

"Anything to declare?"

Since Bastien was incapable of repeating his earlier joke in English, he made do with a laconic *"No"*.

"Please stay in the car," said the official, walking back to his cabin.

Bastien waited until he was out of earshot.

"Erika told me they only inspect one vehicle in ten," he whispered. "We're surely not going to be the ones they . . ."

Even before he finished his sentence, the customs official

305

pointed to his colleague, who until then had stayed in the background. The man came over, carrying a metal rod about fifty centimetres long. The flat rectangular tip was covered in a kind of mini cotton sock.

"Hands on your knees, please," he said in English.

"He's asking you to put your hands on your knees, papa."

Bastien did as he was told and the customs officer rubbed the sock all over the steering wheel, before disappearing into his booth. Bastien recognised the apparatus: he'd seen it used in airports.

"It's fine. They're looking for explosives or drugs. There's nothing to be afraid of, okay?"

These last words were for Jade's benefit, and Bastien turned in his seat to repeat them.

"There's nothing to be afraid of, okay?"

He looked down at his daughter's hands.

"You're shaking, sweetheart. That's not good. Put your phone down and slide your hands between your thighs. We'll be on the boat in a minute. They've no reason to search any more in the front here, still less to ask us to open the—"

"Unlock the boot of your car, please."

"Seriously, papa, I think you ought to keep quiet, because it seems to me you invite trouble."

Bastien pulled the lever under the steering wheel, and the customs official opened the boot. Three pieces of luggage. One of them was a capacious kit bag Bastien had used throughout his police training. Kilani was concealed inside, curled up in a thin duvet to even out the shape.

"We're going to go to jail, we're going to go to jail, we're going to go to jail . . ." Manon chanted in a low voice.

The customs man ran the sample rod over the boot carpet, under the bags and along their zips. Bastien tried hard not to

306

look in the rear-view mirror at what he was doing, but found he couldn't take his eyes off him.

When the English customs officer slammed the boot shut, the three passengers in the car sighed with relief. It was as if they had just been woken from a prolonged bout of sleep apnoea.

The cotton sock had not revealed any trace of drugs or explosives, so they were invited to continue on their way. Of course, Bastien stalled the engine. He glanced sheepishly at the customs official, and finally moved forward.

Before they joined the line of vehicles boarding the ferry, Jade turned round and opened the long black bag a third of the way. A small hand emerged. She took it and gave it a kiss.

In an hour and a half they would be in *Youké*.

Manon and Jade were leaning over the handrails on deck, enjoying the breeze that wafted salt spray over them, spoilt only by a faint smell of fuel. They both had idiotically proud grins on their faces. The wind was making their dresses flap, and they were holding on to their hats.

"Did you open the bag?" asked Manon.

"For the crossing, yes," said Jade. "He's covered by the duvet I put in there."

"Did you give him the water and madeleines?"

"Don't worry, Maman, it's all good."

Bastien came out of the cafeteria staggering a little, three coffees in his hands. He almost spilled the lot over an elderly couple before he managed to reach his family.

"Wasn't there any proper coffee?" Manon asked.

"Sorry, only this pale imitation. We'll survive."

They blew on their scalding drinks, staring at the coastline they were nearing. Standing between her parents, Jade felt quite simply invincible.

"I read on the internet that you're more likely to win the lottery than be born healthy, in a democratic country at peace, with a roof over your head."

"Well then, enjoy it," her father said. "It's not fair, but enjoy it."

50

Dover, UK
Eight-fifty p.m.

Jade had noted down their meeting point the previous evening, and now entered the address on her phone's GPS.

Alkham Road, the car park between Russell Gardens and Kearsney Abbey.

By now Kilani was sitting in the back, clasping Jade's hand as he discovered yet another new landscape. Desert, tents, huts and the violence of the Jungle had given way to fields, woods, meadows and well-tended gardens. Far too much greenery to allow any passing police car to spot them, which probably explained the choice of rendezvous.

Night was falling as they pulled up at their destination a few minutes early.

At nine o'clock precisely, a white van entered the car park from Alkham Road and stopped opposite them, its headlights switched off.

"What shall we do?" asked Jade.

"I don't think they'll get out until they see the boy. The association isn't legal, so they have to take precautions."

"So what do we do?" Jade insisted.

Bastien turned to her, a sad look in his eyes.

"Well . . . I guess we get out of the car and say goodbye to him."

One after the other, Manon slid the two straps of the backpack onto Kilani's shoulders. She put her hands on his hips, then on his cheeks, until finally something inside her gave way and she wrapped her arms round him as though she wanted to make him disappear completely. Her tears began to flow.

Jade was equally distraught, but this time Kilani clumsily wiped her soaking cheeks.

"I'm going to miss you, little ninja," she murmured.

The van doors opened and a woman and man in their sixties got out. She looked like a picture-book granny with permed white hair, while he had the air of a retired school master, with a clipped beard and glasses down on his nose. There was nothing threatening or disturbing about them. Bastien took Kilani's hand and walked towards the couple.

"Is this Kilani?" the woman asked, greeting them warmly.

The man came up, crouched down to Kilani's level, and spoke to him in Arabic. Only a few words, but they were enough to bring a smile to Kilani's face. He nodded, as if he'd heard good news. Then he pointed to the Miller family. The man spoke again in Arabic, but this time his expression was sombre. Kilani understood he would be continuing on his way without them.

"*Euh . . . a thousand euros for the kid,*" Bastien said in English, handing the woman an envelope.

"It won't be just for him. It will be for all the children," she replied.

Somewhat stunned by everything that was going on, Jade translated for her father.

Bastien looked at the woman, pleased at her reply.

"Tell her that's fine."

The man gave him a calling card with the logo of the Sunchild Association, a landline number and an address.

"Can we visit?" asked Bastien.

"Whenever you want, sir."

The retired teacher stooped down to Kilani and reassured him that he could see the Millers again if he wanted to. The van's side door slid open, and the boy jumped in. Manon and Jade bit their lips to avoid crying again. Kilani gave them one last disarming smile.

The elderly couple made to climb back into the front of the van, but before they disappeared Bastien got out his phone and took a photograph of them without asking permission. The flash lit up the car park for a moment, and Bastien turned to say something to Jade. As he spoke, his words became increasingly heated.

"Tell them we'll be coming to see him. Tell them I'm a police officer. Tell them that if this isn't the right address or if the telephone number is fake, I'll find them. Wherever they are, I'll find them. Tell them that!"

The white-haired granny smiled indulgently at him . . .

"There's no need, papa. I think she understood."

To reassure him, the woman laid her hand gently on the arm of this man who, though he hadn't shown any emotion, also seemed on the verge of breaking down.

The Miller family watched as the van pulled away, standing in the car park as if they were the ones who had been abandoned.

Epilogue

Calais police headquarters
October 2016
Two months later

The French government had decided to dismantle the Jungle. It was a stain on the map of France that had become too visible, too embarrassing ahead of the upcoming elections.

Nine thousand adults and a thousand children to rehouse, to sprinkle round the entire country, to dilute as much as possible so they would be almost unnoticeable.

Ten thousand people were being transferred as far away as possible from what was still their main objective: to reach England.

The president had promised that no-one would be left out, and yet the reception and training centres set up without funding or staff were quickly overwhelmed. Soon, mini jungles began to pop up everywhere. And more than a thousand migrants returned to Calais.

As if to mark the announcement of the closure of the Jungle camp, a few new posts were created at Calais police headquarters – for the first time in years. This morning, the BSU finally got a new recruit, gardien de la paix Foued Smadja. A product of the estates on the outskirts of Paris, son of second-generation immigrants, wearing a cheap-looking new suit to create a good impression. His first posting as a police officer in the north of France.

After being introduced to commissaire Dorsay, he was escorted to the BSU office, where the head of the group was waiting for him.

"These are the other members of your team: Erika Loris and Ruben Corval."

His new colleagues waved a greeting.

"And I'm lieutenant. Not Bastien, not Miller, not sir, simply lieutenant. We'll see about first-name terms later."

Erika winked at Corval just as Passaro pushed open their door.

"Sorry, Bastien, but I've just had a call from our patrol. They're in the Jungle."

"There is no Jungle anymore. What on earth are they doing down there?"

"They were called by the workmen. A digger has just uncovered a cemetery."

Miller quickly decided how to allocate his team.

"Okay. You head over first. I'll meet you down there with Corval. Smadja, you stay here with Erika. We'll keep you up to speed."

"Can't I come with you?" the new recruit asked, anxious to please.

"No. you spend the day here with Erika. She'll tell me what she thinks of you. I trust her judgment more than I do my own."

The diggers had demolished the huts and tents, reducing them to debris that a little further on was piled into mountains of plastic, fabrics and clothes, destined to be condemned to the flames once the wind died down.

There was nothing left on this vast stretch of land of anything hope had built there. Nothing except the hole around which the workmen were still standing, hypnotised by horror.

Corval parked their patrol car at the entrance. Even before he had switched off the engine, a gull had settled on the bonnet.

"Those damned rats of the air!" Bastien moaned. "I can't stand them."

Corval scared the bird off with his arm, and the two men headed towards the team of first responders.

"Could you gather the details, Ruben? I'd like to have a look in the Jungle."

"No worries, Bastien. Take your time, I'll look after everything."

The day after driving Kilani to England two months earlier, Bastien had returned to the refugee camp with one of Manon's photos of Adam in his pocket. He had shown it all over the Jungle, but no-one had spoken to him. Nobody wanted to talk to a cop.

Now he was back, on this stretch of land between two worlds, where the sand dunes stood as serene as ever. No more migrants, no more aid workers, as if the problem had been solved with the wave of a magic wand. Probably the decade's best disappearing act.

A few minutes later, Corval joined him, notebook in hand.

"Apparently there are several corpses, not all of them complete. I took it upon myself to call the police judiciaire in Coquelles, and they're sending their forensics people."

"I don't suppose anybody saw anything?"

"Not much. Only a strange guy carrying a machete who came out of the forest and scared the workmen stiff. He even touched the bodies, but then he disappeared again."

"What did he look like?"

Ruben leafed through the pages of his notebook.

"Yeah, I wrote it down, wait a sec . . .Tall, Arab, around forty years old, filthy, creepy, machete, scar."

This last word brought Bastien up short.

"Scar? Where was it?"

"One of the workmen said it was on his cheek under his left eye. Another says it was on his right temple."

Bastien surveyed the forest bordering the Jungle. He had searched it for days. Even if he hadn't found him in the camp, he and Adam were friends, and he would surely have come to find him. The Syrian had marked out a path from the Jungle to the scorched front door, leaving a mark Bastien had never had the heart to clean off . . .

But above all, and this was something the young police lieutenant was sure of, Adam would never have abandoned Kilani.

"Well, boss? Does that mean anything to you?"

With one last look at the forest, Bastien turned on his heel.

"No. I don't believe in ghosts."

OLIVIER NOREK served as a humanitarian aid worker in the former Yugoslavia before embarking on an eighteen-year career in the French police, rising to the rank of capitaine in the Seine-Saint-Denis Police Judiciaire. He has written six crime novels, which have sold two million copies in France and won a dozen literary prizes.

NICK CAISTOR is a translator from French, Spanish and Portuguese. He has won the Valle-Inclán Prize for translation from the Spanish three times, most recently for *An Englishman in Madrid* by Eduardo Mendoza, published by MacLehose Press.